VICIOUS HEARTS

A STANDALONE DARK ROMANCE

CARA BIANCHI

Copyright © 2023 - Cara Bianchi

Cover © 2023 - @covers_by_wonderland (Instagram)

All rights reserved.

No part of this book may be reproduced in any form or by any electronic or mechanical means, including information storage and retrieval systems, without written permission from the author, except for the use of brief quotations in a book review.

TRIGGER WARNINGS

It's my responsibility as an author to be clear about any possible triggers in this book. Your safety and mental health are very important, so please don't read this story if you may be adversely affected by the following:

- **graphic and extensive descriptions of sexual acts**, including the use of sex toys (consent is not discussed but stops short of being dub-con)

- **praise kink and sexually degrading language**

- **sexually-charged physical violence**, including slapping, spitting, pinching, spanking, biting, and the 'hand necklace'

- **genre-typical violence**, specifically shooting and stabbing

- **body mutilation.** Brief and not graphic (aftermath rather than event)

- **child murder in the context of a serial killer.** This is not graphically described but is a key plot element, so references are regular

- **peril involving a young child**, both on the page and described. This does not include sexual or other abuse but may cause distress to some readers

- **abduction of an adult**

- **suicide** (aftermath depicted on the page)

- **mentions of pedophilia, child abuse, child murder, and human trafficking** (not on the page or described in detail)

- **alcohol** consumption depicted on the page

- **drug references** (specifically heroin, amphetamines, LSD). Drug use is depicted on the page briefly in one instance

- **references to mental illness** (specifically schizophrenia and bipolar)

- discussion/depictions of **narcissism, toxic empathy, gaslighting, emotional/psychological abuse**

A quick word on consent and safety in relationships:

This book and the characters depicted herein are in no way intended to represent safe or healthy relationship dynamics, particularly how they handle their kinks.

If you are interested in exploring any of the practices described in this story, please don't use my book as a primer! I encourage you to do your own research and put your physical and psychological safety first.

Thank you and be safe!

This book is dedicated to all of you slutty good girls who want to be railed by a much older man. A man who praises and degrades you in equal measure and loves you like it's his job.

An honorable mention goes to Bosch, the company that brought us the Tassimo coffee maker. Without it, you would not be reading this. I would have died.

Enjoy yourself, you horny creeps. I love you all.

Cara xx

CONTENTS

Prologue	1
Chapter 1	19
Chapter 2	27
Chapter 3	29
Chapter 4	38
Chapter 5	50
Chapter 6	59
Chapter 7	70
Chapter 8	83
Chapter 9	94
Chapter 10	104
Chapter 11	111
Chapter 12	114
Chapter 13	124
Chapter 14	133
Chapter 15	145
Chapter 16	155
Chapter 17	168
Chapter 18	177
Chapter 19	180
Chapter 20	187
Chapter 21	196
Chapter 22	203
Chapter 23	206
Chapter 24	215
Chapter 25	229
Chapter 26	239
Chapter 27	243
Chapter 28	251
Chapter 29	260
Chapter 30	263
Chapter 31	275

Chapter 32	284
Chapter 33	296
Epilogue	311
Mailing List	325
Also by Cara Bianchi	327

PROLOGUE

Ben

I *'m losing my mind.*

The woman I'm obsessed with is inside the beach house next door. *Alone.*

This week has been hell. I avoided Roxy whenever I could, but it's fucking challenging to dodge someone at a wedding when there are only two guests—you and them.

I thought this trip would be a pleasant change of scenery, but the tension was unbearable. Just being close to her does things to me.

The newlyweds, Leo and Ali, flew home with their little daughter this afternoon. I booked an extra night at the resort, certain that Roxy would leave with them and I'd finally get some peace. But she stayed too, and I haven't left my villa since I saw her walking past, toting a string bag of groceries.

I stand at the open patio doors, watching as a flash of pink lightning splits the sky over the sea. Thunder rolls like a growl of judgment from above the clouds.

Hawaii is paradise, then suddenly the heavens open, and you're screwed. Although the torrent outside is deafening against the palm fronds, I'm comfortable here and dry as a bone.

Vodka blurs the edges enough to keep me from losing my shit. The glass in my hand is ice cold, and I press it to my temple, trying to calm the throbbing there.

I don't hear the knock at first, but eventually, the insistent sound penetrates my thoughts. I go to the door and look through the spyhole.

It's Kai, the resort manager. When I open the door, I immediately realize something is amiss.

"What's up, buddy?" I ask.

"I'm sorry, Mr. Benedikt."

Kai sighs and steps aside. Behind him stands Roxy, her suitcase in her hand.

"Her roof has a bad leak. It's flooding. We're booked up, so I can't offer this young lady another villa, but she tells me you are friends and are both leaving tomorrow. It doesn't seem worth transferring her to another resort under the circumstances, and she assures me she will be okay with you?"

I glance at Roxy. Her eyes are as wide and innocent as ever, the same pale blue, like a clear winter sky. Her blonde hair is fluffy and unkempt, flyaways framing her pretty face.

My eyes slide back to Kai.

"I told you I didn't want to be disturbed, Kai. I distinctly remember telling you not to bother me with anything less than a world-ending emergency."

"Don't be such a dick," Roxy interjects. "I'll sleep on your couch. We're flying home tomorrow morning anyway, so what difference does it make?"

"You're bothering me," I reply. "I want my peace."

"What, so you can drink bison grass vodka, stare at the rain, and brood?" She smirks, her eyes flashing up and down my body. "While half-naked?"

I had given no thought to my shirtless state. Why should I? It's my fucking villa. I should just tell Kai to take her to another resort. But she's here, wet and cold, with nowhere to go.

Do I want her to go? *No.* I do not want her to be anywhere other than sitting on my face.

Don't think about that now, for fuck's sake.

When Roxy got out of the hospital, I kept running into her. I'd visit Leo and Ali, and she'd be there. Walk through her neighborhood, and I'd see her. I could have thought about *why* I was always going places where she might be, but instead, I started to distance myself. I turned down so many invitations that I stopped receiving them anymore.

A wedding is different, though. I didn't know Roxy and I were the only guests until we were already here, so I had to make the best of it.

But Roxy does not need a man like me in her life. Just because she likes the look of me, thinks I'm funny, enjoys my company—so what? She's young. She'll forget all about me before long.

These are the thoughts that stopped me from calling her on many a horny night. But now I'm warm and buzzed from the vodka, and the storm has charged the air with a hot, humid feeling that's making me want to forget all the promises I made to myself.

I hear my voice.

"Whatever. Come in then, get dry."

Roxy darts past me before I have a chance to change my mind. I shoot Kai a glare, and he shrugs.

"That girl is most persuasive. And Mr. Benedikt, I have to wonder—why wouldn't you want a beautiful young woman staying the night with you?"

"Just don't bring me any more. This one is plenty for me to handle, thank you."

He nods. "*Aloha ahiahi*, Mr. Benedikt."

"As you say, good evening."

I close the door behind him and rest my forehead on it, drawing a deep breath before turning around.

Roxy isn't there. She's in the bathroom. Her suitcase is open on the floor by the couch, and I hear the shower running.

She's naked behind that door. Naked and standing under the rainforest shower head, water running down over her—

I shake my head hard, trying to banish the memories I've visited so many times.

I first met her in the hospital. It was awkward—I shot her in the thigh while trying to kill my best friend. That was a shitty day at work, but we're Bratva. People get killed over less, yet forgive far worse, so it's not surprising that we all made up in the end.

When I first saw Roxy in the hospital, I intended to apologize and get out of there, but I kept returning. Again and again, I sat in her little room with her, playing cards and watching television. She didn't ask why I was there, and I didn't think about it. I just told myself it was guilt that brought me to her. She needed some company, and I had nothing better to do since I was suddenly unemployed.

Roxy doesn't belong amongst criminals. She's too breezy, too bright and sweet. Those qualities prevent me from putting her out of my mind.

I hate myself for it, but when I'm horny, it's always Roxy I envisage. Her tan skin, her full curves, and the abundance of soft flesh that I go fucking wild for.

She's so sweet, so sassy with her flirty little mouth. I have a deep urge to sully her, to drag her down to my level. It's easy to imagine her bruised and ruined, begging for my come, and my mind plays the scenes like a filthy showreel whenever she's near me.

She's way, *way* too fucking near now.

My cock is hard and sticking out lewdly in my pajama pants. I reach into my waistband and grab it, working it a little to ease the pain, and it throbs against my palm.

The shower stops, steam billowing from the crack in the bathroom door. I hurl myself onto the couch, arranging my body and the cushions to hide my arousal. It occurs to me I should probably have put on a shirt, but it's too late for that now.

Roxy emerges from the bathroom. She's wearing shortie pajamas, her thick thighs and round ass filling them out perfectly. Her skin is flushed pink from the heat of the water, and she's styled her hair in two neat dutch braids.

I suppress a growl. *Fuck.* She looks *so* hot like that. *If I got a hold of those braids, I could just—*

"Can I get a drink?" Roxy asks. She gestures at the bottle on the table.

I cough. "Yes," I wave my glass, "but you can get one for me while you're at it. The icebox is in the top of the refrigerator."

I look out of the open patio doors at the rain, still falling in thick sheets. Roxy is about to bend over to get the ice, and given my frame of mind, I'm not sure I won't be cock-first across the room before I can stop myself.

Roxy sits beside me and nudges my shoulder with the glass. The cold of it shocks me, and it's only then I realize I'm covered with a thin sheen of sweat. Whether it's proximity to her or the humidity, I don't know.

I glance at her leg. The puckered scar on her thigh looks more prominent, picked out pale against her bronzed skin.

Roxy sees where I'm looking and sighs. "You know it wasn't your fault," she says. "You got mixed up in something and didn't have the right information. That happens sometimes. I'm alright. You're alright."

I decide to change the subject.

"So, your villa flooded?"

"As Kai said, the water was coming in the roof," she shrugs. "I got back from the restaurant, and the bed was soaked, the couch too. I was out for a while, so it had the chance to get really bad."

She's lying.

She's too young and inexperienced at bullshitting people to understand how to go about it. I asked her a closed question —it only needed a yes or no answer. But she started giving details. I decide to stay quiet and see what she says next.

The truth-teller does not need to convince, but when people lie, they need feedback from the other person to tell whether their deception is working. In the absence of anything to go on, a liar will babble.

Sure enough, after a sip of her drink, Roxy continues.

"Seeing as you weren't taking my calls or responding to messages, I asked Kai about you. He told me you'd asked to be left alone."

A long pause. She turns to look at me, but when she sees she has my full attention, she retreats, not letting me have her eyes. If she was in an interrogation, I could reduce her to an anxious, cooperative puddle in no time.

She knows she's carelessly given away her motive here. Next, she'll attempt to steer me away from it.

"Not that I wanted to see you by then," she says. "So I went to the seafood buffet, had something to eat, and returned to find the place wrecked. I ran down to the concierge station, and Kai said he'd have to move me somewhere else, but I didn't want that, so—"

"—you got him to bring you here. With your stuff. None of which is wet, I notice."

Roxy is now all too aware of the possibility that I don't believe her. Her eyes scan my face, looking for something to latch onto, but I'm well-practiced at not giving anything away.

"You don't need to be so fucking rude," she snaps.

Ah. The classic deflection argument. Get me on the defensive, hoping I'll forget to ride this train of inquiry into the station.

"Alright, I'm sorry." I sip my drink. My erection has faded, and I stretch, setting the glass on the table as I shift. "But it's hardly convenient that you're here. You're gonna have a shit-awful crick in your neck tomorrow, just in time for an eleven-hour flight."

"If you're worried about my neck, you could give me the bed." She smiles at me, twirling her braid around her finger. "Or, you know. A bunk-share between good friends. That could be fun?"

Her neck? I *was* thinking about that, actually. I wanna squeeze it while I fuck her.

My cock twitches and I tense my thighs, trying to discourage it from getting hard again.

Roxy returned from her grocery shopping trip about three hours ago and didn't go out again. I know this because she has to walk past my villa to get anywhere—it's the next one along, the last in the row. And I've been watching ever since, checking to see whether she went out again. Her dinner story is a fabrication.

"What did you eat?"

"Lobster from the barbeque. It's my favorite. Chardonnay with it."

Too much detail again. I pity her inability to lie convincingly.

Could she have gotten onto the roof of her villa and trashed it herself? Probably. They're only bungalows. She could have dragged the patio furniture over and used it to get up there. Ripped up the palm fronds and smashed through the tile just over her bed. So it was bad enough that she couldn't stay there, but not so bad that her stuff got ruined too.

This was her plan all along. So whatever happens next isn't *my* fault, is it?

I pick up my drink and throw it back.

"Fine," I say, waving my arm at the bed. "You make yourself comfortable. I'm gonna freshen up, and then I'll get in too. If you want me to take the couch, I will, but I hope you fucking appreciate it since you're the one who's imposing."

"I thought we might talk a little more," Roxy says, standing up as I move. "I have questions, Ben. I want to know why we were friends and then we weren't."

"There's nothing to say." I turn in the bathroom doorway. "Leo is my only friend, and because of my stupidity, I nearly killed him. You had a serious injury and a traumatic experience at my hands before we even *met*, so that tells you plenty. You really want a friend like me?"

She doesn't reply, and I realize my tone is harsher than I intended. Still, she shouldn't be here, but she is, and she has to take me as she finds me.

"Just go to bed, Roxy."

∼

Roxy

Ben takes his time. I know he's hoping I'll fall asleep, but I'm not gonna let that happen.

Is this a dumb thing to do? *Absolutely.* But I want him *so* bad.

Kai is a helpful concierge. The best. And a few dollar bills—a few hundred—did a lot to enhance his customer service skills.

The resort was full, but when Ben booked another night, Kai booked me to stay, too. And when I asked for a sledgehammer and told him what it was for, he only said he would have to invoice me for the damage to the roof. I'm sure I overpaid, but it was worth it.

Because *fuck me. It worked.*

I turn off the bedside lamp and snuggle under the sheet. The patio doors are open, and outside, the thunder mixes with the crashing waves until it seems like the tempest might come in and drown us.

When I was in the hospital, I lived for Ben's visits, and after I got out, I spent a ton of time with Leo and Ali, always hoping Ben would drop by. I saw him plenty of times, and we'd talk, but that hospital room had been like our little world. We were never the same.

But I'm not a fool. I saw things. A lick of the lips, a shift in his sitting position. His hands would twitch and flex when I got near him, as though he was fighting the urge to touch me. Those blue eyes—a deeper shade than mine—moved over my body.

He avoided me, made excuses, and distanced himself. Then he got rude and dismissive, hoping to offend me and throw my attention.

I tried to take that on board. Truly I did. But then we were together in beautiful Hawaii, attending our best friends' wedding. It was okay until they left yesterday, and I couldn't distract myself anymore.

Benedikt Voratov wants me. I know it, and he knows it too.

∽

I'm dozing when I feel the mattress shifting. As I wake up, I realize it's Ben, getting into the bed beside me.

I lie still, my eyes closed. Despite my bravado, I thought he'd sleep on the couch, but I was wrong.

I feel the heat coming off him as he settles, and I steal a look, expecting to see his back. To my surprise, he's facing me. His eyes are closed, his head resting on his arm. His bicep muscle is bunched and big enough to make an effective pillow.

I've never been this close to him before. He smells faintly of toothpaste and his aftershave—citrus, with an earthy spiciness beneath it. I have to find out what it is so I can buy myself a bottle and indulge in his scent whenever I like. The warmth of his breath reaches me, and I breathe it in, reveling in it.

I could reach out and touch him. But now I'm here, I can't do it.

Ben has dominated my fantasies for so long. If he rejects me, that will all be ruined.

But that was the deal, wasn't it? That's exactly how I justified this to myself. I need to know whether there's something here, and if there isn't, I can move on.

No. I can't do it. I misjudged this situation. Lying here, I feel like a dangerous creature slumbers beside me.

I'm gonna move to the couch myself in a minute, and when I'm sure I can sneak out, I'll leave. Get an earlier flight, book a charter, anything.

I count to sixty in my head, then open one eye. Ben's chest rises and falls steadily, and he hasn't moved. The mattress doesn't make a sound as I slowly turn away from him, my foot reaching for the floor. The rug is soft as my toes make contact, and I sit up, perching on the edge of the bed.

"You coward."

I freeze and turn, looking over my shoulder.

"You connive your way into my bed, only to chicken out when you get here?" Ben's sapphire eyes pierce me. "Roxy, you're here because you want to be. Have you changed your mind?"

"No," I whisper. "But something about you scares me."

"It fucking *should*." The low rumble in his voice makes me feel weak. "You think you know me, don't you? Well, you don't. I'll break you in two and not care if you hate me for it."

The thunder seems louder than ever. My heart hammers in my chest, and my pussy flutters a little, despite his harsh words.

Holy shit. Is this why he's been avoiding me?

"Can we just fool around a little?" I ask, my voice quivering.

"Are you out of your fucking mind?"

Ben is on his feet, walking fast around the bed. He kneels on the floor before me, his hands on my knees, and I shiver at his touch.

"You are *so* naïve, Rox. Do you know who 'fools around?' Fools. I'm not a fucking fool. I'm a man sixteen years your senior who wants to fuck you damn hard. Believe me when I say I'm not gonna be leaving space for Jesus."

He pushes my legs apart so he can press his body between them. He seems suddenly huge, his muscles flexing beneath his skin as he leans into me. My breath catches in my throat as his lips brush against my earlobe.

"Stop it with the innocent act," he says. "You came here because you want me in your little pussy. Don't you?"

I nod. He chuckles and licks my lower lip.

"I'll need to get it good and wet first, *charodeyka*."

Ben's hand is between my legs, his fingertips teasing the seam of my shorts. He rubs my sex for a minute before kissing me deeply, his tongue invading my mouth. I gasp as he presses more insistently against my pussy, my clit pulsating against his touch.

"What a little slut you are," he murmurs against my lips. "You want *my* kind of rough? Because that's how I do it."

He tugs at my shorts, dragging them down my legs until they are wrapped around one ankle. I wear no panties underneath, and as he parts my legs again, he pushes me back until I'm resting on my elbows.

With my legs wide apart and my hot pussy on show, I feel incredibly vulnerable. Ben has no such qualms. He lets out a low moan of appreciation as he places his hands on my inner thighs, pushing them wider apart and opening me up for his attention.

"So pretty." He glances up at me from between my legs, and a smirk of satisfaction breaks out on his face. I'm panting already, my pussy juicy and desperate for touch.

Can he tell I've never gone this far with anyone before? I've had nothing more than the occasional kiss and fumble, and not with anyone I felt was deserving of my virginity.

The *last* thing I am is a slut, but I want to be *his* slut.

His face drops out of sight, and I feel the tip of his tongue delving between my pussy lips. I bite my lip and moan gently.

"Don't you dare be fucking quiet." He kisses my clit, and I jump. "If I'm gonna do the wrong thing, I'm gonna do it right, so I wanna hear you. Grab my hair, whatever you gotta do, but find your damn voice."

With that, he sticks his tongue into me, and I squeal. It feels so good to have his mouth on me. Better than I imagined, and I imagined it a thousand times. All those hot nights alone, my fingertips moving as I chased relief. Thinking about Benedikt Voratov's tongue lashing my clit, just like this.

His fingertip pushes against my entrance, providing a welcome pressure. He moves it around but doesn't enter me, gathering my moisture, and I watch as he brings his finger to his lips, sucking my juice from it.

I do my best to relax, but my nerves are shot. I drop flat on my back as he presses my clit with the thumb of his other hand, easing his finger into me as he does so.

"I knew you'd be tight, but *fuck*," he says, licking my clit again. His saliva runs down and adds to my natural lubrication, easing his way as he pushes his finger deeper. "It's a good job I made myself come earlier because otherwise, I might not hold back."

"You don't have to," I gasp. Ben's finger is deep inside me now, and the ache I feel is replaced with a satisfying fullness as he moves, slipping in and out of me. "You make me feel so good."

He continues fingering me for a minute or two, and I wind my hands through his hair, moaning as he drives me toward my orgasm. I feel the rolling tension deep in my abdomen, and my pussy clutches at his finger, trying to feel more.

This is too much for him, and he suddenly pulls away. I sit up on my elbows again and watch him as he stands, shedding his pajama pants as he goes.

He's lean and muscular, his shoulders rounded out by heavy lifting. My eyes scan his torso, and I see a long, jagged scar from his hipbone to just below his left pectoral muscle. I didn't notice it before. It's flat but silvery as it catches the light. I follow the scar back down again, blanching at the sight of his cock.

I own a dildo, sure, but I've never seen a real one in person. Ben's erection is thick and straight, reaching out for me, and it seems enormous. Maybe they all seem huge the first time?

He sees the look on my face and laughs. "Don't worry. You want me. You said so yourself. It might hurt a bit, but not for long, and then you'll be begging me to fuck you deeper."

I frown. "Oh, my God. Did Ali tell you I'm a virgin? Why would she *do* that?

Ben stares at me for a long moment. When he speaks again, his tone chills my blood.

"You're a virgin?" He rubs his face with his palm. "Are you fucking *serious*?"

I sit up, reaching for him, but he steps back.

"What difference does it make?" I ask, but he's already turning away, pulling his pants on again. "What is your problem? I'm an adult. It's up to me when I—"

"Yeah, it's up to you, fine." He's back over at the couch, splashing the now-warm vodka into a tumbler. He downs it in one. "But it takes two to tango, and I'm saying no way. Now get out."

I freeze. How can it be possible that he was eating my pussy a minute ago, and now he's telling me to leave?

He's still speaking, half to himself.

"I can't fucking believe I allowed myself to do this. For fuck's sake. You're a virgin, and you were gonna give it up to *me*."

I stand up, feeling exposed, with nothing covering my lower half. I snatch up the sheet, wrapping it around me.

"I didn't know you were the sort of man to get precious about taking my honor," I snap. "And in case you can't tell, I'm being sarcastic. So I'm a virgin? Whatever. It doesn't define me. If you just carry on and do what you were about to do, I won't be a virgin anymore, and you won't have to worry about it."

"You don't get it." He slams my suitcase closed and carries it into the bathroom, dumping it on the floor. "This is not some fade-to-black romantic scene. I don't do that. You can only give it up once, and you'll regret letting me take it."

"I won't!" I block the bathroom door with my body, but he picks me up by my waist and sets me down again without breaking stride. "I don't care how rough you are. Do you have any idea what I've pictured you doing to me? Don't talk to me like I'm a child!"

"Get dressed and get out, Roxy." Ben picks up the vodka bottle, but not the glass. "I'm not who you think I am, and this isn't happening. Do you understand?"

My face feels hot, and my eyes sting with tears. I blink them away.

"Fine."

Ben stalks out onto the patio, closing the door behind him. Ten minutes later, I'm dressed and ready to leave, but he's still staring out to sea.

I steal a last look at him as I open the villa door, but he doesn't turn around.

1

Six months later...

Roxy

Valentine's Day. My least favorite day of the year.

I volunteered to work today so I could distract myself, but I can only write so many case notes before I feel compelled to put my head in the shredder. Before my best friend Ali got married, I could indulge in whining with her, but now there's no one to complain to anymore.

As per any other Friday, I have a date with a glass of wine and a movie. When all else fails, David Bowie in *Labyrinth* is my happy place.

I know what my problem is. I'm always at work and studying the rest of the time—no headspace for a relationship. And, of course, there's the other reason, the one I've spent the last few months trying not to think about.

Ben totally humiliated me. Not a day passes that I don't remember his face as he turned away, dismissing me even though we'd shared the most erotic few minutes of my life. But it's not as though I was that surprised. Except for Ali, everyone I cared about rejected me in one way or another. I should be grateful he didn't take more from me before he cast me aside.

I still hate myself for wanting him, and this stupid cutesy holiday is doing nothing to help. Luckily for me, he's out of town.

All the files have been stamped and put away, the referrals processed, and tomorrow's visits are on the board. As I walk out the door, I see a young man walking by, holding a red foil heart-shaped balloon.

I check the locks and tuck the keys into my bag. Shivering, I pull my collar up against the wind and head toward the park.

As a trainee children's counselor at Always Home, I get the donkey work, like coffee runs and data entry, but I wouldn't change a thing. If the charity had existed when I was a kid, I'd have been far safer. Maybe I'd have had a shot at finding a new family instead of ending up in juvie and clinging to Ali for so long.

I think about the murders and feel even colder.

Six children, all aged between five and nine, bled pale and left in marshy areas or shallow water.

New York City homicide was the first to call him The Dollmaker. It's a stupid, frivolous nickname, but the gutter press loves that kind of thing, and once they got hold of it, the name wouldn't go away. They stuck with it even after the suspect was arrested and convicted, and they had a real name to use.

Simon Farraday confessed to being the serial child-killer. He operated along the East Coast from Massachusetts to Savannah but actually lived and worked not far from here. A cable repairman with a wife and baby son.

The trial was brief but sensational. His family did not attend —reporters parked their news vans on the Farraday's front lawn, but in the days after the conviction, they left one by one.

The Farraday house stands empty, a battered realtor's board face-down on the unkempt lawn. No one is trying to sell it anymore.

The neighbor to the right has moved their fence closer to their own property, as though to put more distance between their peaceful home and the murder house next door. Scavengers have stolen the garden ornaments, but the windows are boarded up.

The front door to the Farraday house is cracked an inch. Maybe some hobo is sheltering there.

Usually, I avoid walking this way, but today I'm too cold and tired to care. I take a left, heading toward the park's top entrance. I quicken my pace as I pass below the wrought-iron arch and into the park.

The wind seems louder, as though it's being funneled. I clutch my collar, holding it closed to keep my neck warm. Along the path to the south side, and then it's six blocks to my building.

Takeout, TV, early night. Sounds like a plan. I can probably—

A hand claps over my mouth. A sweet, suffocating smell engulfs my nose and mouth, and I try to kick out behind me, but my legs are already failing.

My thoughts are racing. My pulse hammers painfully hard as my body's stress response floods my system.

It's chloroform it's too strong oh Jesus it'll kill me I'm having a heart attack –

I don't know whether my attacker isn't well enough prepared or just watches too much true crime, but as he tries to pull me to the ground, he realizes I'm not going to lose consciousness after all. I catch a glimpse of a completely blank face, and it takes me a moment to understand that it's a mask.

Pain explodes at the base of my skull, and I know nothing more.

∼

I cough into something—a tight band around my face, covering my mouth. I'm lying on my side, a scratchy carpet beneath my cheek, and I'm zip-tied at the wrists and ankles.

The chloroform stung my eyes, but I suspect the blow to the head is responsible for my blurred vision. The nausea could be anything.

I push my legs straight and meet resistance. It's apparent that I'm inside something, and as I come around, I realize it's the trunk of a car. A car that is moving.

A bubble works its way up from my stomach, and I belch, wincing at the sour taste.

Keep calm. Keep it together and think.

The rolling sensation in my gut subsides for now. I turn onto my back, wincing as the back of my head hits the carpet. There's an open wound, but I don't know how bad it is or how much blood I've lost. My breath hitches in my chest, my head spinning as the carbon dioxide level in my blood rises.

I roll onto my side, trying to get in a safe position in case I throw up. As I move, the car hits a bump, and my injured head hits the side of the trunk. My vision swims, and I blink hard, trying to stay awake.

Gravel under the tires. A door opens and closes, footsteps crunching over loose stones as my abductor retreats. Where is he going?

I hear nothing except vehicles passing, and after a minute or so, I decide to risk pulling the trunk release lever. If I *don't* try it, I'll die for sure.

I scramble around with my bound hands and find the lever. The trunk pops open, a splash of light dazzling me.

The night air is cold but welcome. I breathe deeply through my nose, and with some effort, I roll onto my back and sit up, my abdominal muscles burning with the exertion.

I'm in a small parking lot beside a derelict diner, set back from a road I don't recognize.

I raise my hands to my face, feeling the gag. It's only tape, and I pick the edge with my nail until I can tear it away. My head is pounding, but a revelation breaks through, skewering me with terror.

Chloroform. Zip ties. Duct tape.

The Dollmaker used them all.

When Simon Farraday was arrested, I was allocated as a family liaison volunteer, spending time with his wife and helping her navigate the circus around the killings. From what she said about him, I started to wonder.

Farraday is mentally ill. Shortly after his conviction, he started talking to his feet and getting into arguments with people that weren't there. He's extremely paranoid and distrustful, said to be features of his illness.

He talks to *me*, though. I'm the only one he trusts because I looked after his family. His medication does nothing to stabilize him, and most people think he's a sick man who did sick things.

But I believe he's holding something back. Something important.

He cannot appeal unless he's declared legally sane, at which point he could instruct an attorney and demand a retrial. He's too unwell, though, and he's not getting any better.

The murder investigation needs to start from scratch. The whole thing stinks.

Now the real Dollmaker has come for me. I get it—he's gonna murder me in the hope that the appeal will peter out if I'm not there to drive it.

I don't want to die I don't want to die I don't want to die–

Wait.

In theory, I know how to get out of zip ties. Leo told me, but I've never seen it done.

Pull it as tight as possible first. I clamp my teeth around the loose end of the tie on my wrists, dragging it through the locking mechanism until the plastic bites into my skin. I raise my arms above my head and pull them down hard, winging out my elbows and pulling my shoulder blades together. Pain sears through my wrists, but the zip tie does not break.

Try again.

I keep trying, barely noticing my tears. Whether I'm crying with pain or fear, I don't know, but I have to keep at it. He could come back any minute.

I pound my clasped hands against my hip bone, and the zip tie breaks neatly. A few half-squats make short work of the binding at my ankles, and I'm away, sprinting for the road.

I don't look behind me. I'm terrified I can hear his breathing, but it's just my own.

I hurl myself into the bushes at the edge of the verge and lie still, trying not to pass out again. My head is in agony, blood still running down my neck.

Incredibly, my phone is still in my pocket. Why the hell didn't he take it?

I dial 911, my hands shaking. I can't tell the operator where I am, but she says an ambulance will be able to find me if I get out from under the hedge.

I roll into the light just as unconsciousness settles over me, smothering my thoughts.

I don't want to die.

Not yet.

Not ready.

Not

ready

to

go.

2

The Dollmaker

I can't believe she's not there.

It doesn't matter how many times I look. Open the trunk, close it, open it again, and the outcome is the same. Dead space where there should be Dead Roxanne.

Dead Roxanne isn't the same as Living Roxanne. The living one has thoughts, plans, and knowledge, but the dead one is nothing.

No, I'm wrong. Dead is *less* than nothing, especially if no one identifies your body. Then you're just a rotting hunk of meat, returning to dust over time. Unmourned. It's the better way —the natural order, untarnished by mawkish notions of love and grief. And if you're weak enough to be overpowered by someone like me, you deserve everything you get.

Nature makes no concessions. There are no participation trophies, no marks for trying your fucking best. If you're not intelligent, fast, or strong, you'll die, so you should. Some things—and some people—exist only to give the best of us something to trample on our way to the top of the pile.

I had intended to bury Dead Roxanne deep and far from home, hoping she'd just fade into the earth, leaving her friends to wonder. It's pleasant to imagine an alternative to reality. Maybe she went to Italy like she said she would someday. Perhaps she just wanted a new start. But no need to find out for sure that she's nowhere and nothing.

But now Living Roxanne has run away, stealing Dead Roxanne's tranquil fate. What a fucking bitch.

Too little chloroform, maybe. Certainly not firm enough bindings. I didn't adjust my methods to account for Roxanne being an adult. Smashing someone's head was a new experience for me. So much blood. It was kinda interesting, watching it bubble from her skull like a geyser. I thought she'd have bled out by the time we got here.

She must have woken up when I stopped. This is what happens when I try to busk it. One call of nature, I failed to check the trunk before setting off, and that's all it took to make my situation so much worse than it was.

I speak to Momma and tell her what I've done. She tells me not to panic and to go home.

The morning will come, and with it, Living Roxy or Dead Roxy. It can't bring both.

The Dollmaker is in prison. No one will believe her.

As for me—what do we do when we don't succeed?

We try again.

3

Three days later...

Ben

I dump my bag on the floor and look around.

My plants are dead, the leaves hanging limply. I should have asked someone to water them.

Who was I gonna ask? I went to the roof of the fucking *Earth* to get away from people. One person in particular.

Six months it's been. I went straight from Hawaii to Mexico to climb Pico de Orizaba and get my head out of the game. Then I didn't feel like going home, so I didn't. I kept getting on planes and kept climbing. I'm only here now because I'm low on funds, but part of me thinks I should have kept going until I eventually fucked up and froze to death on some treacherous slope.

The red light flashes on my answering machine. It's crazy that I still have a landline, but I like to give the impression that I'll get back to people eventually, and I refuse to enable voicemail on my cell phone. I press the playback button.

"You have ninety-nine messages," the machine trills.

That's the maximum. *How many times did it record over itself?*

I never told anyone where I was going, but besides Leo, there's no one I care to hear from. I have yet to speak to him since his wedding. It was awkward as fuck, and I don't know how to address it. I suspect it was Ali's doing that Roxy and I ended up alone together in Hawaii, but what good would it do to throw accusations around now?

What happened was all on me. I let Roxy in, tossed out all my reservations, and gave myself permission to indulge my selfish whims. It was only when she said she was a virgin that I came to my senses.

She told me she wanted to go to Italy for a while, maybe travel around Europe. If I'm lucky, she's no longer kicking around here.

"First message." The machine clicks. I reach for the buttons again and tap a couple.

"Delete all. Are you sure?"

I press once more to confirm, and the red light goes off.

The air feels stale, like on an airplane. I've had enough of that sensation recently, so I open the window. The breeze is welcome, but the dirge of the city's endless grind isn't.

The television remote is on the table, and after a few attempts to turn it on, I realize it's still switched off at the outlet. I flick the power on and settle down on the chair again, rummaging through my bag for water as the local news anchor goes through the motions.

"Simon Farraday, better known as sadistic killer 'The Dollmaker...'"

He isn't a sadist. He's just a sad weirdo, like I said he would be.

"...is recovering after a vicious assault at the hands of a fellow patient at Kirby Forensic Psychiatry center, Wards Island. Farraday was allowed to mix with the other violent and dangerous patients, a risky decision considering the nature of his crimes."

No shit. The fucked-up little weasel deserves a beat-down, and I'm glad he got one.

The news lady is still talking.

"Detective Tate Hillard gave a statement this afternoon."

The shot cuts to Tate. He looks tired, but he always does. Trying to be a good cop in this shitty world will put years on a man's face.

"Farraday is under guard in the hospital at the moment." Tate's eye's dart sideways, then back to the camera. "I'd be lying if I said I cared about his well being, but vigilante behavior in maximum security is a serious issue, and the notoriety of the criminal has no bearing on the matter. Thank you."

I know what he *wants* to say. He wants to laugh his ass off and make a personal request to finish the piece of shit off with his bare hands.

My cell phone is ringing. I switch off the television, swipe my thumb over my cell phone screen, and put it to my ear.

"Freddie."

"Benedikt, you slippery motherfucker." Freddie is as annoyingly jovial as ever. Can someone have a punchable voice? "Finally got your feet on the ground again?"

Freddie Dubois is my handler and the only person I contacted before disappearing. Even then, it was only to tell him to leave me the hell alone. Literal fucker that he is, he never tried to call me again, but he's obviously had someone on the lookout for me. He probably knew I was coming home before I even left Europe.

"I've been climbing mountains. I didn't go to Mars."

"You may as well have done," Freddie huffs, "but I'm not interested in your little holiday. Are you still soul-searching or can I put your name on the board?"

He has this way of talking about his agency like it's a Burger King.

Mezhdunarodnaya Komanda Ekspertov, or MKE for short, roughly translates as 'International Expert Team.' It's a suitably vague term, but essentially it's an organized crime skill bank—ex-cons, terrorists, assassins, mobsters, money launderers, and hackers. You name the service you need, and as long as you can pay, Freddie Dubois can procure a professional to assist. He's a recruitment consultant of sorts, but one who keeps a harpy knife in an ankle holster and could deliver you a nuclear warhead like a pizza.

When Detective Hillard joined the precinct in our territory, we made it known that he needed to make friends with us as his colleagues had. He refused to play ball. But idealists like him are not usually cynics, which makes them gullible.

Hillard was shopping for a freelance profiler who could move fast on The Dollmaker case. Freddie had his ear to the ground, so when he heard, he brought the issue to my attention.

I was local, available, and had the correct skillset. I had to fudge my qualifications, but other than that, I got the gig legitimately and on merit, posing as a private investigator and forensic criminologist.

The *kommissiya* were delighted. In his panic, Hillard took his eye off the ball and ended up in the one place he didn't want to be—the pocket of the Bratva. I did the job straight, but by the time he realized I had mob connections, it was too late. If Hillard's most celebrated and successful case were tainted with the knowledge that the Bratva was involved, it would call into question every collar he got in his many years of unimpeachable law enforcement. His career would be a dumpster fire, and he'd go out in disgrace.

Now he has to keep on the right side of the mob, and I'm back in the good books. Kind of. I could have capitalized on my success if I hadn't disappeared for half a year just because a woman messed up my head.

"Freddie, I just got back. Not yet, alright?"

"Come on, you gotta need a payday," Freddie laughs. "How much of your fee did you give to that charity?"

All of it.

"Some. I like to do a little bit of good now and again."

"Yeah, right. The Dollmaker was caught and convicted, and you got paid. Then you vanished. Did I offend you with what I said that day we were fishing?"

"I don't remember what you said. We were drunk as fuck."

That's a lie. I *do* remember. I was trying to haul in a marlin, and he started telling me to embrace the person I am and let love in. To take a chance on the girl I was obviously obsessed with instead of thinking I was too messed up to be anything more than lonely. I distracted him by hauling that big fucker of a fish right into his lap.

He had no idea what he was talking about, but it got to me. *Everything* was getting to me around that time. With the murder case done and dusted, I was restless.

When the wedding invitation came, I was glad of the distraction. A week in paradise might have helped to quieten the constant chatter in my head.

But it didn't. Not with Roxy there.

"I'm glad you're back," Freddie says, breaking the awkward silence. "Give me a call when you've pulled your head out of your ass, okay?"

"Got it."

I hang up and swing my feet onto the couch.

Relationships are a terrible idea for a guy like me. I have enough insight to know that I can't resist manipulating people. So what if I'm obsessed with Roxy? It's not as though that's healthy.

I'm a man with a freak on my back. A sweet girl like her can't stand up to that.

I close my eyes. The city's colors are too brash and bright after spending so long in nature, and I have a headache.

~

Roxy

"You were out for three days. You had a seizure shortly after you arrived, so we put you in an induced coma."

The flowers beside me are looking limp. Someone put them in water when they were fresh but never topped it up again, and the heads of the gerberas bow as though they're praying for me. The card beside them reads, 'much love from everyone at Always Home.'

The doctor is pissed that he's not holding my attention. "The paramedics found you unconscious at the roadside, two hours from here. Luckily, you had some identification on you, and we could bring you to a hospital near home." He frowns. "What happened to you?"

I've been awake for a few hours, but this is the first time anyone has asked me that question.

"Have the police been here?"

"No," the doctor replies, "but if you need to speak to someone, we'll call them."

The Dollmaker planned to kill me. He drove me miles out of the city to dump me somewhere. Whatever I do next, I'm not telling this doctor anything.

"I think someone tried to mug me," I say. "I was hitchhiking. I'll report it myself." I shrug in an I-know-I'm-dumb way, but the doctor isn't amused.

"We're waiting for a liver toxicity screen to come back," he says. "We ran various tests while we kept you under." He picks up my chart and looks at it. "You have a concussion, but observation suggests no long-term damage. We thought you'd need a blood transfusion, but it looked worse than it was. Eighteen dissolvable stitches in the lower occipital area of your head, and you now have what one of the younger residents told me is a 'nape undercut.' Very fashionable, by all accounts."

He pauses and sees I'm not laughing.

"Liver function results were borderline, hence the in-depth screening." He narrows his eyes at me. "Do you do drugs?"

Fuck no. But I don't want to get into a conversation about chloroform.

"Um, sometimes?" I lie.

"Well, don't." The doctor shakes his head, raising an eyebrow at me. "Anyway, we're confident you will be able to have your catheters out this afternoon, and if your test results are better, you can leave after your evening meal."

I can't afford all this. But there's no way I'm sending the bill to Leo and Ali, no matter how much Ali would want me to. She's rolling in money, but I don't like accepting charity.

"Thank you, doctor.' I yawn. "I feel exhausted. Is that normal?"

"Sure." The doctor stands up, slipping the chart back into its holder at the foot of my bed. "You're still adjusting to being awake. I'll leave a discharge notice with the charge nurse, conditional on you being fit to go and your liver tests returning with levels in normal parameters." He waves his pen at me. "Take better care of yourself. Clear?"

I give my most solemn nod. The doctor walks away, leaving me to rest.

I touch the back of my head, feeling the shaved patch where they had to stitch my head together. Split like a watermelon by a man who could have killed me but didn't.

I close my eyes.

The Dollmaker is still out there. And no one knows but me.

I have to get out of here.

4

Twenty-four hours later...

Roxy

My cell phone starts ringing as I hit the bell again. A female officer comes to the desk and sighs when she sees me.

"Wanna get that?" she asks.

"Get Hillard. I know he's here. I saw him arrive."

She looks me up and down before turning her back and heading into the bullpen. She crosses the floor and raps on the door of a small office.

I snatch the phone from my pocket and answer it.

"Hi, Moira."

"Rox, you're out! Why didn't you tell me?"

Moira Coffey is one of the trustees at Always Home, and she's like a mom to me. Her husband, Senator Coffey, was shot dead by Leo after the senator got mixed up in something that wasn't his business. Not to say he didn't deserve it —Coffey was a pedophile, known to hold horrible little parties for his dodgy friends. His wife and young son, Eddie, were taken hostage while all the craziness went down but released unharmed shortly after it was over.

Moira knew nothing about her husband's activities. She was mortified when the truth came out, and she's now a staunch advocate of victims' rights, giving her patronage to children's charities across the nation.

"I was home last night, but I went straight to bed. I only woke up an hour ago."

"Jesus. I'm sorry I didn't know. Oliver had me shredding old files for what felt like an eternity."

Ah yes. The scourge of the annual 'big tidy.'

My manager Oliver is the type never to stop something once he starts. So if he wants to reorganize the filing system, we're doing it until it's done. The fact that he technically works for Moira makes no difference—he can strong-arm her into anything. I think she likes to feel useful.

"Rather you than me," I say. "Will you tell him I will be back next week? I need to sort some stuff out."

"What happened? The hospital wouldn't tell us anything. We weren't even allowed to see you."

"I got mugged on the walk home from work. They stitched me up, but I had a fit, so they kept me asleep while they checked me over. I'm fine now. Just a little bit achy."

I rehearsed this little speech a few times to ensure I could keep my voice level and not trip over any of the words.

I glance up to see Detective Hillard walking toward me. I'm surprised he didn't put up more of a fight. He flips the flap on the desk and beckons me through.

"Gotta go, Moira. Let Ali know I'm okay and tell Oliver I'll come by the office later."

I put my phone back in my pocket and extend my hand to Hillard. He looks at it and turns away, throwing the words over his shoulder.

"Come through, Roxanne, and stop the bullshit."

∼

Detective Tate Hillard isn't my biggest fan.

Since I finished my counseling course, I've been working towards criminology and forensic psych credits. That's why I'm allowed to volunteer as an advocate for prisoners and psych hospital inmates, and that's how I met Simon Farraday.

I didn't believe Farraday was The Dollmaker. He's too disorganized, too scatter-gun. Despite his calm and cooperative demeanor throughout the trial, his poor mental health was cited as the reason for his sickening actions. No motive ever emerged, and he never volunteered one.

The jury was dazzled by Farraday's graphic taped confession but outside the courtroom, there were rumblings about gaps in the prosecution's case. It made no difference—he was found legally insane and couldn't be sentenced to death. Arguably an indeterminate period in a psych hospital is worse, and many said that was the hell he deserved.

When the family liaison work ended, his wife Lois took her child and moved out of the area under witness protection, swearing never to return. I went to give Farraday the news in person because she asked me to, and he took it hard. Really hard. He was on suicide watch for a fortnight, and shit got weird. Rambling, crying, talking to nothing. He pulled out his eyelashes, worried they were 'picking up signals.' Farraday's lawyer tried to speak with him, but he was never lucid enough to instruct, which is where I came in.

Farraday appointed me to assist him, as is his right. Hillard can't reasonably refuse to engage with me, but he's a master of malicious compliance, and I never *quite* get what I want. I've been needling him for months, asking for files, evidence reviews, and transcripts. It's a colossal waste of everybody's time.

Hillard gestures at the chair in his office, and I sit, pulling off my scarf. He sits behind his desk and fiddles with his nameplate, as he always does.

"What is it today, Roxanne?" He looks at me, steepling his fingers below his chin. "You want to know what brand of cheese was in Farraday's refrigerator when we arrested him? Do you have a burning desire to check whether we offered him a selection of fine wines during his interrogation?"

I smile. "Wine and cheese haven't yet made it into the Bill of Rights, but I can dream of a better world."

I'm rewarded with a smirk. I caught him on a good day.

"Can I have one of your Lifesavers?" I ask, holding my throat and swallowing hard. "My mouth is dry. I know you keep them in your secret drawer."

He rolls his eyes and reaches for his vest pocket, extracting the key. He unlocks the drawer and takes out the bag, holding it toward me. I peer inside and take a red candy.

"Come on, kid. I need to know what it's gonna take to get you out of my office. I only came by to pick up the show tickets for tonight—if I flake out on my wife again, there will be a domestic homicide in this area tonight."

I lean forward and fix my eyes on Hillard's.

"Detective Hillard," I begin. "Tate. I know for sure that Farraday isn't The Dollmaker, okay?"

He narrows his eyes. He's heard me say this before, but he can see something has changed.

"You know? How can you possibly know?"

I want to hold his gaze, but I can't.

"I got abducted when I left work," I say. The words rush out too quickly, crashing into one another. "The kidnapper chloroformed me, hit me, zip-tied me, the works. I woke up in the trunk of his car, miles away from home, and managed to escape."

Hillard's expression doesn't change.

"Roxanne, Farraday sat opposite me in the interrogation suite and told me things I can never unhear. He had the final victim's fingers in a fucking *jewelry* box. Did you know that?"

I nod my head.

Somehow, I knew this would happen. It's written all over the detective's face—he doesn't believe me.

"*Something* happened," Hillard says, "and we'll look into it, but you must drop the idea that The Dollmaker is still at large. Even as a copycat attack, it's laughable. The Dollmaker didn't hit his victims, he didn't drive hours away to dump them, and most importantly, he didn't let them get away. He was too smart for that." Hillard fixes me with a stern look, but then his eyes soften. "Forgive me for saying this, but you're not exactly his type. There's no logical reason for a child murderer to move on to adults."

"What about the work I'm doing with Farraday's review?" I ask. "Farraday can't file his own appeal, but as his chosen representative, I can push for a formal evidence review—there's precedent in law. What if the real killer just wanted me out of the picture so that the case would go nowhere and Farraday would rot in the hospital?"

Hillard doesn't respond. Instead, he pinches the bridge of his nose with his fingers. I press my lips together to fend off an outburst of profanity.

"Fine," I say, trying to keep the frustration out of my voice. "I was abducted. What are you going to do about it?"

"We'll make some inquiries as soon as we have a statement from you. Think very hard about what you want to say."

This man thinks I'm a fantasist. That I've invented a kidnapping story to cover up for some mundane street mugging incident.

Why? To draw *attention* to myself? To risk prejudicing the entire process by getting the case re-examined under false pretenses?

I start coughing, working up into a bad choking fit. Hillard darts around the desk to my side, slapping my back as I convulse until my breathing begins to calm.

"Can I have a glass of water?" I ask. "I'm sorry. I'm still hazy from it all, and I guess I'm just running my mouth."

Hillard looks at me for a beat too long, and I don't think he believes me. He knows I'm holding back.

Then he stands, heading for the door.

"Sure thing, kiddo. Those Lifesavers sure didn't live up to their name this time. Just sit tight, and I'll be back in a minute." He closes the door behind him.

I know I have to move fast.

I have no choice. If I do nothing, I am just waiting for the killer to return and finish the job. If Hillard isn't going to take me seriously, I have to go around him.

The request for the candy got Hillard to unlock the drawer, and the fake coughing fit got him out of his seat. The only thing left was to get him out of the room, so I asked for a drink, and off he went, leaving the drawer accessible.

Easy as one, two, three.

Hillard's desk drawer contains a black address book. I know it's there because I burst in on him once, and he put it away fast, locking the drawer and pocketing the key. I also know that he has refused point-blank to give me specific vital information that might be in that little book.

There is a criminal profile included in The Dollmaker case file. It's dated before Farraday was apprehended but had no signature or details of the profiler.

The person described in the profile bears no resemblance to Farraday, and it wasn't submitted as evidence in court—one of many things that don't seem right. Someone advised Hillard, but then their contribution was shelved.

The secrecy around Hillard's silent partner makes me highly interested in them. Despite their essential role, they are the only person involved in this case that I still need to meet and speak with. Maybe they will listen to me, help me lean on Hillard. After all, their profile would be pulled apart at Farraday's appeal, and they have their reputation to consider. It's the only card I have left to play.

I scoot around the desk and snatch the book, skimming it. There's a sticky tab sticking out, marked BV.

What does that mean? I flick to the page.

Profiling and acquisition, DM murder inquiry.

Ah. *Now* we're talking.

Evidence file delivery address: 274 Mott St., Nolita, NY10012. 12a.

I put the book back and return to my seat, muttering the address again and again in an effort to remember it. Hillard reappears only moments later, a glass of water in hand.

"I'll give you the statement now if you have time," I say.

Hillard's expression sours, but he manages a smile. It doesn't reach his eyes. "Whatever you say. But it's a new case. There's no way I'm even gonna *mention* The Dollmaker in connection with this incident, and neither are you. Is that clear?"

I nod. Hillard hands me the water and holds the door open for me.

By the time I get done at the station, the sun is low in the sky, but I'm not going home.

∼

Ben

I'm cooking a steak and listening to Bowie when the intercom buzzer sounds. I turn off the music and look out of the window, craning my neck to see who is at the door.

It's a woman with fair hair and a long coat. I can't see her too well, but she's obviously anxious—her hands pull at her hair, winding her fingers through it. She bites the tip of her thumb before jabbing at the bell, setting the intercom jangling again.

I pick up the handset.

"Yeah?"

A distorted voice, too loud in the speaker. "I'm sorry, I'm not sure who I'm looking for. Are you a profiler?"

How does she know that? It's not like I take out ads. I need to find out what the fuck she wants.

"Come in, and I'll explain." I press the button, and the main door unlocks. I glance outside and see her walking into the building.

I pull a sleeveless t-shirt over my head and think quickly.

No one is supposed to come to my fucking door. Freddie offers me the jobs, I take them, or I don't. Who the *fuck* has been giving my address out? This woman didn't even call me first.

A firm knock. I flip my steak onto a plate and head for the door.

On the coat hook hangs the holster that cradles my pistol. I retrieve the gun, lifting my shirt to tuck the weapon into my waistband. Suitably prepared, I open the door.

I *wasn't* prepared. Not for this. Not for *her*.

Roxy isn't even looking at me. She's rummaging through her haversack, shuffling papers.

Her hair isn't as light a blonde as it was when I saw her last. Her skin has paled, and she has purplish circles under her eyes. As I look at her, she seems to hold herself strangely, as though she's in pain.

She's fucking *gorgeous*.

Every time I see her, I'm dazzled all over again. And I haven't seen her since that night. The night I've played in my head a thousand times.

After a moment or two, she looks up. Her face is blank for a moment, but then her light blue eyes flash with recognition, and her lips curl into a sneer.

"Oh, for fuck's sake," she says. "Of course."

"What the hell are you doing here?" I ask. "I got back yesterday, and you're on my doorstep?"

"Believe it or not, this isn't a social call," she says, pushing past me.

Fuck this. The last thing I need is to be dragged into some drama with Roxy at the center. It can only lead to trouble.

End this quickly and get her out of here.

"What do you want?" I ask, closing the door.

I move back into the kitchen area and pick up my wine glass. Roxy has already helped herself to my armchair and is pulling out files, flicking through them.

"I'm working as a trainee counselor now at Always Home, you know. The kid's charity? I'm also volunteering in the justice system, advocating for prisoners."

"Fucking fascinating." I sip my wine, resisting the urge to chug it. "You barged in here to give me your updated resumé?"

Roxy shoots me a look but ignores me. "One of my clients is Simon Farraday. You know, the—"

"—The Dollmaker. I know."

"Right. Except Farraday isn't The Dollmaker, and I know it for sure." She continues to rifle through her documents. "I've been helping with his appeal, and the only person who still needs to give me their two cents is the profiler."

Roxy stops what she's doing and looks at me. I realize I'm tapping my toe, a tic I get when I'm stressed unless I consciously focus on overcoming it. Roxy glances from my face to my foot and back again.

"You're the fucking profiler," she says. She slaps her hand on the table, skimming a stack of photos onto the carpet. "I can't believe I didn't catch on sooner. Bratva fixer, the man with the connections, the insights. Always knew how to get people to do what you wanted. So now you're working for the law?"

"Not quite," I say. I sit on the couch, cradling the wine glass in my hand. "I picked up a freelance gig. I have every right to do that."

"Simon Farraday has rights, too," Roxy says, frowning. "He was found to be criminally insane and locked away in a hospital, probably forever. The case was bullshit from the start. How can a crazy man's confession be treated as the headline piece of evidence in a murder trial?"

"Why not? He knew things about the murders, because he was the murderer. Simple as that."

"He didn't do it."

I narrow my eyes at her. How dare she imply that my profile is wrong? I gave Hillard my report, and The Dollmaker was in custody and singing like a bird just a few days later. What's that if not a perfect result?

"Yes, he fucking did, Roxy. I have nothing to contribute to your little crusade. Take your amateur theories to someone who cares."

I look into my glass, swilling the wine. I'm waiting for a snarky comment, hoping she'll say something rude so I can feel justified in tossing her out on her ass. Nothing.

When I look at her, she's shaking.

5

Roxy

I cannot believe this is happening to me.

At this time of life-or-death crisis, I run into Benedikt.

I didn't know he was back. I didn't think he would ever come back at all. But here he is, the last person I want to be near.

But he's the only one who can help me.

"Please just shut up and listen to me," I say. I squeeze my eyes closed, but it's too late, and tears run down my cheeks. "I think your profile was accurate, but the man is innocent. The Dollmaker is still out there. At least hear me out."

Ben raises an eyebrow at me. He stands up, and for a moment, I think he'll come over and hold me. He taps his toe again.

"Do you want some wine?" he asks. "It's Rioja, so it's good stuff."

"Yes, please."

I wipe my face with my sleeve. Ben sets a glass down in front of me and gestures at my coat.

"I'll hang it up. Otherwise, you won't benefit when I throw you out."

I manage a smile, but he doesn't return it. *Damn. He's so hard to read.*

He puts my coat on a hook near the door. As he walks back toward me, he lifts his shirt and pulls a gun out of his sweatpants. He places the pistol on the table like it's the most natural thing in the world.

I never get used to seeing firearms. Leo and Ali don't leave theirs on display because they have a kid, but you'd think I'd be desensitized. After all, I've *been* shot. By Ben, and not intentionally, but still.

"Do you have to leave that there?"

"This is my home, and you barged in," he replies, stretching out along the couch. "So I don't consider you a guest. Deal with it."

His shirt hitches a little, revealing his taut lower abs. A sliver of hair is just visible above his waistband.

No. Have to stay focused.

"Tell me what you came to tell me, Roxy. Then I'll give you as much time as it takes for me to explain why you're wrong. Okay?"

Fine. Be a dick.

I open a file.

"Simon Farraday was not a suspect before you provided your profile," I begin. "He wasn't known to any victims or their families, as you predicted, and he had no significant priors. No flashing, no child molesting, no attempted abductions, no stalking."

Ben is looking at the ceiling. I continue.

"He was swift to confess. Extraordinarily co-operative. He did everything the police asked him to do and didn't waste time or dick anyone around."

"I know. It was a good thing, too." Ben turns his head and looks at me through half-closed eyes. "What's your point?"

I glance at the report in front of me. I've read it so often I practically have it memorized, but I don't want Ben to know that. "Your profile suggests a subject who is a malignant narcissist. A good mimic that could show performative empathy but didn't understand the real thing. Someone like that wouldn't have many close relationships, but nothing in Farraday's personal life matched up. He was married with a child and had friends he'd known since his childhood."

Asshole. Lying there like he's the only one who can know anything.

"Farraday didn't revel in his confession," I continue. "He didn't withhold information or drip-feed interviewers to force them to keep engaging with him. He showed no grandiosity or desire to be seen as better than everyone else. He just cried a lot."

Ben sits up. He stares at me for a few seconds, and I let the thought take hold.

Something about what I'm saying is bothering him. *Good.*

"Your profile was submitted but dismissed as incorrect and irrelevant because it didn't fit Farraday. Did you know that?"

He doesn't reply, but his silence suggests he did *not* know that. His features are impassive, but his eyes grow stormy as he digests what I'm saying.

"I think Farraday was framed." I watch Ben's face, still looking for a reaction, but he gives nothing away. "The evidence against him was inconsistent. There was no suggestion that he was a menace to society either—he took his medication and turned up for work every day. His wife was horrified, and no one who knew him ever said they'd suspected him."

"That's not unusual," Ben says. "People don't like to admit it when they've known someone for years, only to find they misjudged them and had a monster in their midst."

"You'd know, I guess."

I didn't mean to say that, but it's too late to take it back. Ben's face, already stony, seems to close up even more.

He gets to his feet and storms over to the coat hooks, snatching up my coat. He drapes it over the back of the armchair before picking up his glass again, draining the wine in one.

"Take all this to Hillard and Farraday's lawyers. It's none of my business. The right guy was caught, and I got paid. I'm sorry if he regrets it, but he doesn't deserve a pass. Six little kids aren't getting a second chance. Why should *he*?"

I'm crying again. I can't help it. Ben looks at me in confusion.

"Jesus, Roxy. Why does this *matter* so much?"

I try to reply, but my words catch in my throat.

"Find your voice. Come on."

He said that to me that night in Hawaii. Because he wanted me to cry out when he made me come.

I cough and compose myself. "Okay. Firstly, I don't want to see an innocent man suffer and more kids get murdered when I might be able to stop it. And secondly, The Dollmaker is still out there. I know it for sure."

I turn around in my chair and lift my hair, exposing the nape of my neck. My fingertips trace the raised edges of my head wound.

Ben says nothing for a moment. Then, without warning, he hurls his wine glass at the wall, shattering it into a million razor-sharp shards. If they hurt his feet as he moves toward me, he doesn't seem to care. He's beside me in an instant, his hand in my hair, the other cradling my head as his thumb touches the stitches gently.

He's tender with me, so careful, but I feel his muscles tensing. I'm reminded of the raw strength I felt when I lay next to him in his bed.

His voice is low and calm when he speaks, but the simmering rage is impossible to miss.

"Who is the soon-to-be-dead cunt who hurt you, *charodeyka*?"

"I don't know," I whisper. "But God help me, Ben—I gotta find out."

"How did you escape?" he asks. He sits next to me on the armchair, pulling me back toward him until I'm resting against his chest. His hand cups my cheek, my tears running over his fingers.

"Luck. And carelessness on my abductor's part."

"And you think it was The Dollmaker? Why?"

"Same *modus operandi*, mostly. But I'm not his usual victim type, so it's got to be for practical reasons rather than for fun. He must have planned to kill me to shut me up and keep Farraday where he is."

Ben's fingers are on my neck, and his thumb grazes my lower lip. His movements are slow, as though he doesn't realize he's doing it. His other hand holds my hip, kneading it.

"How dare he," he murmurs. "How dare that slimy piece of shit lay a finger on my girl. I swear to God, Roxy, I'll make him beg for your mercy. He'll bleed rivers under your fucking feet."

∼

Ben

I need to let go of her.

She's in no state to handle me even if I was on an even keel. And I'm not. I can feel the ropes that hold me in place whipping loose, the broken parts of my mind thrashing to get free.

Seeing Roxy hurt, knowing some bastard injured her, frightened her—it makes me want to do something terrible. But holding her like this, feeling her softness against me? It's gonna kill me.

My hands aren't interested in my nobler intentions. My arm steals around her waist, pulling her ass into my lap as my hand holds her neck gently. My cock is hard in an instant as I feel her gorgeous body against me.

Someone hit Roxy and hurt her badly enough to leave a permanent scar. No one should have had the opportunity to mark her but *me*.

I can't let her go, not now. I'm feral with rage and horny as all fuck, because my brain is wired wrong, and I'm capable of feeling both simultaneously.

I keep my eyes closed, trying to just *feel*. All I want is to lose myself in her.

"So you'll help me?"

I open my eyes to see hers, wide and pleading. I could get used to that look.

I push my thumb between her lips, feeling her tongue against it. My cock lurches in response, and I'm struck by the urge to pin her down and fuck her innocent face. That'd stop her talking.

"Yes. You're talking about a copycat, but it doesn't matter. You're in danger, and I'm not gonna stand by and—"

Roxy leaps to her feet and wheels around to face me. I notice her flushed cheeks, her peaky nipples reaching me through her shirt.

"You don't believe me?" she asks, throwing her hands in the air. "Is it impossible for you to be wrong? Because last time I checked, you nearly murdered my best friend and yours, shooting me in the process because you had the wrong information!"

She can't know that her fury is fuelling my lust for her, but it is. I stand, towering over her, and close the space between us. She steps back but doesn't realize how close she is to the wall until she bumps into it.

"Don't mess with me, Rox." She reaches out with both hands to shove me in the chest, but I snatch her wrists, pinning them to her sides. "Look at me when I'm fucking talking to you."

Roxy tilts her head up, jutting her chin at me defiantly, but I see the fear on her face. She's scared enough without me frightening her, but God help me—my cock twitches at the sight.

"You are staying with me," I say, looking into her eyes.

"No." She holds my gaze. "I'm gonna swing by work, and then I'm going home."

I raise an eyebrow. "It's not a question. We're not discussing it. I will find who hurt you and make them beg you for mercy."

"Okay, I'll stay. Now let me go."

I release her wrists and step away, turning quickly and heading into the bathroom. I splash my face with cold water.

I don't know what I'd have done if she had argued with me. My anger was already getting me fired up, but she was simultaneously enraged and terrified, and it was almost too much for my libido. A few seconds longer, a word or two of sass from her lips, and I can't be sure I wouldn't have fucked her ragged there and then.

The irregular sound of the running faucet takes me out of my head for a minute. Focusing on the changes grounds me, and I feel more in control.

I can't tell Roxy I'm obsessed with her. She has enough psychos in her life already, and I have nothing to bring to the table but my own madness and dysfunction.

When I come out of the bathroom, Roxy is nowhere to be seen. My steak is on the floor, lying in a small blood splatter.

Oh great. So she wants to play? I have many games to share with her, but she might not like them.

6

Roxy

It's dark, and I shouldn't be out alone. Insane as it may be, the danger out here seems preferable to whatever just happened.

Ben and I both know I'll go back to him. I need his protection and his help. He's already involved in this shitshow, and without him at my side, I'll probably disappear. But I don't know what scared me more— his possessive rage or my reaction to it. When he grabbed my wrists, something inside me wanted desperately to yield to him. Right then, I'd have done anything he asked me to do.

We were friends once. Then something shifted in him, and I didn't understand it.

I'm approaching Always Home's offices when I see Oliver walking out of the front door. "Hey," I say, opening the gate as he turns around.

Oliver's glasses are too big for his face, and behind them, his eyes seem wider and more owl-like than ever. "Roxy! Moira said you were out of the hospital. I didn't expect to see you today. How are you feeling?"

"I've had a headache for days," I reply as he pulls me into a hug, "but I'm used to it now."

"I raided the petty cash and sent you some flowers," he says. "I hope you liked them."

"Sure did, thank you."

"I hope you're not gonna take any more risky walks." He looks in the direction of the park. "This neighborhood is going to the dogs."

"I guess so." I look over his shoulder at the door. "So, who's still here? I see you're not locking up."

"Ali said she'd stay back tonight and try to get ahead of the big filing adventure. She's in the back office, up to her ears in forms."

That's not like Ali. She'd rather be doing sessions and group work with the kids on our caseload. The records must be a total mess.

After what happened last year, all the agencies we work with are being extra vigilant with referrals. When the case broke, there was a lot of negative press about how little was done to protect those kids. Now no one wants to be accused of not doing things by the book, and Oliver writes up the details of every single referral that is called in to us, so the paperwork piles up fast.

"She has the keys," Oliver says. "Don't hurry back to work, Roxy. You're an asset to this organization, and I want you here, but *not* at the cost of your health. Rest up and take care, okay?"

Oliver could take a massive salary, but he doesn't. He has a tiny apartment and a crappy sedan, and he likes it that way. As the operating director of the charity, he's obliged to do little except appear on the news, but he's always here, getting his hands on the actual work. Before taking the manager's position at Always Home, he raised over fifteen million dollars for charitable causes worldwide, and he's still at it, organizing sponsored bungee jumps and other crazy stuff. It's because he never knew his own parents, and he wants to give something back. Occasionally he can be a bit of a dick, expecting us to be as committed as he is, but Ali nor I are up for a tandem skydive.

"You *need* me back," I grin. "Otherwise, you have to suffer Ali's terrible coffee. Unless you fixed the machine?"

"It needs a repair guy to look at it."

"Oliver, it needs a *priest*. Have you heard the noises it makes? It sounds like it'll demand your soul for a macchiato."

Oliver laughs. "Okay, I'll deal with it. G'night, kid."

~

Ali sits on the floor, surrounded by papers and cardboard files. She has sheets of square stickers beside her, with colored circles to add to the front of the files. She looks tired and pissed off.

"Hey, what's the deal?" I ask. Her head whips around when she hears my voice.

"Back at you, Rox," she says. "What am I gonna do with you? I can't believe this happened!"

Seeing that expression of concern on her face makes my heart sink. I know it so well.

I met her in Juvie, and she kept me by her side when we left. Held me when I cried about the loss of my parents. She cared for me for years, protecting me from people who might take advantage. Even when she was pregnant with Luna, she worked and got mad at me when I took the same risks she was taking every day.

She wanted better for me. Still does.

I want to tell her the whole truth, but it's my responsibility this time, not hers. She's happy with Leo and has her own family—a family I cannot put at risk by involving them in this shitshow. Luna is only four. The Dollmaker could come for her.

Ali catches my expression. "I'm sorry," she says, getting to her feet. "I'm glad you're okay, but I'm a natural worrier. Are you back at work already?"

I take the sheaf of paper from her hand and smile. "Nah, but I'll help you out here for a minute. I just wanted to see a familiar face. Otherwise, I'm gonna be resting and doing some work on Farraday's appeal."

Ali's expression sours as she slaps red stickers onto files. "Rox, I know you think Farraday is innocent but has it ever occurred to you that you're just a sucker for the crazies? You want to see the best in someone who's, you know—not right in the head." She has the grace to look a little uncomfortable. "No one would blame you, but it could lead you astray."

I pull out a drawer and put all the files with 'A' surnames inside. "I know what you're saying, but trust me. I know enough to be certain."

"Okay," Ali shrugs. "I take it you reported what happened to the police?"

"Yeah, you might hear from them. I dunno. Anyway," I say, trying to sound casual, "Benedikt is back from his travels."

"He is?" Ali exclaims. "How do you know?"

"We...ran into each other. Actually," I avoid looking at her, "I'm gonna be spending a lot of time with him, I think."

"Oh really?" Ali can't keep the salacious tone out of her voice. "He's crazy about you. Did you know that?"

Crazy, maybe. About *me*? Possibly. But it's more complicated than that.

"He's helping me with the appeal stuff, that's all."

"Whatever you say."

I brush some dust off the top of the filing cabinet and sneeze. "Promise me you'll vacuum," I say, my voice nasal as I pinch my nose, fending off another sneeze. "I know this place is a charity, but our second-hand Dyson works fine as long as someone, you know, turns the damn thing on and moves it about."

Ali grins. "You got it. Enjoy your convalescence and get some rest between whatever else you're doing."

The archway over the park entrance never scared me before, but tonight it looks like the gaping maw of a shark. The lamps are bright enough at the threshold, but the light is lower inside the park, the shadows long.

I nope out of there and set off on the more time-consuming route. It will take me along the sidewalk and through the more built-up area but add a solid ten minutes to the journey. In my eye-line, a jogger crosses the park grass, a small dog struggling to keep up on stumpy legs.

I hold my counseling appointments here quite often. I've found it's less intimidating for the kids than the classic claustrophobic office setting. We sometimes sit and have ice cream on the swing set, talking things over.

I feel a surge of anger.

I refuse to let the fucking Dollmaker frighten me away from the park I love. The bastard doesn't have that power over me.

I take my keys from my purse and arrange them between my fingers, a jagged edge sticking out between each knuckle. Feeling more confident, I pass under the arch and along the path to the south exit, closest to my apartment.

The breeze has picked up to a gale, and I regret my choice of outerwear - a leather jacket and scarf weren't too bad in the daytime, but now I'm struggling to prevent the cold from biting at my limbs. I wrap my coat around me and bundle my scarf, trying to get it to cover my ears before I remember that I need to be listening for trouble.

The path drops away down a small hill, and as I descend into the sheltered spot, the wind drops too.

Then I see it. A rustle in the bushes to my right.

It's a dog. It's a dog or a bird or a cat or a rat...okay. Get it together, Dr. Seuss.

I squeeze my fist around my keys as I pass the line of shrubs. Nothing happens.

Picking up the pace now. I can see the exit I want, just a couple of hundred yards away.

A hand on my arm, hot breath in my ear.

"Boo."

I turn quickly, punching my assailant in the thigh with the keys. There's a sickening wet sound as his skin breaks, and I let go, leaving the keys embedded in his flesh. He releases my arm, and I realize who it is.

Ben is looking at his leg, frowning. He grabs the keys and pulls them out.

"Why did you do that?" I cry. "I just got through telling you I was abducted, and you decided to follow me and pull a stunt like that?"

"I told you—you're staying with me." He tosses me the bloody keys, and I catch them. "*You* came to *me* looking for help, remember. You don't get to decide what that looks like."

He gets to his feet and stands in front of me. He places his fingertip under my chin and lifts it so I have to look at him.

Ben

My blood is up for all the wrong reasons. Stalking Roxy through the park was a fucking stupid thing to do, especially given what she told me, but I wanted to scare her. I wanted to see it on her face, in her eyes, so I could drink it in.

But as I look at her now, I can see something else. Something *more*.

Back at my apartment, when I touched her head injury, she seemed to quicken rather than shrink away, and the next thing I knew, she was in my arms. She pulled away quickly, but not before something undeniable had passed between us.

When I grabbed her just now, her fight-or-flight mechanism kicked in, and she lashed out hard. Now she looks confused, angry, and frightened all at once, but I'm sure she's as hot for me as I am for her. Something about me makes her want to run, but that same thing stops her from pushing me away.

"I admire your spirit, *charodeyka*, but you better get this through your head." My gaze drops to her lips and throat before snapping back to her eyes again. "Believe me when I say that I'm not your sanctuary. Fuck around with me and see how safe you feel. I don't have the strength to resist now that you've hurled yourself into my life again, so don't blame me if you don't like what you get."

This is so fucked up.

Roxy has experienced tremendous trauma and is afraid for her life. She came to *me* for help. I want to protect her from anything and everything that could hurt her, but only so I can own her fear and feed myself on it.

She's terrified of me, I can feel it, and it turns me on to a degree that is absolutely fucking obscene. Her sweet, kind nature makes it all the better. It's all part of my unique blend of psychological traits, and it's not healthy.

In Hawaii, I found out she was a virgin, and it totally threw me—enough to prevent myself from fucking her and claiming her as mine. I told myself I didn't want her to waste her first time on me. But the truth is, I want to be her first *everything*. I'm too selfish a person to throw away a second chance.

I hold her chin firmly and pull her closer. She doesn't fight. She's limp in my grip, eyes wide and fixed on mine.

Oh, sweet Jesus. This girl wants *whatever* I have to give. She has no idea what that would entail, but she's in my thrall.

"Nothing to say?" I murmur.

"I told you I wanted you," Roxy whispers. "Nothing has changed. I don't care if you hurt me. I've been hurt so many times, I barely feel it anymore."

That pulls at me. I want to find everyone who has ever offended her and throttle the life out of them. The thought brings a surge of fresh fury.

I slide my hand over her mouth, my fingertips digging into her cheek as my thumb presses her cheekbone. She could fight me, but she doesn't.

Not now. Not here.

I push her face away, and she stumbles backward a little. We stare at each other for a moment.

"Where were you going?" I ask.

Roxy is panting slightly. She swallows hard, trying to steady herself. "My apartment is just over there," she tilts her head. "I need to get my stuff, and I want my own car. "

"So let's go. You can park it at mine."

The path we're walking on is dotted with pools of light from the lamps. It's pretty, but the visibility is poor.

"So, is this where it happened?" I ask as we reach the exit.

Roxy shakes her head. "It was on the other side, near the park entrance. I was walking and never heard a thing. He tried to chloroform me, but it didn't work, and that's when he hit me."

Roxy's attacker fucked up with his administration of chloroform. He didn't realize it wouldn't induce unconsciousness, so he had to hit her to knock her out.

Typically for a copycat, he had the method correct but not the detail. He may not have been a copycat anyway. It could be a coincidence.

If I've learned anything in dealing with people, it's that our species' natural tendency to look for patterns can and will lead us into trouble. Happenstance has a sense of humor, which is why it's not true that there's no smoke without fire. There's always smoke, but when you look closer, often the only thing getting burnt is *you*.

It's not right, somehow. There's a haze in front of the data like I'm trying to see it through a fogged-up window.

The quiet voice of doubt speaks up.

Or Roxy could be right, it mutters. *Maybe Farraday isn't The Dollmaker, and something very fucked up is happening.*

7

Roxy

We're back at Ben's place within the hour. We didn't say much while we were at my apartment, but he wouldn't let me carry my own bag. When we headed back, he made me drive in front of him.

He stands at the balcony door, watching the night. He has his back to me, the muscles corded and tight. He rolls his right shoulder every now and then, and I wonder if it hurts him.

I remember him getting this way when he visited me in the hospital after he shot me. He would stop talking and stare out the window as though burdened with something. Never let me in, never allowing any weakness to show. Stoic, aloof, and still as a monument.

I have to say something.

"Ben, I—"

"No more bullshit, Roxy." His voice is stern as he looks over his shoulder at me. "This is not your opportunity to be cute with me. You're lucky to be alive as it is. If you make me angry, you're gonna distract me, and I need to concentrate on the problem at hand."

His expression is stony, but I see his eyes soften as he looks at me.

"You think I'm cute?" I ask.

"Yes. That's only part of the problem." He sighs as he steps away from the window.

"Problem? Ali says you're crazy about me. Don't pretend it's not true."

Ben sits on the couch beside me and stretches out, putting his feet on the coffee table.

"Okay. Let me make something crystal clear to you," he says. He palms his hair, running his fingers through it. "I *am* crazy about you. But there's nothing cute about it."

He's not looking at me. I wonder whether I should respond, but I decide to let the silence do its job.

Ben continues. "I'm useful to the Bratva because of the way I think. I can narrow the field and identify our enemies. Get the job done. And when someone needs persuading, I'm excellent at figuring out how to hit them the hardest."

"What does that have to do with me? With us?"

Ben turns his head slightly, giving me his cornflower-blue gaze. "My mind doesn't work like most people's. I'm good at manipulation. I do it for work but also because I *like* it. I enjoy the power it gives me. You're young and inexperienced. You'll bring out the worst in me, and I'll hurt you just for kicks."

"Your self-awareness does you credit," I say, dropping my head onto the back of the couch, "but you're not unique. There's some Machiavellianism in us all."

He smiles at me. "You pay attention in your forensic psych classes, don't you? So, let's pretend I'm your teacher."

Oh my God. I didn't know how much that concept would appeal to me until he said those words.

I sit up cross legged and face him, regretting the choice of posture immediately. If my pussy soaks through my pants, he'll see. I pull my knees up instead, wrapping my arms around them.

"Okay, I'm listening. Teach me."

The words sound a little breathy, and Ben gives me a lopsided grin of satisfaction.

Dammit. He knows he's turning me on already, and he's barely said a word. He turns to face me, moving closer as he does so.

"Impress me with your insight, *charodeyka*," he says. "How do we understand other people's motives and desires, even when we haven't met them?"

"A person's behavior always leaves an impression. We can take that impression and trace it back to the source."

He leans forward, his eyes sparkling in the low light. "Yes, but *how*? Think hard now."

Vicious Hearts 73

I'm grappling for an answer. It's not that I don't know—I've spent hours with criminology textbooks. But Ben's attention is so singular, so all-encompassing. It's like I'm hypnotized, unable to grasp my thoughts because he has a hold on my mind.

"Empathy," I say.

He moves nearer still, and I shift back into my cross-legged position. I can smell my own arousal and hope I'm imagining it.

"Good girl. You're quite right."

Oh shit, don't call me that.

"I can feel empathy, I think, but I can switch it off if it's getting in my way," he says. "Don't get me wrong. I'm capable of caring, sometimes *too* much, and definitely not in a healthy way. What would you call that?"

"Psychopathy," I reply. "Maybe an insecure attachment style."

"Precisely." Ben nods. "No one ever cared to diagnose me formally, but I'm not wired up right. With my affection, there's all, or there's nothing. I veer between the two, and it makes me a fucking nightmare to be with."

He's trying to tell me he's bad news. God knows what's wrong with me, but every word he says drags me deeper.

I catch the scent I remember from Hawaii. When did he apply it? He wasn't wearing it earlier.

This is what he's talking about. *Manipulation*. Olfactory memories are strong—he knew his aftershave would jostle my memory and invoke the hot, dreamy atmosphere of that night in his beach house.

Ben's gaze drops to my lips, my neck, my cleavage. My skin heats up at his attention.

"I *see* you, Roxy." He reaches for me, his fingertip trailing from my cheek to the hollow of my collarbone. I shudder at his touch, my nerves over-sensitive. "You're scared of me, but you fucking love it. So do I. I've never seen anything hotter in my life."

I should say something, but I don't wanna break the spell. His intensity is mesmerizing.

"Not my fault if you wanna learn the hard way," he says, his voice low. "You want me to teach you? Give you an education?"

I nod.

Without warning, his hand wraps my throat, and I gasp. It's such a sudden escalation that I freeze, unable to respond. He bares his teeth at me, a low moan escaping him.

"Fuck, I wanna ruin you," he murmurs. "Pleasure you until you're delirious, cover you in spit and blood and come until you're as low and debased as you can get. Do you think you can handle that, Rox? Because the thought has obsessed me since the moment we fucking *met*."

He leans close and licks the corner of my mouth, his breath hot on my cheek.

I can't speak. Ben's grip on my neck is tightening, his fingertips pinching the sinew. I should fight him, hit him, *anything*, but instead, I reach into the waistband of my pants. My clit is chafing against the seam, desperately in need of attention.

He isn't the gentleman lover of my naive teen dreams. He's not gonna hold my fucking hand. No poetry, no flowers. I saw a glimpse of it in Hawaii— something raw, elemental, and rough.

Benedikt Voratov wants to take me apart, body and soul.

The intercom buzzer slices shrilly through the atmosphere, snapping us back to reality.

I withdraw my hand, and Ben lets go of me, sliding off the couch and picking up the handset.

"Hang on," he says. He replaces the handset and opens the apartment door, heading downstairs.

I sit motionless. My neck throbs painfully where Ben's fingertips pressed into me, but my pussy throbs even more.

After what happened in Hawaii, I felt humiliated— even more so when he didn't come back, and I couldn't talk to him about it. I dated one guy, but couldn't hold a candle to Ben, and I didn't even contemplate having sex with him. I *did* spend a lot of time with my dildo, trying to fantasize about anything and anyone but Ben.

It was useless. I couldn't come without imagining Ben touching me, fucking me. I couldn't keep from wondering what *his* kind of rough might be, and just like that, all my masturbatory thoughts switched from sweet lovemaking to dirty, nasty sex. But only with *him*.

I didn't travel to Europe as I planned. Instead, I signed up for extra studies, telling myself *that's* why I was staying.

Not waiting for Ben. *Not* hoping he'd come back for me.

But now he's here, and he *does* want me. He always did. But his desire is made of something filthy and base and primal. He doesn't *just* want to fuck me. He wants to devour me, subsume me. And I want him to do it.

Ben reappears with two paper grocery sacks.

"I forgot to tell you—I ordered takeout. You still love seafood?"

I smile. "Only if you have cold white wine to go with it."

He pulls a bottle of Chardonnay from one of the bags, condensation beading the glass. "I remember someone telling me this was good with lobster."

⁓

Ben

"I haven't eaten a meal since just before I got out of the hospital," Roxy says, tipping fries onto her plate. "If I'm lucky, I'll have dropped a few pounds."

I frown. "What? Why?"

"Because I haven't been eating."

"No, why would you want to lose weight?"

Roxy pinches a roll of flesh at her waistline. "I have it to spare. My body seems to be preparing for a famine. When Ali and I were poor and lived on instant ramen, she got skinny, but I stayed chubby."

I'm aghast. Doesn't she understand that her thick thighs and rounded little stomach are driving me fucking batshit crazy?

Objectively, I can see why Roxy might envy her friend. Ali's gorgeous, a lithe, lean beauty, but she doesn't do it for *me*. No one held my attention since I set eyes on Roxy.

When I first met her, we were in adjacent rooms in the hospital. I wasn't staying—I was resting after getting the bullet removed from my shoulder. But I knew she was in a pretty bad way, and it was my fault, so I decided to apologize.

She was weak from blood loss and the anesthetic, but that didn't dull her shine. She was still radiant.

When I introduced myself, she laughed.

"You shot me!" she exclaimed. "Because of you, I missed the whole drama!"

I told her I didn't mean to do it.

"I know," she said. "It's over now."

I was bowled over. This bright, sunny girl, smiling, despite her horrible experience. Prepared to forgive, willing to forget, just like that.

I talked about my part in it. How I'd thought I could be Pakhan. My willingness to fuck over my closest friend and kill his woman, and how that willingness evaporated when I realized I'd been duped.

I found Roxy easy to talk to, but that's because she mostly listened.

When she got out of the hospital, and I saw her around, it didn't feel the same. I regretted telling her so much about myself. Combined with my attraction to her, it was as though she had taken something from me, even though I'd given it of my own accord.

"You look furious," Roxy says. "What did I do wrong?"

"Don't talk yourself down, Rox." I top up her wine glass. "If the delivery guy hadn't shown up, I'd have fucked you so hard that your ass would have left a permanent dent in my couch."

"That's sweet. I think."

I enjoy her blushes. What a delightful contradiction she is. How she stayed a virgin for this long, I have no idea.

Roxy puts down her fork and sighs. She rubs her eyes with her fists like a child.

"I'm so tired, Ben. I feel dirty, and I ache all over."

I stand and reach my hand to her. "As luck would have it, I have a bathtub. A huge one with claw feet. It looks like it belongs in an enchanted castle."

She starts laughing. "Why?" she asks, taking my hand. "What the hell is that doing here?"

"It was here when I moved in." I pull her to her feet. "I kinda like it, so I never had it removed."

"I love the idea of you sitting in the tub with a glass of wine and your loofah."

I grin. "Don't fucking tell anyone. You'll ruin my reputation. It's between you, me, and Mr. Quackers."

"You don't *really* have a rubber duckie, do you?" she asks, bursting into fresh giggles.

"Nah, I was kidding. But if I did, that's what I'd call it." I kiss the back of her hand and turn away, heading for the bathroom. "How hot do you like it?"

She smiles. "Bordering on scalding, if you please."

I arch an eyebrow. "Dangerous. I like it."

∽

It's gonna happen tonight. I know it.

I have to at least fucking *try* to keep myself in check for now. Roxy needs to unwind. It's not just the fear and confusion of her predicament—it's *me*. I'm getting to her. So as much as I want to join her in the bath, I'm gonna leave her be.

I take a giant slug of the wine and put the glass down on the table. In the drawer below the tabletop is the case file. Two cardboard covers, and between them, as much evil as you could hope never to see. Statements, transcripts, photos, psych and pathology reports, the works. Hillard turned it all over to me when I got involved.

I always keep things. You never know when it'll come in useful.

I open the cover and see Simon Farraday. A man with a powerful jaw, a receding hairline, and strangely, kind eyes. The same mugshot was printed in every newspaper up and down the country.

Roxy believes this man is innocent, with the zealotry and fervor of a true idealist. I admire her for that. I never believed in much except myself and my own interests.

Hillard's signature is at the bottom of Farraday's confession. He signed off every page because he ran every interview. He didn't want his men to suffer through it if they didn't have to.

I had my share of run-ins with the cops over the years, but most of them were either on the Bratva payroll or I had something on them that ensured they'd stay out of my business. Hillard is a different kind, though. He tolerated the mob influence that corrodes his city and poisons his precinct, but he wouldn't partake. Then I got involved in his most important case and brought the Bratva into his business. A shame for an honest cop who'd stayed clean for years.

The Bratva community keeps me on the fringes because I was involved in a coup against a Pakhan. I tried to take a violent shortcut to seize power that wasn't mine. And although I backtracked when I discovered I'd been lied to, my actions have marked me.

Despite my usefulness, I doubt I'll find a way back to the world I called home for so long. But I wonder—if I'd known I'd be pushed out regardless, would I still have helped Leo and Ali? Or would I have done whatever the fuck served me best? I could have killed them and taken over from Paval Gurin, just like the old bastard promised me.

No. I have my limits, and killing innocent people is beyond the pale. That's why it mattered to me to see The Dollmaker put away.

An idea occurs to me.

What would it be worth to the *kommissiya* if it turned out that Hillard's most significant case *was* a complete fuck-up? He'd be fired, and they could use their leverage to get someone better in his post—someone who *wanted* to play nicely with the Bratva. I'd get some appreciation for *that*.

I still think the man who attacked Roxy is a copycat. But you never know.

I flick through the file, my eyes moving over things. Words. Names. Faces, some of the living and some of the dead.

The photos are the worst. The bodies are just lifeless mannequins, there to serve a need. No vitality, no presence, just shells. That's why they call him The Dollmaker.

Of the six children killed, only the third body was identified. He came from a very respectable family, but the others were street kids. The media went crazy over it, but despite an intensive police effort and a public campaign, none of them were named.

When Farraday was arrested, he said he'd picked them up off the streets—just plucked them, like he was picking grapes. It seems he was good at spotting the right kind of victim, and it burns me to think that they died afraid and alone, with no one looking for them.

I remember the father of the third victim. The wife told Hillard her husband was at a meeting at the time of her son's abduction, and the alibi was sound. But I hated that fucker as soon as I set eyes on him.

When I was doing my background check on the case, I went to see the parents. The mother kept saying I had to talk to her husband, but he was dismissive when I finally got hold of him. He kept saying his son would still be alive if he had not been playing in the street when he was meant to be in his room. I seethed to hear him callously blame his dead son for his own murder, as though the poor kid deserved it somehow.

Bad shit happens to bad people too. Victims are not saints, and neither are the bereaved. They're just people with their traits and peculiar ways of responding to grief.

Fate rarely gives you your dues. The truth is that we're all riding the sharp edge of dumb luck every day. No one deserves to die, and no one deserves to live—the universe is indifferent. Why do we strive to believe otherwise?

A sound from the bathroom reaches into my thoughts, and I close the file. I tilt my head and listen.

Roxy is sobbing. A weary, heartsore whimper, punctuated by sniffing as she tries to hold herself together.

I go to the bathroom door and knock.

8

Roxy

My fingertips brush against my stitches. The wound is closed and healing well, but it's still a little bit tender.

A knock on the door. "Rox? You're crying. What's wrong?"

He'll think I'm an idiot. It sounds so fucking stupid.

I try to swallow my sobs and level my voice, but when I speak, my voice cracks.

"I can't wash my hair. I can't see what I'm doing and I'm afraid to touch my head."

The handle squeals as it turns. I gather the bubbles in my arms, piling a wall of foam in front of me, and duck low in the water. Ben's face appears round the doorframe.

"Why knock if you're just going to walk in?" I ask. I wrap my arms around myself, covering my breasts.

"I'll wash your hair for you."

It's not a question, and he doesn't wait for an answer. Instead, he picks up a glass from the basin edge and takes out his toothbrush, setting it down. I watch as he walks around the bath, rolling up his sleeves as he goes, and then he's behind me, out of sight.

"I don't need you to–"

"Shh, *charodeyka*." His hands are on my shoulders, kneading them. "You've had a fucking shitty few days. Be a good girl, and let me help you."

The knots in my muscles melt away under his touch. The same hands that gripped my throat are now loosening the tension, moving firmly over the sore spots. I sigh and lean back on his chest.

"Why do you want me?" I whisper.

"Because you're an angel," he says. His hand steals into the water, and he finds my nipple, pinching it gently. "Every woman I ever knew had a hard, cruel edge to her, but that's because the Bratva made them that way. You're not from that world. You're tough but not cold, and you have faith in people." He pauses, removing his hand from the water and picking up a bottle of shampoo. "And you're *so* fucking hot. I mean, what sort of a question was that anyway?"

I want him. So what if he's no good? I thought I *had* love and safety once, only for them to be ripped away. I'm not holding out for that again. He'll leave, and he'll let me down, but for now, he's here.

I smile as Ben tips the warm water over my hair. He puts his palm on my forehead as though he's checking my temperature, pulling my head back gently, so suds don't sting my eyes as he works the shampoo through the strands. He massages my scalp, careful to avoid the tender area, and rinses the lather away.

"You tell me what you need, Rox," he says, "and I will make sure you have it."

A thought occurs to me. *Shit*. It's been a while since I shaved...well, anywhere. I keep my underarms smooth, but my legs are fuzzy. And my bikini line? The less said, the better.

Ben stands up and picks up a large towel from the rail. He holds it by its corners.

"Out."

I frown. "Ben, I'm not gonna get out of the bath with you in here–"

"Roxy." His expression darkens. "The only reason you're not full of my come right now is that I was considerate enough to get you some food. You wanted a bath, and you got one. Now it's my turn to get something *I* want, and you know what it is. Do you think I can concentrate for a fucking *second* otherwise?"

The light reflects in his eyes like two tiny stars. His gaze is unwavering, intense.

I stand, the water running off my skin. The chill air hits me, and I try to cover myself with my hands.

"I'm sorry," I say, cupping my mound. "I'm not exactly presentable."

Ben's eyes scan my body. "You're beautiful. But you're not *comfortable*. Hang on."

He passes me the towel, and I wrap it around my body, grateful I'm covered. I try to step out of the bath, but he raises a hand and stops me.

"Stay there. I'm gonna shave you."

I clap my hand over my mouth in shock, nearly dropping my towel. "Oh *no*. Ben, that's so–"

"What?" He has a can of shaving foam in one hand and a cut-throat razor in the other. He flicks his wrist, and the silver blade appears. "I'm good with this, I promise. I've never cut anyone unless I meant to do it."

He sits on the rim of the bath and swings to face me, his feet in the water. His face is level with my pussy, still covered by the towel.

"Put one foot up here," he taps the rim beside him, "and hold that towel out of the way."

"I feel so stupid. I can't."

"Come on." His voice is soft and coaxing. "You want to be a good girl for me, don't you?"

His hand slips beneath the towel, warm on my thigh. He lifts my leg, and I settle my foot in a good position. I hold the towel out of the way and close my eyes, shy of his scrutiny as he takes a good look at me.

I hear the sound of the shaving foam can as he piles the foam into his palm. Then it's cold against my skin as he smooths it where he needs it.

I open my eyes, looking down at him. He's concentrating on what he's doing, using his thumb to hold the skin taut. He swipes the razor through the hair on my mound, and I feel the coldness of the blade against my newly-exposed skin.

"Stay still," Ben says. I feel his breath against my pussy lips. "You don't need to do anything. I'll move you where I need to."

I tense my legs, trying to stop them from shaking. He chuckles and kisses my inner thigh.

I'm getting wet. Ben might not be able to tell because I'm soaked from the bath, but I can *feel* it. His fingertips flex against my skin as he maneuvers the razor, removing the fuzz and leaving me smooth and super-sensitive.

"I intend to bury my face here before the night is through," he murmurs, "so I'm gonna shave you *very* close. Do you trust me?"

"Yes."

"Good girl. You're doing so well."

My pussy gives a little involuntary pulse deep inside. It's *so* hot when he talks to me like that.

He uses two fingers to gently part my pussy lips so he can pass the sharp edge over my most intimate places. He laughs as he dips the blade in the bathwater to rinse it off.

"Your pussy tells it like it is, *charodeyka*. You're glistening like a jewel." He grazes my clit lightly with his tongue. "Let me get done here. I wanna feel you come on my tongue more than I wanna fucking breathe."

I'm warm and comfortable, the pillows under my head.

Ben settles beside me. He's shirtless and wearing pajama pants, just like he was that night in Hawaii.

Usually, I'd be more abashed about my nakedness, but we're beyond that now. He touched me so carefully, exposing places no one else had ever seen. There's nothing more to say, nowhere to hide.

Dangerous, harsh, tender, intimate. Ben is all these things at once. He confuses me, but I want him. There's no getting away from it.

My nipples are large, and when they're stiff, like right now, I swear I could hang my coat on them. Ben rolls one between his thumb and forefinger, teasing a moan from my lips.

"Try to understand, Rox." Ben doesn't smile as he fixes his eyes on mine. "I want you too much. It's why I wouldn't do this before, why I kept my distance." He touches his fingertip to each bruise on my neck. Bruises made by his hand. "I don't usually fuck people I care about because I might hurt them. And I care about *you* to the point where I had to put entire continents between us to ensure I stayed away."

"I don't care if you *do* hurt me," I whisper. "All I want is you. I never wanted anyone else. I tried to get over you, I really did, but no one else I dated could ever take your place."

He lowers his face to mine, touching his lips to my ear. He kisses me, his tongue reaching for mine as he lowers his weight onto me, his cock digging into my thigh.

Then he stops, pushing back onto his hands to look at me.

"Rox, did you fuck anyone?"

His tone jars me out of my reverie, and I furrow my brow, confused at his sudden coldness.

"No. I mean, I had opportunities, but it didn't happen."

He scowls, and a surge of fury strikes me.

"You have no right to be angry." I push at his chest, but he doesn't move. "I offered myself to you, and you turned me down, threw me out, and disappeared for months. Was I supposed to take that some other way?"

"So?" Ben's eyes blaze with jealousy. "I'm still fucking furious that you even *considered* letting anyone else touch you."

His possessiveness is so unreasonable. But although he's frightening me, there's no arguing with my pussy as my wetness soaks into his sweatpants.

"You nasty girl," he murmurs. "You like making me angry, don't you?"

"Yeah. Ever since you got mad at me and threw me out, I've thought about it so many times." I shudder as he moves, shifting so his erection grinds against my sex.

"Ever made yourself come while you think of me?" he asks.

"Oh God, yes." I reach up and wind my hands through his hair. "Every time I touched myself, I imagined you fucking me."

He lowers his face to my neck, kissing the sore places. "Good. Because every time I jerk off, it's to thoughts of you. You were mine from the second I set eyes on you, and anyone who doubts it can fucking take it up with me if they dare." His lips enclose my nipple, sucking gently. "That includes you, by the way," he says as he pulls away. "I'm not just gonna be your first, Rox. I'll be your *last*, too. After tonight, there won't be an inch of your body you can call your own."

I'm not stupid. I know that's obscenely controlling of him. But he doesn't give a shit how crazy he seems to me. He's obsessed with me and doesn't care what I think. It just *is*.

Ben is moving down my body, running his tongue toward my navel. He dips into it, and I jump. His hands grip my thighs, pulling them wide as he settles on his front, his face inches from my sex.

"*Sladkiy Iisus*, Roxy. Such a pretty little *devstvennik* pussy." He touches my smooth outer lips, parting them with his fingers. "I can see everything. So wet and pink. I wanna know—when you make yourself come, what do you do?"

I swallow hard. I'm so turned on that I can't think straight. All I want is for him to eat my pussy until I come so hard he almost drowns.

"I...I use my fingers. And I have a...a..."

"A what? Tell me. I love toys." Ben presses the pad of his thumb on my clit, moving it in tiny circles, and I moan, arching my hips. He puts his other hand on my abdomen and shoves me flat on my back again. "Tell me what you did while you thought about me. I wanna hear your pretty voice say it."

I draw a deep breath.

"I fucked myself with my dildo and wished it was your cock."

Ben grabs my thighs with a snarl of satisfaction, his grip vice-like. I squeal as he buries his face in my pussy, his tongue delving inside me. He rubs his nose on my clit, and bolts of pleasure zing through my core.

It's as though he's devouring me. He takes my clit between his lips, sucking it softly at first before stepping up the pressure. He snarls and bites the soft flesh of my thigh hard enough to make me scream.

He moves away, sitting up on his knees. My wetness shines on his face. He kicks off his sweats and kneels between my parted thighs, hard cock in hand.

I wondered whether I'd made him bigger in my imagination or my memory was faulty, but no. It really is that big.

Ben uses his other hand to gather my wetness, rubbing it onto his cock. He strokes himself idly, sighing as he massages my pussy juice over my stomach and breasts.

"I take it I can come where I want?" he asks.

"I'm safe," I reply.

"Good. Because you're gonna be a fucking mess when I'm done with you." He touches my lips with his wet fingertips. "Here. Taste how slutty you are."

His fingers invade my mouth. They're lubricated with my arousal, slipping easily over my tongue. I gag as he moves his fingers deeper, coating them in thick saliva. He withdraws and smears my spit all over my face.

What do you want, baby?" He rubs the head of his cock against my clit, making me gasp. "Ask me nicely, *charodeyka*. Come on."

I don't know what I want. My pussy aches with longing, but I don't want this to end.

Ben seems to read my mind, laughing as he pulls me closer. He works my clit gently with his thumb again, and my pussy responds with a gush of lubrication. The smooth head of his cock eases into me, slick against my wetness as he stretches me.

"Last chance to stop me." His voice is heavy with tension. "Because once I'm inside you, I can't promise I'll be gentle."

I'm beside myself. I don't give a shit what he does as long as his cock is in me while he does it.

"Just take me," I say, shuffling my hips as I try to move him deeper. He runs his hand over my body and reaches for my hair, taking a handful in his fist. He holds me in place so he can look at my face.

"Eyes on me."

I fix my gaze on him as he eases his cock into me, his thumb still massaging my clit. I grit my teeth and exhale slowly, relaxing to take him. My clinging pussy gives way to his hardness, and he clenches his jaw, his mouth falling open as he rests his hips on mine.

"So fucking tight." He shifts a little, opening me up, and I gasp against his shoulder. Despite my readiness, it's a stretch to take him, but his small movements are helping me to relax. The sting gives way to a deep, languorous pleasure that makes me feel warm all over.

Ben is still looking into my eyes. He lets go of my hair and puts his hands on either side of me, propping himself up so he can see me properly.

"Touch yourself while I fuck you," he murmurs. "Come on my cock, like the good girl you are."

I reach between my legs and find my clit, sighing as he pulls out of me. He growls and grips my thighs, pushing them wider apart, and thrusts back inside me hard, making me cry out.

"Am I hurting you?" His hand wraps my throat again, and he leans his weight onto me, pinning me down. I nod as best I can, and he leans close to my ear as he bottoms out in my pussy again. "Good. I know you like it. You want to be my fucktoy, don't you? If you want me to stop, prove it. Take your hand off your pussy."

He *is* hurting me, but there's no way I'm gonna do anything to stop him. The pressure on my neck is a lot, but it's nothing compared to the incredible sense of fullness as he surges in and out of me. The sensation starts to build deep in my core, and I work my clit harder, chasing my climax.

Ben isn't being gentle, not anymore. His hips smash into mine as he fucks me, his grip on my neck ever tighter. I open my mouth to scream as I come, and he shoves his fingers inside, cutting off the sound. My pussy spasms, and I writhe on his cock, biting his knuckles as pleasure smashes through my body.

Ben snatches his hand from my mouth and lets go of my neck, grabbing my legs with both hands. He holds me still as he unloads into me, his come flowing into the crack of my ass.

9

Ben

I pull free of Roxy and stand up, turning my hand to examine it in the light. My knuckles are bleeding from where she sank her teeth into me.

"That'll probably scar," she murmurs.

She looks gorgeous. Naked and a fucking filthy mess, just like I dreamed. Her face is smeared with saliva and perspiration and her own wetness. My come is pooling beneath her ass, and I notice new bruises blooming on her throat.

I know it's wrong, but I love it. It will remind everyone, including her, that she's spoken for.

I fucked her, came inside her, and marked her. She's *mine*. I tried to keep away, but it was meant to happen.

I didn't lie when I said I cared about her. Otherwise, I would have fucked her back in Hawaii and not given a damn. But my obsession with her isn't the good thing she thinks it is.

Sure, the girl is a freak. I gave her a taste of the rough stuff, and she fucking loved it. But I can get a lot rougher in more ways than one. I have a read on her, and I suspect she's a romantic at heart, one who might convince herself she can let me have my way for a while and then smooth me out, get the wedding ring, and all that shit.

Best not to dwell on what happens when she realizes the truth.

Roxy sits up, looking dazed, and I smile.

"You good, *charodeyka*?"

"Yep." She rubs her face and grimaces. "Ew. I'm disgusting. I was all clean too, and look what you did!" She crosses her legs and blushes.

"I like you better dirty," I say. Something about her sudden coyness is getting me going all over again. "You can get clean later. I wanna make you come on my tongue like I said I would."

She stands up. "But I'm all full of your—"

"I know." I lie flat on the bed. "Sit."

She frowns. "I don't understand."

I tap my chin. "Right here. Your come, my come—I don't care, I'll eat it all."

Roxy doesn't move.

"I'm too heavy," she says. "What if—"

"You're not too fucking *anything*," I say. I grin at her. "If I die, I'll die happy. Just do me a favor and tell people the truth. It'd be too good a story to waste." Roxy giggles and I raise my eyebrows at her. "Now sit facing my feet and keep your balance."

She assumes the position, and my cock thickens as I take in the view. Her fleshy ass feels fantastic in my hands as she settles her knees on either side of my head, her dripping pussy inches from my face.

I shift one hand, gathering some of my come from her thigh, and massage it into her asshole. She jumps and I laugh, spanking her lightly.

"*All* your holes are mine," I say, teasing her tight rosebud. "I will fuck the hell out of this, too, but not now."

I dip my tongue into her pussy, tasting our mixed fluids on my tongue. She's sullied now, and it's fucking *beautiful*. Her clit is slick and smooth between my lips as I suck it gently.

"Ohhh, Ben," Roxy says, leaning forward and gripping my thighs. Her fingertips dig into me, and she quivers as I do my thing. "I'm too sensitive."

"No, you're not," I murmur against her. "Hang on and push past it, *charodeyka*. Be a good girl, and trust me now."

Fuck, she feels good. Her luscious curves all around me, hot pussy spasming around my tongue. My cock is growing hard again already.

She's losing herself now, grinding her hips as she rides my face. I push two fingers into her, enjoying the feel of my come lubricating her newly-fucked little hole. She flexes her spine, opening herself up to me, and I keep up the pressure while I work her clit. My fingers press the spongy spot inside her, and she groans.

"I don't know how you're doing this," she says.

"Skill," I say, pausing to lash my tongue over her clit. "And remember—I've dreamed of doing this to you, Rox. You feel better than I could ever have imagined."

She's coming. I don't know what tipped her over the edge, but it doesn't matter. Her pussy gushes over my fingers and onto my face, and I pull my hand away so I can grab her ass and hold her still. She shrieks as I move my lips over her clit, pushing her through and past her climax until she's a shivering wreck.

Roxy rolls onto her back beside me, her blonde hair streaked with sweat and tangled beneath her head. She's breathing heavily, her eyes closed.

I get to my knees. My cock is painfully hard again, and I want to come all over her pretty face.

"You wanna be my good little slut?" I ask.

Roxy opens her eyes. "I can't take any more, Ben," she whispers. "I need a break."

I grasp my cock in one hand, a handful of her hair in the other. "Look at me," I say, pumping my hand. "I'm gonna mess up your beautiful face so every time I look at you, I can remember what you looked like when I ruined you."

She smiles at me and opens her mouth. I rub the head of my cock against her tongue as I stroke myself.

Holy shit. I thought it would take longer, but my climax is already hurtling toward me. I yank her hair, pulling her head back and exposing her neck. The bruises are purplish, her pulse moving beneath them.

The sight pushes me past the point of no return. I snarl as I release onto Roxy's face and neck, thick ropes of come catching in her eyelashes and running over her marked throat.

I lower my face to hers, and before she can react, I whip my tongue over her from collarbone to chin, picking up my come as I go. Taking her slick cheeks in my hand, I kiss her hard, pushing my release into her mouth as her lips crush against mine.

∽

For the second time this evening, I wash Roxy's hair. The shower feels good, sluicing away all the filth we made.

Except it could never truly be gone. Even if she washes off every atom of me, it changes nothing. She belongs to me now, and I'm gonna see that everyone knows it.

We get dry and settle in bed, her head on my shoulder.

"So, who's the guy?" I ask.

Roxy nuzzles sleepily into my chest. "What?"

"The guy you dated." I try to keep it light, but I can't suppress the razor-sharp edge to my voice. "I need to know. Some disgruntled ex might be behind all this bullshit."

"You think I was dating The Dollmaker? No, you don't," she sits up, pulling the sheet around her, "but you *do* still think I'm wrong and that someone is just fucking with me."

"Get mad. I don't fucking care. Who is it?"

She glares at me. "You only want to know because you're jealous. You don't think he's a threat to me at all."

"Not anymore, he isn't. If he gets in your face or mine, I won't hesitate to fuck him up."

Her face softens. "Look, he's not someone you need to worry about. We went out a few times, it was weird, and then we had a huge bust-up. Now we avoid each other. He hasn't got a role in all this, so keep him out of it, okay?"

Roxy lies down beside me and closes her eyes. I watch her for a moment, thinking about pressing the matter but decide to drop it for now.

I'll get the information I want anyway. That's what I do. And I'll make up my mind about whether he's relevant after I've ensured the fucker knows his place.

~

Roxy

I got the message at eight a.m. I don't want to explain this to Ben until it's over because I don't know what it's about yet. I need to handle it without my Bratva boyfriend throwing his weight around.

Is he my boyfriend? The word sounds infantile. Lover? Fuck-buddy? Is this…what's that stupid word…a *situationship*? We're certainly not 'just talking.' The dull ache in my core is evidence enough of that. I'm glad I used a dildo in my self-pleasure escapades, or he could have hurt me.

He's a confusing mix of tenderness and cruelty, like an iron fist in a velvet glove. I'm off balance, unsure of what to expect, but his command of my body excites and scares me. The contradiction in him holds my attention, even though I know he's dangerous to me.

He's so possessive, so dominant, yet everything I didn't know I wanted.

But I'm inexperienced, and he knows it. He tried to warn me, even as he seduced me with his words. What seemed so alluring last night seems messed up in the cold light of day, but I don't care, and that's what troubles me most.

I'm looking in the mirror near the front door and adjusting my scarf when Ben appears in the bedroom doorway. He catches my eye in the mirror and smiles.

"And where are *you* going?"

"Work called me in," I say, picking up my purse. "It's nothing, just a meeting."

"Then it doesn't matter if I come along, does it?"

"You can't come with me to work." I turn to glare at him. "I mean, nothing is stopping you from being there. It's an open-door place because it's a community hub. But I don't need you. It's broad daylight, and I'll be with people I know. You said you wanted to spend some time with the case files this morning until I can get in to see Farraday."

Ben looks me up and down. "You are wearing a pencil skirt and pumps when you usually go to work in jeans. I know that from the photos on the walls of your apartment.

He's talking about my collection of press clippings. Oliver, Moira, Ali, and I, with giant cheques and cheesy grins.

"So I felt like dressing up a bit."

"Nuh-uh." He steps to me and uses his finger to move my face to one side. "Your earrings are plain studs, and your hair is up in a tidy bun. Sensible black blouse, minimal makeup. No perfume. But do you know what truly gives you away?"

I shake my head.

"Your eyes. They're darting, anxious-looking. Understandable—you've got plenty to be anxious about." His mouth curves into a smile, and I wonder whether he means the situation overall or just himself. "But you're more grounded than that. It would take more than 'just work' to set you off, but I don't think you lied about where you're going. So you want to look serious and professional today, which feels like you're protesting too much."

Fuck him. I *hate* him reading me like this. It's more violating than anything he could do to my body.

I want to hit him with some cutting retort, but it won't come to me. As much as I try to keep my expression neutral, I can't do it, and he sees my anger.

"You're in trouble at work, aren't you? You got the call this morning to attend a meeting urgently. If you knew before now, you'd have mentioned it or had a lie ready to cover yourself."

"Bingo," I say icily. "I don't know what the issue is, but Oliver called and said an official complaint was made against me. He can't tell me who made it, but I have to respond and make my case to the trustees."

Ben narrows his eyes. "I *am* coming with you, Rox. Let them see you're not alone. I won't let anyone push you around."

∼

It's too early for Ali to be at work. I knew it would be the case, but I wish she were here for me to talk to before I face the inquisition.

Oliver is fussing around behind his desk, trying to cram files into an already overstuffed drawer.

"I'm sorry about all this," he says. "I have a protocol to follow, I'm afraid. I'm sure it'll be fine." He looks up at Ben and smiles uneasily. "And who is this gentleman friend of yours? Have we met before? My memory is atrocious."

"We haven't met, no." Ben stands up and the two men exchange a handshake. "Benedikt Voratov. It's good to meet you, Mr. Buckley. Roxy has told me all about you."

No, I haven't. What's he doing?

"There's not much to tell," Oliver shrugs, accidentally knocking over a stack of pamphlets. "This office is too damn small—I'm always looking for new premises. I desperately need space to keep things *safe*. I just try to keep the place running smoothly and keep Her Majesty happy." He scuttles into the back office, closing the door behind him.

"What's he talking about?" Ben asks.

"He deals with every referral personally," I reply. "Makes notes and starts a new file for each of them, then has nowhere to put them. That's why it's mayhem."

"No," Ben says. "I mean Her Majesty."

"Oh, I *see*. He's referring to Moira Coffey. Remember her? The senator's wife. She's our most prominent trustee and really put the organization on the map. She'll be in my corner today."

"Ah, I remember now." Ben frowns. "Does she know the Bratva brought all that heat down on her husband?"

"Shhh!" I lower my voice. "No. She and her little son Eddie were kidnapped and released. That's all she knows. Her husband had a lot of enemies, and no one cared to try very hard to work out what had happened to him, so she let it be—she was trying to distance herself from the whole affair, it's understandable. Ali got a clean slate, so our Bratva connections are unknown too. If you keep from shouting about them, maybe they'll stay that way."

The door buzzer sounds, and Moira sweeps in, dusting hailstones out of her hair. She's statuesque and chic as always in a Chanel winter suit, her heavy overcoat sweeping the floor.

"It's foul out there, just foul," she says. "Good morning, sweetie. Let's get this over with, shall we?"

She ignores Ben and opens the meeting room door. I look inside to see the other trustees are already waiting for me. Ben takes a step toward me, but Moira shakes her head.

"I'll look after her, I promise."

Ben glances at me, but I shake my head. I turn away and head into the meeting room, Moira at my heels.

10

Roxy

"I can't get into details, but you've been called out for poor judgment."

Oliver is looking at the form before him instead of at me. This isn't his natural habitat—he'd rather supervise a lemonade stand or lead a fun run. But he's the manager here, and he has to do this.

Moira sits beside Oliver, her face stony. At his other side, Hillard taps his badge on the table at his other side as though to remind everyone he's the law. Here, he's just another trustee, but he doesn't seem to realize that.

"What poor judgment?" I ask.

Oliver opens his mouth, but it's Hillard who speaks. "You encouraged a mentally unwell man—a man who confessed to a series of hideous murders—to believe he is innocent and should appeal his sentence. That's misguided and dangerous, Roxanne. I tried to warn and guide you, but you wouldn't be dissuaded."

I fix him with a stare. "Do you *know* Farraday, Detective Hillard?"

Hillard shrugs. "I know enough. I sat with him for hours in those interviews, and I'll never be the same."

"As you said, he's unwell." I sit up straight in my chair, trying to project confidence. "And that was—"

The door opens behind me, and for a minute, I think it's Ben. The latecomer takes a seat beside Hillard.

"When did Mr. Fisher join the organization?" I ask.

"Graham, please," he says, flashing me a grin. "I think we're past the formalities now."

Graham Fisher's son was the third to die at the hands of The Dollmaker and the only victim to be identified. I met him in a victim support session at Always Home when everything calmed down.

His wife couldn't walk the streets where the killer had taken her son. When Graham refused to consider leaving the area, she left him and moved upstate to be near her sister.

I shouldn't have responded to his advances, but I wanted a distraction from Ben, and I thought Graham might be cut from the same cloth.

He's not as handsome, but he has kind eyes and a rakish sense of humor. I admired his ability to laugh after everything he'd been through. But he got weird, calling me endlessly and making unreasonable demands on my time.

At first, I was understanding—he'd been through a lot. His father was a distant figure in his life, and his mother, though doting, wasn't very supportive. But Graham turned on me when I didn't want to sleep with him. Called me a prick tease, a gold-digger. He's a big-shot executive pretending to work in his father's import and export business, and I guess he wasn't used to hearing the word 'no.'

The last time I saw him, he pinned me to the wall and wouldn't let me go. I kneed him in the balls and threw him out of my flat. Now he's here, sneering at me over the desk.

Of course, he must have made the complaint against me. Way to make it obvious.

"Mr. Fisher is our newest trustee and our biggest donor," Moira says. "We're delighted to have him." She turns to Graham. "Glad you could make it."

Graham isn't looking at her. Instead, he fixes his gaze on me.

"Roxanne, you *know* how much I've suffered since Max died. You also know what Always Home means to me. I think your support of Farraday brings this organization into disrepute." He shrugs. "This is a children's charity, a counseling service. A place where vulnerable young people should feel safe and supported. And you, a prominent member of our staff, are working to undermine the conviction of a man who murdered children.."

Am I gonna play this card? I have to.

"You and I were in a relationship," I say. "*I* ended it. I think you're motivated by bitterness and hiding behind your status to get what you want."

"Roxy," Moira says, but I won't be swayed.

"You're a rich man with connections. You're also a victim of crime. I'm sorry for what happened to you, Graham, but it's not fair for you to lash out at me. Farraday has rights, and I want to see that he's treated fairly, that's all."

Graham pushes back his chair and stands up. "I'm not listening to this," he shouts. "You get this girl in line," he jabs a finger at me, "or *I* will."

He storms out, slamming the door behind him.

"I'm sorry about that, Roxy," Moira says, rolling her eyes. "I'm sure he'll calm down."

I look at Hillard. "Don't you have anything to say?" I ask. "He threatened me."

"No, he didn't." Hillard turns to Oliver with a sigh. "Let's just wrap this up. I have places to be."

Oh, do you? Finding my abductor not on your to-do list?

"Okay." Oliver looks at me and marshals his courage, drawing a deep breath. "Roxanne Harlowe, you are suspended from work until further notice. You cannot undertake any activities on behalf of Always Home. We have no jurisdiction over your volunteer work in justice. Still, for the sake of your career with *us*, you should consider whether it's in your interests to continue supporting Farraday."

I look at Moira, but she has nothing to say. I catch her eye, only for her to look away.

When we come out of the office, Ben has gone. I call him but get no answer.

What the fuck is wrong with him? He insists on coming with me, only to run out on me afterward?

Hillard raises an eyebrow at me. "You need a ride to the prison?"

I frown. "What?"

"Figured you'd want to tell Farraday in person that you ain't gonna bother with him no more." He smiles. "Only polite. And I'm going there anyway. Got some probation paperwork to sign, may as well get it done now."

∼

Ben

The car I've been tailing pulls up outside a large house with wisteria growing outside. I drive past and park on the opposite side of the road.

The man is oblivious. He has the lack of self-awareness that only the rich and cosseted can afford. He thinks he can bully people and get away with it, and maybe that's true, but not today. Because today, he yelled at my woman, and there's no way I can let that go.

I'm impulsive at the best of times, but as I expected, claiming Roxy has brought out the worst in me.

My phone pings in my pocket, and I glance at the message.

Suspended from work. Gone with Hillard to visit Farraday. You are an asshole.

Direct and to the point. Still, at least I know where she is. I knew she'd go to the secure hospital at the first opportunity, but I'm glad she's got Hillard with her.

I get out of my car and head up the path to the house. The paneled glass in the front door is familiar, and as I press the doorbell, I realize where I am.

Graham Fisher sees me through the window and glares at me. The ignorant prick didn't even see me ten minutes ago when he stormed past me and out of Always Home. He takes his time coming to the door.

"Good morning," he says. "And what can I—"

I shove him inside and close the door behind me. I pin him to the wall, his neck scrawny in my hand. He's gibbering like a moron, so I deliver a sharp punch to his solar plexus, and he wheezes, sinking to his knees.

"Now I'm gonna talk, and you're gonna listen," I say. "Roxy's work means the world to her. She cares about justice and wants to see the right person behind bars for The Dollmaker murders. She doesn't believe Farraday did it and wants the justice system to treat him fairly." I pick Graham up by his collar and set him on his feet. "But I don't give a fuck about any of that, and neither should you. Because Roxy is mine." I slap his cheek and he yelps. "Do you fucking understand me? *Mine*. You get in her way again, speak to her, or in any way upset her, and I'll take you apart."

I let go of him and head for the door. As much as I want to fuck him up, it won't do Roxy any good. Her job is hanging by a thread as it is.

I'm halfway down the garden path when he says it.

"I fucked her, you know."

I stop.

"She doesn't *look* like a whore. That pretty face—she seems kinda classy. But once you get her naked, she's a tramp. Gagging for it. Did you find that?"

Don't rise to it. He's lying.

"Pretends not to like it, doesn't she? But she loves it, really. All sluts do."

Does it even matter whether he's telling the truth or not? *Who am I kidding?* Of *course* it fucking matters. Roxy was evasive when I asked who she dated. Did she lose her virginity to this smarmy cunt?

Graham puts his hand in his pocket and extracts some lint, rolling it in his fingers. "You know," he laughs, "Vivienne did me a favor when she left me. I got some fresh blonde pussy and a ton of sympathy in the bargain. Pass Roxy back my way when you're done, okay?"

My feet are moving before I can register my anger. All I see is a mist of white-hot rage. I slug Graham hard in the face, his nose crunching beneath my knuckles, and he stumbles back into the hallway. He scrambles to his feet and slams the front door, locking it just as I reach it.

I punch through the glass, sending splinters flying. When I peer through the hole, I can't see Graham.

But I hear him laughing.

I take a few steps back, ready to kick the door.

11

The Dollmaker

I have to concede that Roxanne is very much Living.

The complaint against her is a valuable tool. I'm glad I thought of it. If the busybodying little cunt can't take a hint, maybe concern for her job will make her think twice.

She made me angry. Fucking mouthing off like that. Most people who'd narrowly escaped being murdered would be too traumatized to make a nuisance of themselves, but here we are.

I never considered what would happen if I *failed* to kill her. It's never happened, so why would I bother planning for it? It's a bit like asking whether I have the appropriate weapons in my house for a zombie invasion or something equally implausible.

Unfortunately, lack of foresight on my part means that Living Roxanne has new urgency and motivation—things I intended to snuff out at the wick and bury with her body. Judging by her behavior, she isn't taking the threat from me seriously enough.

And what's with the wildcard? The big handsome Russian who I've fucking dealt with *before* is now Roxanne's fuck-buddy. It won't be easy to make the little bitch disappear, not with that pretty-boy Cossack sniffing around her precious little pussy. I've clocked his weakness, though—he adores her. Quite possibly loves her. It seems he's willing to make stupid decisions because of it, so we'll see what transpires. I'd bet he'd be less keen on putting his cock in her if she was cold.

Still, other people's over-reactions are always a rich seam to mine, and risky though it is, it's worth my while to see how far idiots can be pushed before they do something moronic. The Russian isn't smart enough to learn when to take a hit.

Roxanne needs to leave Farraday alone for his sake. The sad bastard knows damn well what will happen to his wife and baby if he opens his trap. But Roxanne's dogged insistence on fighting his corner would get a result in the end, if only to shut her up. I don't want him to struggle in a new environment with different carers. He needs to stay in Kirby hospital, where the mad cunt belongs.

I'm not mad. I'm perfectly alright. My Momma says so, although she gets the look in her eye that I've seen many a time. Frightened little faces, looking at me the way Momma does when she tells me it's not my fault. That I'm fine, really. It's *society* that made me this way. And Papa. As he would say, when you're wealthy and connected, you can do whatever you like.

I'm okay. I'm self-interested and tend to see the worst in everything, but deep down, I'm a good person.

I'm sure Roxanne would be a better person deep down too. All I need to do is put her there.

12

Roxy

"Hello, Roxy. Thank you for coming."

I never saw Simon Farraday so composed. He's clean, his blue jumpsuit devoid of the usual stains, and his hair is nearly combed. The stitches in his face look sore, but he's healing. A medication cup sits on the table before him, the pills still inside.

"How are you doing, Simon?" I ask.

"Other than my face being split like a baguette, I'm actually on good form," he says. "It's not as bad as the press made out. My fault, anyway. I got cheeky with a guy I thought was my friend, but there you go. This place is *full* of crazies."

I smile. "You win some, you lose some. You look well, all things considered."

He leans closer to me over the table, so the guard in the corner behind me can't hear him.

"I *am* well," he says. "You wanna know why?"

I raise my eyebrow. "Go on."

"Whenever I can, I'm dodging my medication. I've been flushing it instead."

"Why?"

"My key worker was on sick leave last week," he says. "He pre-filled my prescription, but there was a mix-up, and I missed two doses. You know something?" He drops his voice to a whisper. "I never felt better. So now I dodge it whenever I can."

I try not to react, but I don't understand. How can he be this calm if he's *not* taking his pills?

"It's really not good that you're not complying with the program," I say. "Even if you do seem very...normal."

"I know." He sits back in his chair and smiles benignly. "But I won't be asking for anything to be changed. The rules are different for me."

"Simon, I know for certain you're not The Dollmaker. This is the first time I've seen you like this. What happened to you? How did you get mixed up in this?"

"You mean, why did I confess to something I didn't do?" He sighs. "I got in financial trouble, and I couldn't tell Lois. I promised her I wouldn't get in a mess again. We were about to lose the house. Someone offered to bail me out, but the price was too steep. I tried to back out, but it was too late. Lois still got the money, though."

"Who, Simon? Who did this to you?"

"I can't tell you. My family's lives depend on it." Farraday looks suddenly pained. "Now that I can think straight, I *need* you to back off. No appeal, no trying to get me out of here. The scrutiny is dangerous."

"You didn't kill anyone. Why are you willing to take the rap?"

"When I was psychotic, I don't remember feeling anything but fear, but you would always talk to me. You looked after Lois too, and I appreciate that. But I don't think my tormentor anticipated your tenacity in drawing attention to my case. He likes me the way I am, in my little cage. I can keep my head down and see out my days in the knowledge that I'm keeping up my end of the bargain."

I knew it.

Someone framed him for the murders, and he confessed so the investigation wouldn't need to rely on solid evidence. Because had they looked for it, they wouldn't have found it.

Farraday sees the turmoil on my face and smiles at me. It's wonderful but terrible to see the man under the madness.

"I know what you're thinking, but there's no point," he says. "Lois left me and took Jamie with her. No one will believe you *or* me, and even if they did, my family would be murdered before the appeal got off the ground."

Tears fill my eyes. It must be torture for him.

"Stop trying to help me, honey," Farraday says, his expression serene. "I'm done for. I've accepted it."

"The real killer came for me," I whisper, "but I escaped. I think he wanted to kill me because then you'd have no one supporting your appeal, but it looks like he's getting his way without having to do a thing."

Farraday shakes his head. "I'm so sorry that happened on my account. You're a good person, Roxy, but you can't save everyone. Leave and don't come back. I'll kick off and act crazy again, say I don't wanna see you anymore. No appeal, no nothing. Maybe you'll be safe then."

"I won't let him get away with it. I have someone willing to protect me and help me find out who's behind all this, but it'll take time."

Farraday glances at the paper cup between us. "Do me a favor and stash those pills. That orderly behind you is half asleep, but he's supposed to make sure I take them. He might search me."

I have my back to the guard, and he can't see what I'm doing. I tip the paper cup into my palm and tuck the capsules into the inside pocket of my jacket.

Suddenly, Farraday is on his feet. He can't do much as his legs are manacled to the floor, but he still cuts a scary figure as he towers over me. He slams his fists into the tabletop.

"Fuck off and leave me alone!" he yells. "Don't come near me, don't talk to me!"

I push my chair backward and away from the table in panic, but I see him wink.

The guard is behind Farraday in an instant. He pulls a nightstick from his belt and smashes it into Farraday's calves, sending him to the ground. An orderly escorts me back to the waiting area as guards descend on the room, restraining the innocent man they believe to be a killer.

So much for justice.

~

Farraday's calm lucidity is more terrifying than his psychotic ramblings. I'm wrung out when I wander into the visitor's lounge.

To my surprise, Hillard is still here. He sits on a scruffy armchair, picking at the foam through a hole in the threadbare fabric of the seat.

"Are you waiting for me?" I ask.

"I brought you out here. Only fair I take you back unless you want a ride in the hospital transport." He grins, but the smile doesn't reach his eyes. "How's our boy doin'? You done the smart thing and said your goodbyes?"

He's enjoying this too much. The man liked seeing me squirm this morning, and now he wants to watch my face while I admit to abandoning Farraday. Still, I'm not about to tell Hillard the truth. Even if he *wanted* to help, the real Dollmaker would go after Lois Farraday as soon as the case was reopened.

"I told him I couldn't be involved anymore. He took it badly."

Hillard sniffs. "Best to leave it alone now. The sick asshole just wanted your attention. He doesn't get any other hot little pieces to look at."

He shoots me a quick look, and I realize that something got away from him just then. An unpleasant aspect of his character that he usually keeps under wraps.

I've only had coffee today, but it crawls in my stomach.

"Have you made any progress on *my* case yet?" I snap. "Only you seem to be here running errands instead of leading the investigation."

Hillard shrugs. "I passed the case off to another lead, Detective Landon. He's co-ordinating the case. Do you know him?"

I've met Cliff Landon, yeah. He asked me out when I was at the precinct one day, waiting to see Hillard. When I told him no, he laughed and said he was joking.

Are all the cops around here assholes, or do I just bring that out in people?

A crackle of a radio, and Hillard is already walking away, slapping open the door. The sunlight stings my eyes, and I shield them with my hand as I scurry after him.

"Goddammit," he's saying. "No, just keep him in a cell. I'll be back soon." He slips the radio back into his belt holster and throws open the driver's door of his car.

"Get in," he barks. "I know where your man is."

Ben

"Okay, okay!" A voice cries. "I'll let *you* in, but I'm not letting *him* out until Hillard has spoken to him."

A buzzer sounds, and the cell door opens. I'm face-to-face with my good friend Leo, who looks ready to break my jaw.

"You, get lost," he says, shooing away the junior officer escorting him. "This isn't Alcatraz. You wanna guard us, go down the other end of the corridor, and be scary there." Leo turns to me. "I left you fuck knows how many messages for months, and you don't respond. Then you call and leave a message telling me you're in custody?"

I shrug. "I didn't know who else to call. *Izvini, tovarishch*. And stop bitching. We're not married. I've been here for hours, waiting for you to show your face."

"Sorry is not gonna cut it. You wanna tell me what you're playing at?"

"I broke the nose of some cunt called Graham Fisher, then when he locked me out of his house, I kicked the door down and dragged him out of the understairs cupboard, but the cops showed up before I could stomp the fucker into mush."

Leo frowns. "Graham Fisher? The guy Roxy dated?"

I drop my head into my hands and groan.

It had to be him.

"If that piece of shit fucked my woman, I'll go back and fuck him up some more."

Leo throws his hands in the air. "Good work, Benedikt. You came back here to do *what*? Mess around with Ali's best friend *again* after what you did in Hawaii?"

I glare at him. Roxy told Ali, and she told Leo, presumably. Did they set up a sewing circle, too?"

"I'm glad you're here, Leo, but you don't have the full story."

Leo has the sense enough not to interrupt. I only take a few minutes to get him up to speed.

"So Roxy was abducted by a man who may or may not be The Dollmaker," he says, tapping his finger on his palm as he makes each point. "The guy sent down for the murders may be innocent. Roxy has been suspended from work because someone complained about her, and in response to that, you made the sensible decision to go and beat up a guy. In broad daylight, at his fucking *home*."

"You're gonna give me shit for trying to protect a woman?"

Leo knows what I'm talking about. He went through something similar for Ali, and we *all* nearly got killed in *that* incident.

I've been arrested before, but one phone call was all it took to get out. I'd call my Pakhan, he'd knock heads together, and the cops would turn me loose immediately, usually with a few apologies thrown in. But Pavel is gone, and I'm bang to rights. I figure I'll be able to talk my way out of it, but if Graham Fisher is determined to press charges...

The things Graham said got to me, and I lost control. It was stupid and reckless. I should never have gone after him in the first place, but the man put his filthy hands on Roxy. I was already itching for a reason to throw down on him, and his shitty attitude in the meeting was all I needed.

I have to get out of here in case the incorrigible prick decides to take the matter up with Roxy. Graham is a bigger problem than the so-called Dollmaker at this point.

"I know this isn't Bratva business," I say, "but I need a bailout."

"Actually, that ought to be easy." Leo grins at me. "Did you think no one was keeping tabs on you? When you disappeared, I got in big fucking trouble for losing track of you."

"Why would anyone give a shit that I got my ass arrested?" I ask.

"Two things." Leo sits on the bunk beside me. "Firstly, the Bratva couldn't get an angle on that guy Hillard. So when he needed a profiler, Freddie saw an opportunity to do the Bratva a solid. Sending you in as a Trojan horse gave us the leverage we needed, making *you* valuable."

Ah. Hillard totally ignored my fucking profile anyway. Farraday handed himself in, the evidence was there, and my valuable contribution was filed and forgotten.

"Hillard was fucking pissed when he found out," Leo continues, "but it was too late by then. It's in his interests to get you out of his hair as soon as possible."

I nod. "Okay, got it. What's the second thing?"

"Fyodor Pushkin doesn't entirely *trust* you." Leo stands up, looking out the door and along the corridor. "But you have a lot of information in your head. Every snitch, every slimeball thug on our payroll, every dirty politician or cop or judge. A lot of knowledge that you could decide to sell or trade."

So the Bratva will protect me because they think I might sell them out if they don't.

"Thanks a fucking bunch," I say. "Why don't they just take me out?"

Leo holds his hands in a supplicating gesture. "You've kept your hands clean since the whole thing with Pavel, and you got Hillard under the cosh, so you're not on anyone's shit list right now. Don't take it too seriously. It's nothing personal. You called me, I called Kal Antonov, and he told me to come down here and bail you out on his authority. He's the Pushkin-Antonov Pakhan now, so—"

"You degenerate bastard Russians!"

Hillard appears in the doorway, apoplectic with rage. "I just got off the phone. Apparently, I have to let this fucker go!"

"Charming." I get to my feet. "I thought you and I were friends."

"That was before I found out I'd been fucking played like a fiddle by your criminal buddies," Hillard snarls. "What good did you do anyway? It was *me* who caught The Dollmaker, not you. I'm better than *all* of you bottom-feeding lowlives!"

Leo and I stare at him. He rolls his shoulders and sniffs, regaining his composure. "Anyway," he says, his voice suddenly placid, "you got what you wanted, didn't you? I have to look the other way and ignore the shit you get up to, including this unprovoked assault. I don't know what I'm gonna tell Graham, but I guess I'll think of something."

He steps aside, letting Leo and I walk before him as we leave the holding area.

"I need a ride to get my car," I say to Leo.

He nods. "You got it. What about Roxy?"

"I'm right here," Roxy says.

I look up to see her sitting at a desk in the bullpen, her expression poisonous.

"What the fuck is your problem?" she asks me.

13

Roxy

Ben closed up like a trap as soon as he saw me. Not a word passed between us on the drive back to his apartment.

He's washing his hands, ensuring no tiny slivers of glass are embedded in the cuts. He has new injuries to add to his collection—nicked and bruised knuckles from punching through glass, perfectly complimenting his dodgy shoulder and punctured thigh. And, of course, the bite marks I left on his other hand.

I suspect I've been getting the silent treatment so he can blow up at me in the privacy of his own home. What gives *him* the right to be mad? He's the one who abandoned *me* in my time of need, only to go off and cause even more problems when he's supposed to be helping me. He'd say he was protecting me, but it's just territoriality. A toxic desire to assert himself and claim me as his.

As far as anyone knows, I have abandoned Simon Farraday. He will not be appealing his sentence. Does that mean I'm now safe? *No, it doesn't.* Because serial killers aren't ordinary people. They don't think that way.

And besides, I still have to contend with Benedikt.

It's not a coincidence that you can't spell *intoxicating* without *toxic*.

Waiting for him to speak to me is terrifying, yet delicious. I'm pinned to the couch by my own fear, not daring to move or speak, yet my clit throbs, trying to get my attention.

Ben walks over and sits in the armchair opposite me, fixing me with a cold glare. His eyes seem almost as pale and icy as my own.

I wish he wasn't so fucking sexy when he's mad.

"That Graham guy said he fucked you, Rox. He called you a whore."

My mouth falls open. Jesus. It doesn't excuse what Ben did, but that's more provocation than I expected.

"Ben, I—"

He holds up a hand, and I fall silent.

"I went after him because he was yelling at you in the meeting," he continues. "I planned to ruffle his feathers, but he goaded me. I don't regret what I did for a second—just thinking about it now makes me fucking angry all over again." He drops his head, kneading his temples with his fingertips.

"I dated him," I say. "I never had sex with him, I swear. I wouldn't let him touch me. That was the whole issue. He's weird and creepy."

He looks up at me, his eyes narrowing. His expression is so harsh, but I feel myself quicken, and I wonder if there's something seriously wrong with me.

"Come here."

I stand awkwardly before him, unsure of what to do. "You left *me*, you know. You just went off and—"

"I'm sorry, *charodeyka*. I really am." He takes my hand and drags me to my knees. "I thought you'd lied to me. Tell me who you belong to."

"You."

I shouldn't say it. It's twisted.

Ben is sixteen years older than me, with a vicious temper and a severe impulsivity problem. His behavior today only proves how dangerous he is.

But I've spent too long fantasizing about him, thinking about what he meant when he whispered filthy things to me on that stormy night. What *his kind of rough* might be.

A firm hand. Tight grip. Slaps. Spanks. Bruises. All my holes filled, aching, ruined.

He undoes his zipper and sits on the edge of the seat, freeing his erection. The horny slut in my head takes the wheel.

Who needs a hero? she whispers. *To get the attention of a good guy, you'd have to compete with things like conscience and honor and the greater good. Benedikt Voratov has no such distractions—*

all this man wants to do is fuck you in every hole and own you forever. In return, he'll fight the world for you and lose no sleep over it.

Is Ben a monster? *Possibly.* He freaks me the fuck out. The way he talks, the things he does. The way his hands feel on my body.

But I love it.

He pulls the pins from my bun, and my hair unravels, falling over my shoulders. He gathers it together, bunching it up in his fist. He gets to his feet, his cock in his other hand.

"Did you let that guy touch you?" he murmurs, rubbing the swollen head on my lips. "Because I wasn't around to give you what you needed, did you settle for him? Did he do this?"

He yanks my hair, making me gasp, and then his cock is in my mouth. He's hard and hot, his girth stretching my lips. He lets go of his shaft and slaps the bulge in my cheek.

"Hard to speak with your mouth full, huh?" He buries both hands in my hair, digging his fingertips into my scalp, and I grip his thighs to keep my balance. "Let me help you, baby." I gasp as he pulls out of my mouth. "What would you like to say?"

"I never let Graham touch me," I gasp, trying to get my breath back.

"Good girl." Ben slips a hand onto my chin, holding it in his fingers. He rubs his thumb on my lower lip as I look up at him. "I'm very pleased to hear that."

He pivots from fury to tenderness so quickly, making me feel dizzy every time. He's capricious yet fascinating, as damaged people tend to be.

He pushes his thumb into my mouth and grips my jawbone, pulling my mouth wide open. I gag hard as he shoves his cock against the back of my throat, coughing around it as he grinds against my tonsils.

"Get me good and slippery," he says, pushing my head toward his hips. "You're gonna ride my cock like the pretty little cumslut you want to be."

I swear I *dreamed* about him talking to me this way. Filled my mind with his voice, calling me dirty names as he claimed my body.

So many things we need to talk about, but everything has fallen clean out of my head. All I know is his surging hardness, filling my tender throat and dragging up thick saliva from deep within.

Ben releases my hair and grips my neck instead. He used his right hand before, but it's the left this time, and I feel the pressure in all new spots. He lets go of my jaw and pinches my cheeks, bridging his massive hand over my mouth so he can slip his cock into the space between. I sigh as he slides his cock against my lips and nose, covering me in my drool and his pre-come.

I feel disgusting, but it's amazing. He snarls and grunts as he pumps his hips, and I stick out my tongue, lubricating his length even more. I love how uninhibited he is—right now, it feels as though he's ravenous for me. Like no other woman in the world could get him this worked up. And I barely did anything except what he told me to do.

Ben stops rubbing himself against my face and pulls me to my feet. He takes me by surprise by kissing me deeply as he tugs my skirt up to my waist.

"I know you think I'm an asshole," he says, nipping my lip with his teeth, "and you're right. But I swear this to you, Roxy—however much *you* regret it, I'll *never* be sorry for making you mine. You can never take it back. No matter how much you end up hating me, I'll always be the man who owns your body."

His hands find my pantyhose, and he groans in frustration. I yelp as he tears at them with his fingers, shredding the fine mesh. He thrusts his hand into my panties, his warm fingertip slipping between my folds.

"Such a tight little hole for me to bury my cock in," he says, rubbing my wetness over my clit. My knees sag, and he wraps an arm around my waist. "I thought as much. So pretty, so lovely, but nasty as fuck when I give you what you want. Are you surprised to discover you're such a needy fuck-doll?"

"No," I say, pleasure melting in my core as he touches me. "I knew I'd be this way. But only for you."

"I like that." Ben yanks down my pantyhose, taking my underwear with them, and puts them on the arm of the couch. He sits, his legs spread, and strokes his cock as he talks.

"I'm gonna have to fuck you now, *charodeyka*. Turn and face away from me. Back up a little, and I'll put you where I want you."

I face the window, a faint cast of our reflections visible in the glass. His hands feel red-hot on my ass as he touches me. He takes my weight as I squat, the silky tip of him hot against my dripping pussy. I moan quietly as he lowers me onto his length.

He feels enormous from this angle. I don't know if I'm still sore from the first time or whether he's just hitting differently inside me, but he fills me so completely that I forget to breathe.

As my ass settles against his hips, he pulls me backward, so I'm lying against his chest. He shifts his thighs, tucking his knees between mine. As he spreads his legs, he takes mine with him, opening my pussy as wide as it'll go.

"That's what I fucking want," Ben murmurs. He holds my neck with one hand, but gently this time, the warmth of his palm soothing the pain. His other hand steals down my body and between my legs, finding my clit again. "Ride me while I play with you."

I move my hips tentatively, trying to find more room inside me, but it's impossible. As I slide along his shaft, I can feel him everywhere—from the depths of my pussy to the tingling nerves at my entrance, everything is alive with sensation.

Ben's fingers work my clit in an insistent rhythm, his breath hot and ragged in my ear. He's muttering obscenities, veering from degrading to praising me and back again.

"Dirty little slut. Such a good girl. You're doing so well taking all of me. Fucking filthy nasty girl. Only I know what your cunt needs. That's it. Keep doing that. That's my *krasivaya angel.*"

Oh God, I love it when he speaks Russian to me.

He relinquishes his grip on my throat, his hand reaching for something. I realize he's picked up my pantyhose and underwear. I howl with need as he takes his fingers off my clit.

"If you want to come, you'll let me do what I want. Open your mouth."

I close my eyes and do as I'm told, unsure of what to expect but willing to take it. Because it's not a matter of wanting to come. I *need* to.

Wadded fabric is stuffed into my mouth by Ben's long fingers. By the time I've registered that it's my panties, he's wrapping my mouth with the leg of my ruined pantyhose. He loops my head three times before holding it taut, my head dropping back against his collarbone. He kisses me over the gag.

"You look fucking amazing. Don't worry. I won't hurt you *too* much. I just wanna hear your muffled moans as I rail you." He releases the tension a little. "You wanna play?"

I manage a slight nod, and he grins, pulling the pantyhose tight again around my mouth. "Good. Because *I* wanna make *you* come really damn hard, and I think this is the way to do it."

He shifts his weight, moving us until we're almost lying flat. I have no choice but to look up at the ceiling. Ben hooks his free arm under the crook of my knees and pulls them up toward my chest.

"Hold your legs up and wide," he says, bumping his cock into me. "This is gonna be rough."

He pulls out of me, hissing through his teeth before pushing back in hard. I cry out and grab my legs, keeping them in position as Ben's hand slips over my smooth mound. He finds my clit again, pressing it as it pulsates against his fingertips.

His cock throbs against my sensitive inner walls as he slides in and out of me. He's talking again, snarled words falling from his lips as he thrusts harder and faster.

"You're all I want. All I need is your juicy pussy riding me. You're a good girl. You want my come. I know you do, you nasty cock-hungry little slut. "

He's pushing me toward my climax with his words as much as his actions. My pussy clutches his cock as heat gathers in my core.

Ben feels the tension and gives a low groan. "Do you wanna come on my cock, pretty girl?"

He doesn't wait for an answer. Instead, he rubs my clit firmly before slapping it with his fingertips, making me yelp into the gag. He alternates between slapping and stroking, my pussy spasming with each fresh sting. My eyes roll as the pain blends with the pleasure, intensifying it.

"Come for me," he says. "Give me those pretty moans, *charodeyka*. No one will ever make you come but me, so let me hear you."

Ben slams into me, and my pussy quivers, squirting as my orgasm wracks my body. He roars triumphantly and grabs my hip, holding me to him as he comes.

14

Ben

I relax my grip and toss the pantyhose aside. Roxy is breathing loudly through her nose, whimpering, and I remove the panties from her mouth.

My body is soaked from my navel to my knees, her come and mine running onto the carpet. I wrap my arms around her body until her chest rises and falls in a steady rhythm, then disentangle myself from her, pulling on my pants as I stand.

Roxy looks shell-shocked, and I wonder whether I'm scaring her too much.

Yeah, right. And this young woman in her early twenties has never read a book, watched pornography, fantasized, or masturbated? Of *course* she has—she told me so. She knows damn well that the shit I'm doing does not equate to romance.

I don't want to think about this thing we have. It's not love—that'd be fucking *banal*. The middle ground on which I never stand.

I'm all or nothing. I have an obsession that has driven out all rational thought.

What am I obsessed with? The fantasy or the reality? Because when I refused to fuck her in Hawaii, I knew that her expectations and mine were worlds apart.

I'm well aware that Roxy is starved for affection, fears abandonment, and wants to belong to someone. She doesn't need to tell me anything specific—it shows in her body language, behavior, and words. Her submissiveness when I fuck her. Already she's embracing things that ought to frighten her, wanting me to take control because her desire is drowning out her common sense.

She wants me. Knowing what she knows, she still wants me to be hers.

It feels damn good.

For the first time in my life, I can imagine the possibility of sharing my dysfunction with someone who's just as screwy but in a way that compliments *my* needs perfectly.

We could be a glorious mess together, and I'd worship the ground she walks on. *Would that be so bad?*

I go to the kitchen and pour a glass of water, bringing it to Roxy. She's sitting on the edge of the couch, her skirt straightened. If it wasn't for her come and mine running down her legs, she'd look respectable. Almost.

"Your hair is a fucking mess," I say. She smiles wanly and takes the glass from my hand.

"At least I could brush mine, and it'd look good," she says. "What's your excuse?"

I frown. "Our guest tonight on 'I Don't Give A Shit About My Hair' is me."

Roxy smiles, a real one this time. "I can see that."

I sit beside her. "A fight and a fuck. Can rely on either one to ruffle me up, but both…"

She grins and nudges me, but there's some distance between us that shouldn't be there.

I wonder whether she's regretting giving up her virginity to me. If she doesn't yet, she will in time. Everyone who gets close to me pays the price.

"It's been a shitty morning," she says, "but at least no one asked me about my bruised neck. I could explain it away, say it happened when I," she raises her fingers in air-quotes, "'fell,' but I'd rather not heap lies upon lies if I don't have to."

"You know what I got up to." I put my feet up on the table. "Tell me what happened when you went to see Farraday."

"He's not taking his medication, but he's lucid. I've never seen him that way before."

She crosses the floor to where her jacket hangs up and fumbles in the pocket, producing two capsules. "Farraday asked me to hide these so the guard would think he'd taken them, but I forgot to throw them out."

"Don't toss them," I say. "Let me see."

Roxy hands me the pills, and I roll them on my palm. "They aren't anti-psychotics, that much I can tell."

"How do you know?"

"Because I've seen every drug there is. I spent some time in psych hospitals."

"As a patient?"

I glance at her, unsure how much to tell her. "Yes. But let's not get into that now."

"I didn't know that," she says. Her eyes betray a certain uneasiness. "You never mentioned it, and no one else told me either."

"That's because no one knows the full story. Leo knows a little. I told Pavel Gurin everything, though, and that's why I never got to train with the *Spetsnaz*. Not in the weapons division, anyway. I trained with the espionage side, specifically in what they used to call *mech razuma*—in English, mind sword. They taught me to take control of my problematic personality traits and find a useful application for them, and the rest is history."

"Problematic?"

I decide to redirect the conversation back to the matter at hand.

"Look." I crush a capsule with my fingertip, and a colorless liquid spills over my palm. "It's a powder suspended in liquid. Do you wanna know what I think?"

Roxy nods. "Very much, yes."

"I think the medication was given to Farraday to induce symptoms of psychosis, not treat them." I dip my finger in the liquid and sniff before touching my tongue to it.

"Is that sensible?" Roxy asks, wide-eyed.

I smile at her. "No, *charodeyka*, it isn't. But I can tell straight away that it's amphetamine—it smells like it. I was into a few things when I was young and stupid. I'll be fine."

"So instead of treating Farraday's psychosis, someone has been swapping out his medication for something that will make him seem crazy—too crazy to be listened to or believed?"

"It certainly seems that way."

I put the broken capsule in the trash and the other on the kitchen counter. I wash my hands in the basin, the simple action distracting me and preventing my mind from running a mile a minute.

"How can we find out what's in these pills?" Roxy asks.

I shrug. "It doesn't matter. The important thing is that Farraday is better without them. You were right. Someone has a vested interest in keeping him inside, and you were threatening that by supporting him. Now that you've backed off, you might be safe."

"I promised Farraday I'd see this through," Roxy says, standing up to face me. "He's an innocent man. And I'm involved now. I won't quit. "

"Neither will I." I go to her, enveloping her in my arms. "You *might* be safe, and that's not fucking good enough for me.

I'm not gonna back down until I'm certain no harm will come to you."

"You can never guarantee that," she whispers. "The world is a dangerous place. You know it."

"It's a shithole," I reply. "Too many sick people, too much corruption. I don't try to swim against the tide. Justice is a fucking joke."

"You're wrong." She looks up at me. "There's a lot of ugliness out there, but there's beauty, too. Goodness, love, faith, hope."

She's so much better than me.

Just a good person, right to the marrow of her bones. Her decency and optimism are what drew me to her. She lights me up, makes me forget the things my memory tries to bury. But the anger always finds an outlet, as this sweet woman is now finding out.

"Some people can't be saved, Rox. They can't be helped, changed, or transformed into decent human beings by compassion and understanding."

Roxy glares at me, jutting her chin in that defiant way I'm growing to adore. "I believe it's worth fighting for what's right," she says. "I'd rather *stand* for something than fall for everything."

I cradle her head against my chest, her blonde hair warm under my chin. We're quiet for a moment, taking comfort from one another.

Roxy's phone beeps. She breaks our embrace and picks it up, frowning at the screen.

"It's Ali, asking if I'm okay. She looks suddenly flustered. "I don't want to talk to her. She'll lose her mind if I admit what's going on. And I need a shower and to look at the case files."

I take her hand. "Take it easy. As you said, it's been a shitty day so far. So let's slow down."

She sighs, giving me a small smile. "Okay. Shower first."

I grin. "We can share. To save water, of course."

∼

The cubicle is small, but the shower itself is powerful. I set the water running, steam building up as Roxy and I shed our clothes.

My plan was to fuck her senseless again, but something about her demeanor gives me pause, and I step into the flow of water, pulling her in with me. She's passive, letting me hold her, but I know something is very wrong.

The shower gel is cold in my hands, and she shivers as I work it into a lather on her skin. She sighs as I run my palms over her breasts, her ass, and between her thighs, suds running down her legs. I touch her stomach, and she shudders, instinctively covering herself with her hands.

"Don't hide your body from me, Rox." I take her wrists and lift her arms, wrapping them around my neck. Her full tits are slippery against me. "You're beautiful. I wish you could see yourself the way I see you."

She's crying. I couldn't tell before, but now I'm looking into her eyes, I can see the tears.

"My father used to call me fat," she says. "It was his way of discouraging me from eating. When you want to spend money on drugs and not food, it makes sense."

I hold her close. Being naked and vulnerable like this makes her feel she can talk to me, and I want to listen. That is, as long as she doesn't try to dig around in *my* head. After what she said about justice, I doubt she'd like what she found.

I talked a lot when she was in the hospital. Not about the things I *never* speak of—my parents, my childhood—but I did tell her other things. About the Bratva, about my life since Pavel Gurin took me at sixteen years old. It's only now I realize that I never asked *her* a fucking thing.

"Your father was an addict? That's a tough way to live," I say, stroking her back.

There's a long silence. When Roxy speaks, she sounds like a child.

"He was bipolar. He wouldn't take the medication, said it was too expensive and didn't help enough. Meth leveled him out better, or so he thought, but it was just a way to justify it to himself."

I wasn't expecting to find we had anything in common. We're different people—her so sunny and compassionate, me with my personality deficits and anger problem. Fascinating how two people experience trauma and respond so differently.

I shut off the water and reach for the towels.

"Do you want to talk about it, *charodeyka?*"

Roxy wraps a towel around her, patting her face dry.

"Not now," she says. "I want to do something normal couples do."

I smile. "So let's go out."

~

I leave Roxy getting ready and go onto the balcony, cell phone in hand.

I'm aware of something knocking at my brain, trying to get my attention. I want to ignore it, but I can't.

Roxy's father was a man with a fractured mind, but she loved him, or at least she tried to. Now she's fixated on redeeming Farraday, a mentally ill man who may *not* be a monster after all.

Is she playing out the same scene again by being with me? Does she think love has to hurt? Because I'm not the man to help her heal. I'm as broken as she is.

I could try. There's no way I can give her up, not knowing what I know. The little girl she used to be is still there, full of light and optimism, and I could never do anything to snuff out the inner strength she doesn't even know she has.

She's *distracting* me, though. I can feel it. The sharpness of my mind is dulled and softened by my feelings for her. I'm not thinking straight.

I close my eyes and try to focus on what I know about The Dollmaker. My thoughts are a jumble of unfinished ruminations and tangled threads, and I recognize a sensation I've felt before.

The whole point of an epiphany is that it's sudden. A revelation that slaps you in the face and changes everything. But my mind is a strange thing.

All the pieces are there. Everything I need to know is bouncing around inside my head, colliding with the millions of other scraps of knowledge and intuition that I have to sift through. Finding the nuggets that have value is like panning for gold.

An epiphany *is* coming. Farraday never felt like the right fit, and it's because I never got *this* sensation—the buzzing tension that comes from knowing a breakthrough is gonna happen.

I tap my phone and call the number Leo gave me. It's the personal number for Kal Antonov.

Kal is the Pakhan of the Pushkin-Antonov Bratva, and the son-in-law of Fyodor Pushkin, head of the *kommissiya*. Being that Hillard and I are no longer sympatico, I need Kal's permission to access resources I used when I worked for Pavel—snitches, info miners, hackers, moles.

No one will give me the time of day without Kal's say-so, but I don't know the guy. He and Leo were *Spetsnaz* buddies, and I'm sure Leo will have vouched for me, but it's Kal I gotta convince.

Kal answers after four rings. "*Da?*"

"*Dobry den'*, Boss," I say, using the common honorific for Bratva leaders. "This is Benedikt Voratov."

"Ah, yes." Kal's tone is cool. "Leo told me you kicked the fuck out of some creep who touched up your girl, and got yourself in trouble with the police. I should be more pissed off than I am, but truthfully, I like your style."

"You know what I'm gonna ask." I look over my shoulder to see Roxy sitting up, stretching her arms above her head. "I'm certain that The Dollmaker is still out there, and the guy in jail was set up for the murders. I need to do some digging."

Kal sighs. "I have a little girl. If anything were to happen to her—hell, just thinking about it makes me want to punch someone." He pauses as though he needs a moment to cleanse the thought from his mind. "Your involvement in The Dollmaker investigation was a useful way to get leverage over Hillard, but that won't change. If the guy sent the wrong suspect to jail, he'll probably lose his job, at which point we might be able to use our influence to get someone more fucking amenable in the job. So on that basis, I can justify letting you run free."

"You can make Hillard give me what I need?"

"I *could* lean on him, but it'd blow the whole thing wide open, and he'd know what was going on. Your woman might get hurt before the cops get their heads out of their asses. They let six kids die and framed an innocent man, so do you want to put your faith in them now?"

He makes a good point. "Can you at least stop Hillard from actively getting in my way?"

"Yep. I'll just tell him to back off. But keep out of fights and don't make problems for yourself."

"Sure."

Roxy frowns questioningly at me through the glass. I turn away.

"Two more things, Benedikt."

"What?"

"Don't tell Fyodor about this. My Papa-in-law is kinda paranoid, and you are persona non grata to him right now. It'll be a lot easier to do what you gotta do and let me cop the flak, but when all's said and done, your standing with the Bratva might improve."

Glad to hear it. It's a fringe benefit at this point, but I'm not complaining.

"Got it," I say. "What else?"

"Criminals like us have rules, but psychopathic sickos are something else." Kal's voice takes on a steely edge. "I can't maintain a sense of order with a guy like that running free. I need no wildcards playing their nasty little games in my territory. If you find that child-murdering shitstain, fucking kill him."

15

Roxy

With some trepidation, I agree to call in on Leo and Ali. I played it down when I spoke to Ali yesterday, but she'll know the score when she sees Ben and me together. I've never been able to hide from her.

"So what?" Ben asks as he shuts off the car's engine. "You're entitled to have your fun too. You don't owe her an explanation."

"What if she asks what we are?"

"Just say you never fuck and tell."

He's pretending to be obtuse, but he knows damn well that I'm really asking *him* to clarify it. I don't want him to act dismissively toward me in front of our friends. They've seen enough of that.

Ben walks around the car and opens the passenger door. I swallow my irritation as he takes my hand, helping me to my feet.

"Occasionally, you can be a real gentleman," I say."

He raises my hand to his face and kisses my fingertips. "Never for long, *charodeyka*, even if I wanted to be. And believe me. I don't."

Charming.

Luna is standing in the doorway to the house, wearing a giant Cossack-style hat. She waves enthusiastically at me, the hat slipping over her eyes.

"Roxeeee!"

Aw. I miss the days when she couldn't quite say my name right. She seems to be growing so quickly. She scuttles down the steps and flings herself into my arms, wrapping my waist with her legs as I pick her up.

"Your dress is super pretty," she says, stroking the velvet sleeves of my gown. "Did you get fancy just to come to my house?"

"Ben and I are going for dinner, but we thought we'd come and say hello first."

Luna looks over my shoulder and sees Ben. She grins at him and cups her hand around her mouth, speaking too loudly in my ear. "Is he your *boyfriend* now?"

Ben tucks a finger under Luna's chin, tickling her, and she bursts into peals of laughter, squirming out of my grasp.

"Yes, I am, you cheeky little *obez'yana*."

Oh. Okay?

I'm shocked at how good it feels to hear him say that. A warm feeling suffuses my body as I catch his eye, and he takes my hand.

"Daddy!" Luna is running ahead of us into the lounge. "Ben called me a monkey!"

Leo is sitting in the armchair, a tumbler of vodka in one hand and a well-thumbed copy of *Dracula* in the other. "Is he wrong, *printsessa*?" he asks Luna.

"No!" she giggles. She runs out of the room again, making monkey sounds, and Leo shrugs at us.

"Last few minutes before her bedtime," he says. "Luna has the zoomies, which is why *I* have a stiff drink." He waves the glass to Ben. "Go pour some for yourselves and top me off while you're at it."

Ben raises a hand. "I'm driving. Is Ali here?"

"Damn right, I'm here!"

∼

I turn to see Ali descending the stairs. She stops halfway and stares at me for a moment. Then she's upon me, wrapping me in her arms.

"You look so gorgeous," she says, "and so *well*. I've been worried about you, but Leo told me to give you guys your space."

"Yep," Leo says. "Nothing worse than someone calling and interrupting when you're trying to get your hands on your girl's—"

"Don't you *dare* say what you're about to say," Ali laughs. "Luna will hear you, and I'll get another note home from kindergarten."

I let go of Ali, giving her a grin. "I'm sorry. But you don't *need* to worry."

"That's right," Ben adds. "Roxy's a big girl now."

"Well, I have to say I'm not as concerned as I might have been." Ali nods at Ben. "Not now that *this* handsome bastard is at your side." She turns to look at Leo.

"Watch it, *tigritsa*," Leo warns, raising an eyebrow at her. She smirks and blows him a kiss before going to Ben.

"You dirty dog. What took you so long?" She hugs him, punching him in the shoulder as she pulls away. "I see your face. Do you even *know* how you look at Roxy?"

Ben shrugs. "No, how?"

Ali smiles. "Exactly the way you *always* looked at her. Like you worship the ground she walks on. Like she's a queen amongst paupers, a goddess amongst mere mortals. Did you really think you could run to the top of a mountain to escape her? It's just further to fall."

Oh my God, Ali. Shut up. You don't know what he's done. The filthy things he whispered as he fucked me...

"Well, maybe a bit." Ben smiles and puts his arm around my waist.

Leo grins at him. "Attaboy, *tovarishch*. So what did Kal have to say?"

"He told me he'd get Hillard off my back long enough for us to see this shit through. We discovered that Farraday definitely isn't The Dollmaker, and they dosed him with acid to *induce* psychosis and prevent him from speaking out."

Leo's eyes widen. "Clever but diabolical. How'd you find that out?"

"This idiot opened one of Farraday's medicine capsules and tasted it," I say. There's an uncomfortable pause.

"Benedikt, you are the smartest person I know," Leo says, shaking his head, "but fuck me, you do some stupid shit."

Luna reappears in the doorway. She's wearing pajamas, a bathrobe, and slippers, but the slippers are not a matching pair. On her head is a Swarovski crystal tiara.

"Can I stay up to be with Roxy?" she asks.

Ali frowns. "Nope. It's late already."

Luna pouts, then brightens. "Okay. Daddy, will *you* tuck me in?"

Leo smiles indulgently at her. "Of course I will. But you can't wear that crown to bed, *malyshka*."

He stands and scoops Luna into his arms. She pouts as he gently disentangles the tiara from her hair and hands it to Ali.

Luna rests her head on her father's shoulder, and I kiss her nose. "G'night, baby girl. We're going soon anyway."

Leo turns in the doorway. "If there's anything we can do to help, let us know." He looks at Ben. "But if experience has taught me anything, it's that events tend to come to a head quickly and painfully." He strokes Luna's hair. "If you gotta choose, protect what you love."

Luna smiles at me, waving sleepily as she disappears from view.

∼

The restaurant is beautiful. A small but comfortable place with warm amber lighting and views of Italy painted on the walls.

"I would dearly love to visit Lake Como," I say, dipping a piece of focaccia into a bowl of olive oil. "My Mom was from Lombardy, and we visited once, when I was very young. I don't remember, but there were photos on the walls of our house."

Ben strokes the back of my hand with his fingertip. "I know. We talked about Lake Como when you were in the hospital, and that's why I brought you here. But you didn't tell me *why* it meant so much."

I'm touched that he remembered. I don't know *what* we talked about back then, but it seems he committed every word I said to memory.

Maybe Ali is right, and he's been fighting his feelings for longer than I realized.

I smile. "Ask me later."

Is this what love should be like? I don't know. I'm so afraid of being abandoned that obsession feels *better* than love—more real, more secure. The frightened girl inside me *wants* Ben's intensity and dysfunction, but the mature, adult Roxy needs a healthy relationship. A man who can keep his cool and guide me as I grow and heal.

Ben said I'd bring out the worst in him, and perhaps he's right. Maybe he brings out the worst in me, too. But I want to reach inside and *know* his darkness, not just experience it.

Right now, this *feels* right. Safe, normal. A glimpse of the potential we have to be happy together.

We split a wild mushroom pizza, Caprese salad, and a bottle of white wine. Ben listens to me as I tell him about my studies and reading on criminal psychology.

"Do you consider yourself an expert?" he asks. "Think about this. We're tracking down a serial killer, but what is Leo? He's *Volk Smerti*, the most feared assassin ever to work for the Bratva. I estimate he killed an average of one person a week for years, putting his headcount well into the hundreds. What do we call him?"

I frown, sipping my wine to buy time to think.

"He has a code," I say. "Sure, he's a murderer, but he killed people who deserved it, at the behest of his boss. The Dollmaker is worlds away from that."

Ben nods. "Agreed. But no one believes they are the villain in their own story, so just like Leo, The Dollmaker has some kind of framework that, in his mind, explains or justifies his actions."

I wrinkle my nose. "You mean he's not just getting turned on by violence?"

"Who says the killer is a he?" He smiles. "*Many* people get turned on by violence, Rox. Despite your makeup and high neckline, I can still see those bruises when the light catches them right. I put them there because I was fucking horny and wanted to do that to you. Did *you* try to stop me? No."

I flush at the memory. *Jesus*. I know what he's getting at.

"So you're saying we're all kinda deviant, it's just on a spectrum?"

Ben swills his wine around in the glass. "Yep. The Dollmaker and I are not different species. It's only a matter of light and shade. I don't know for sure what I'm capable of. Nor do you."

There's a commotion near the bar, and I turn to locate the cause of the ruckus. To my surprise, I see Oliver. He has his back to me, blocking my view of whoever he's with.

"Now you just calm down," Oliver is saying, holding his hands in the air. "There's nothing to be achieved by—"

His companion shoves him aside, and my stomach drops.

It's Graham, a butterfly bandage on his swollen nose. He's walking toward us, wearing the expression I know so well. It's the face he pulls when he's about to lose his shit. Ben stands up as he reaches us.

"You better fuck all the way off, then keep going," Ben says. "I mean it."

Graham ignores him. Ben starts to stand, but I grip his hand harder, and he sits down again. Graham pulls a chair from a nearby table and sits beside me.

"I just want to apologize for before," he says, his smile as false as they come. "Detective Hillard says he's not gonna pursue the assault charge, but he won't tell me why, so I have to assume you are dodgy." He leans closer to Ben. "I'll get my father's people to find out about you, and then maybe there will be consequences."

Ben lets go of my hand. I see it twitching on the tabletop, and I know he wants to beat Graham to a pulp.

"So why the apology?" Ben asks.

"I'm sorry you and I had to come to blows over something as insignificant as this broken, needy little whore." His hand whips out and clutches my arm.

Ben leaps to his feet and punches Graham in the face, fucking up his nose again. Graham lets go of my arm and falls off the chair, blood soaking his shirt.

"You think you can turn *me* down?" he screams at me. "I get what I want. You have no idea who you're dealing with!"

Grabbing the table's edge, he scrambles to his feet, leaving a bloody handprint on the surface. He snatches up a napkin before stumbling away and out the door.

The diners, frozen in place, return to their meals. Ben winces and flexes his hand.

"My knuckles are absolutely fucked," he says. "If I can go a few hours without picking up a new injury, I'll consider it a win."

Oliver comes over to us, all flustered. "I'm sorry," he says, grimacing at the blood on the table. "I was trying to smooth him out. He was furious about the, um, incident earlier today, and he called me demanding I fire Roxy." He takes my hand and pats it. "I'm not going to do that, dear. But do be very careful of Graham. He's...temperamental."

"So am I," Ben interjects. "Don't worry, Oliver. I won't leave her side."

"That's good to hear." Oliver takes a napkin and drapes it gingerly over the pool of blood. "I'm sorry. I can't even *look* at that. Did you go and see Farraday?"

"Yes," I say. "I'm not gonna be working with him anymore."

Oliver sighs. "It's too bad. But you know what they say—don't set yourself on fire to keep other people warm. You worked hard to get where you are. I'm glad I don't have to try and defend your actions anymore. No one will judge you for abandoning a lost cause, and Farraday is as lost as they come."

16

Ben

"I've met Graham before."

Roxy turns to me. "Really?"

We're at Inwood Hill Park, watching the Coots on the river. The restaurant wanted us out, so we paid up and bailed, but I stopped at a dessert place and managed to get some takeout tiramisu.

"I talked to him when I was collecting intel, way back when I got the gig to do the case profile. He was a creep then, too."

Roxy digs into her dessert with a spoon. "He was okay with me at first. Swept me off my feet a bit, I suppose, and I enjoyed the attention, especially since you…"

Her voice trails away to silence. I know what she was gonna say, so I don't embarrass her by making her finish her thought.

"What does Graham actually do?" I ask. "I know it's something in logistics."

"*He* doesn't do much but draw a salary, but his father's business is specifically movement and storage of pharmaceuticals. Laboratory stock, medicines, that sort of thing."

I'm wary of letting my hatred of the man cloud my judgment, but this information is undeniably intriguing.

"Does he have access to the stock?"

She shrugs. "I can't see why he wouldn't. His daddy isn't inclined to deny him anything, so he can probably do whatever he wants." She glances at me as she catches on to my train of thought. "No, you're not thinking about that right," she says. "The drugs that were given to Farraday were illegal."

I lean against the hood of the car. "Think again. Really think it through."

Roxy speaks hesitantly as the pieces fall into place. "The Rx meds would be delivered to the hospital, batched up and labeled. It would be easy enough to swap out Farraday's medication if he had someone under the thumb inside the hospital, but even *easier* at the source. Someone who works for Fisher Pharma."

I nod. "Don't forget the chloroform. He'd be able to get that easily too."

Roxy tosses her empty dessert box into a nearby trash can. "Graham's son was the third kid to die. A big fuss was made about it, and a reward was posted for any information leading to an arrest. You think Graham's *father* might be protecting him?"

"Maybe. But Hillard alibi'd Graham for his son's murder. It all checked out. Graham's wife said he was with her when the kid was abducted, and they called it in straight away."

Roxy drops her head onto my shoulder. "And then she left him," she says. "Maybe she was covering for him all along."

I think of Roxy with Graham and feel suddenly nauseous. "I'm not sorry I hit that piece of shit," I say, sliding my arm around her waist. "If I find out he's the killer, I'll be fucking delighted, because I'll be obliged to murder him with my bare hands."

"Well, exactly," Roxy replies, "which begs the question—why is he getting in your face? He must have known what he was doing this morning when he goaded you, and then he went and did it again this evening."

"Graham failed to control you when you were dating. The Dollmaker failed to kill you. Narcissistic sociopaths don't cope well with failure—I sure don't. Neither do common-or-garden misogynistic losers, so whichever Graham is, he could just be losing his shit and acting out."

Roxy shudders in my arms. "Let's get in the car and warm up," she says. "I'm sick of thinking about all this stuff."

∽

I'm barely in the driver's seat before Roxy is upon me, clambering onto my lap.

"I know it's wrong," she murmurs, reaching for my shirt buttons, "but seeing you punch Graham like that? It *did* something to me. I think you were right—I *am* a little bit deviant."

I shuck her dress up over her thighs, her round ass smooth in my hands. "And I'm a complete fuck-up, *charodeyka*. You wanna get railed by a monster? I'm not complaining."

Her panties are satin, silky under my fingertips as I press against her sex. The heat from her draws a growl from my throat.

"Are you wet already?"

"I've been wet since before we left the restaurant." She licks the shell of my ear, biting the lobe, and my cock lurches.

Naughty little minx. Taking the initiative already.

She's got my shirt open, her hands on my chest. She grazes her nail over my nipple, and I bite my lip. I ease my hand into her panties and touch her smooth mound, slipping a finger between her hot pussy lips.

"Can I do what *I* want?" Roxy asks. She grinds on me, rubbing my hard cock against her ass.

I kiss her, holding her cheek in my palm. "And what might that be?"

She rests her forehead on mine and looks into my eyes. "I wanna be in control," she whispers. "You have so much power over me. I want to take some of it back."

I've never even considered letting a woman take the lead before. But Roxy is not just any woman.

I denied her once, and it nearly killed me. I'm not gonna make that mistake again.

I lift my arms and put them behind me, holding onto the headrest. "Take what you want from me, baby."

Roxy gives a sweet little giggle, and I almost fall apart there and then. I want to shove her into the footwell and fuck her face, but I resist. To my surprise, she slides to her knees on the floor, reaching for my zipper.

"Don't touch me, okay?" she says, freeing my erection. She rubs the tip with her thumb, smearing a bead of dew over the most sensitive spot, before lapping at it with her tongue.

Her movements are agonizingly slow. The sight of her slowly licking around the head, her small hand gripping the base...*fuck*. I tighten my hold on the headrest, fighting the urge to grab her hair and push her warm mouth onto me until she chokes.

After several minutes of this, I'm dying. Every muscle in my body is so tense I feel like I might shatter into a million pieces. As much as I don't want to say it, the words are making a break for my lips.

"Don't fucking tease. Give it to me."

She pauses, stroking my cock slowly as her eyes meet mine. She looks so fucking beautifully slutty in her pretty dress, her lipstick smeared over her cheek.

"What's the matter, Ben?" She arches an eyebrow at me. "You need something?"

"Just get up here and fuck me."

"Your manners are atrocious," she says, swiping her tongue over the head of my cock. I shift my hips, trying to relieve the deep ache in my abdomen.

"I need to feel your tight pussy around my cock," I say as she slowly moves her hand up and down. "This is torture."

"This is what you did to *me* in Hawaii," she says. She stops pumping my cock and grips it firmly at the base, making me moan. "You led me on, only to turn me away at the last minute because you felt some kind of way about screwing a virgin."

"I led *you* on?" Even though I want her more than anything in the world, the audacity is too much. "I know what you did, Rox. I know you wrecked your roof to let the rain in, knowing I'd have no choice but to let you stay with me. Getting changed into that skimpy outfit, with those damn braids..." My words dissolve into a gasp as she runs the tip of her tongue along my length.

"Okay, fine," she murmurs. "But I know you were as hot for me then as you are now. Why wouldn't you just take what you wanted?"

I've asked myself the same question many times and come up with many different answers, but none quite ring true. What should I have said to her?

You're too young. I have nasty, depraved tastes that would frighten you. You want a real relationship, and I cannot give you what you deserve. Don't waste your virginity on me. I'll hurt you in every way imaginable.

"Because I was dangerously and pathologically obsessed with you," I say, closing my eyes. "It consumed me. My desire was too deep, and I feared it'd pull you down and drown you."

"And now?"

I open my eyes to see a haunted expression on her face. The teasing smile has disappeared, concern marring her beautiful features.

"Now I can't let go, even if we both go under. I'd rather drown *with* you than stay afloat without you."

I let go of the headrest, touching her cheek with my fingertip. "If I'm honest with myself, I came home as a test. Could I look at you and *not* feel like I'd die if I didn't touch you again? Then you barged into my life and caught me off guard, but worse—you *needed* me. When I realized someone had hurt you and might hurt you again, I couldn't say no."

Roxy climbs onto my lap, her knees on either side of my hips. I stroke her cheek with my thumb, my fingers rubbing the bruises on her neck.

"And yet, here. Look what *I* did to you." I say, tugging her toward me so I can brush my lips over her tender throat. "This is the *real* me. I don't know how to be any other way, and truthfully, I don't want to change." I bite her neck softly, and she sighs. "You can't pick and choose the parts of me you want. You have to take it *all*. Do that, and I'll worship every sweet inch of your body until you can't say anything except my name."

Roxy grinds her hips, and I reach for her panties, tugging them aside. They are drenched in her arousal, and I can smell the fresh scent of her pussy as she slides along my shaft, lubricating it even more.

"I wouldn't change a thing," she whispers, "except where your hands are. Put them back behind you."

I grit my teeth and acquiesce to her demand, holding the headrest. Roxy shuffles in place, reaching below the hem of her dress so she can move her panties out of the way. The head of my cock catches her slick opening, nudging inside a little, and I drop my head back against the seat. I lift my hips, trying to get inside her, and she surprises me by slapping my cheek.

"Stay still," she says, giggling playfully. "*I'm* driving."

Fuck. I never thought she'd do that. I really wanna slap her back, but there'll be another time. Right now, I'm doing whatever the fuck she tells me to do.

Roxy puts her hands on my shoulders and looks into my eyes as she sinks onto my cock. My mouth falls open as I feel her inner walls give way to me, her warm curves enveloping me. I keep my eyes locked on hers.

"If you're gonna ride me, baby, you'd better go hard," I say. "I can't fucking deal with how sexy you are. Make yourself come, but do it fast."

Roxy kisses me quickly, then sits back, gripping my shoulder hard with one hand. She reaches below her dress, and I feel her fingertips brush my cock as she touches her clit. Her breath catches as she rises up, using her quad muscles to lift her off my throbbing cock before plunging down again.

Sweet Jesus. If I die now, it's all good.

The beautiful woman on top of me is speeding up her movements, the car steaming up as she moans her pleasure in my ear. I want to grab her ass, but somehow I'm enjoying being used in this way. Suddenly I remember what she told me—that she fucked her pussy with her dildo and thought about me while she did it.

That image fucks me up totally, and I'm now hurtling toward the point of no return. Roxy's big ass slaps against my thighs as she fucks me, her pussy clenching rhythmically as her climax builds.

To my utter shock, she grabs my wrists with both hands and pins them to the headrest, slamming her pussy down hard on my cock. She throws her head back and cries out, soaking me with her wetness as her pleasure peaks. Her tight little cunt squeezing me is too much, and I forget myself completely, leaning forward to bite her neck as I flood her pussy with my come.

∽

Roxy

"Alcohol is technically a poison. You know that, right?"

Ben shrugs as he tips vodka into a tumbler. We haven't been back in his apartment for five minutes, and already he's drinking.

"My shoulder is sore, but I don't want to take painkillers," he says. "I like them too much, like everything else." He sees my frown. "Don't worry. My liver is pretty hardy—it must be after what I've put it through."

I want to know about his life. There's something passionate and intense about him that he tries desperately to suppress, but he has a vicious streak, and I want to understand where it comes from. I see it in his eyes when he talks about things that anger him, and I feel it in his hands when he touches me.

He's *deviant*, somehow, and he knows it.

"You said you were in a psych hospital. Why?"

"I did some bad shit when I was a kid. Then I got the blame for something I didn't do. It couldn't be proved, but everyone believed I'd done it. Why not? Like I said—justice is a cute idea, but once you get past a certain age, you learn it's bullshit."

"It's a basic tenet of civilized society," I say. "You make it sound like Santa Claus."

He smiles, but his shoulders sag a little, his eyes fixed on the distant rooftops as he stands at the balcony door. I'm reminded of how he looked when I left his beach house in the pouring rain.

"Anyway," he says, turning around, "that's all behind me now. I wanna know about your parents."

I pull my hands into the sleeves of my sweater and wrap my arms around myself.

Even Ali doesn't know the whole story. I don't know why I'm willing to tell Ben, except he wants to know. I feel his attention warming me as though I'm sitting near a fire.

"My father was so, so crazy. I know it's not a kind word to use, but I can't think of him any other way."

Ben sits beside me on the couch. He watches my face intently as I speak.

"The worst thing is that I can remember us being normal. Mom and Dad were fine. Had a house in suburbia, a station wagon, tire swing. My mom baked sugar cookies for me to take to school." I squeeze my eyes closed, trying to fend off the memory. It's tougher to think of the good times than the bad. "But then my father started to lose it. He would swing from deep depression to insane highs. When he was down, he wouldn't get out of bed, but when he was up, he'd want us to leave, travel around the world, and spend all our money. He'd rage at Mom when she wouldn't go along with it."

I look at Ben. Although he's listening, his expression is one of detached interest. He cocks his head at me.

"Go on, Rox."

"By the time we found out he was bipolar, it was too late—he'd lost his job over his frequent absences, and we had no insurance. My mom got a shitty job as a night clerk at a gas station, and then there were no more sugar cookies. Dad was supposed to be there to look after me in the evenings, but he usually wasn't. He refused to take lithium because it was expensive and fell in with others in a similar situation. They got him into meth, and that was that. The man who lived in my house wasn't my father anymore."

"Where's your mom now?"

I wipe my nose with my sleeve, my vision blurring as tears spring to my eyes. "She wasn't working at the gas station, but she still went out every night. Then she was just *gone*. Strangled and dumped like trash. Only then did I find out my father was pimping my mom out to pay for his drugs, and she'd been too afraid to refuse." The tears spill over. "Dad said my mom got killed because of *me*. The welfare money would have been enough if *I* hadn't needed things."

"No, that's not true, Rox." Ben pulls me into his lap, and I sob into his chest, soaking his t-shirt. "You were only a kid. It's all on your dad. He twisted your mom's love into something ugly. There's nothing you could have done to save her."

His warmth soothes me. No one ever just held me before, not like this.

"What happened after your mom died?" he whispers, smoothing a strand of hair off my face and tucking it behind my ear.

"My father sold me. He owed some money to his so-called buddies, and they wanted a house slave. I'm sure everyone involved knew what they had planned for me, but my father didn't have the balls to do it himself."

Ben tenses around me. I feel the raw power of his body, but instead of fearing it, I melt into him.

"Fuck." His voice is a deep rolling growl. "If you say what I think you're gonna say, then I swear, I'll destroy every one of those junkie cunts. There won't be anything left to find—they will fucking *vanish*."

"It's okay," I say, squeezing his shoulder. "It didn't happen like that. They wanted to wait until I was thirteen before they started selling my body, but I managed to escape one day when they were all strung out. I'd been with them for three years by then. Then I lived on the streets and had a few near misses before the cops picked me up. I went to Juvie and met Ali there."

Ben is holding me almost too hard, as though he's afraid my past might burst in and drag me away. He cradles my head in his hand, his other arm wrapping my waist. My lips meet the hollow of his throat.

"It's personal to you, isn't it?" he says. "You were a child alone with no one looking out for you, just like those kids who were murdered. And Farraday deserves a chance to get his life back. His kid should have the tire swing and sugar cookies, too."

Deep down, I knew this about myself. But he sees through me so easily. It's frightening.

Ben pushes me off his lap abruptly. I almost burst into fresh tears, but then I see his face.

17

Ben

Roxy was right. I shouldn't have tasted what was in the capsules. My fucking curiosity will get me killed one of these days.

It ought to have occurred to me that a tiny bit of amphetamine wouldn't do much, but a drop or two of fucking *acid*?

It's been years since I last took LSD, and that was under duress. The Gurin Bratva boys thought it would be funny to haze me, so they dosed me—at just sixteen years old—and then turned me loose in one of their brothels. I don't remember it, but I knew I wasn't a virgin anymore when I left. I slept for twenty hours straight, and my entire body was in agony. To this day, I don't know what they did to me.

"I'm sorry, *charodeyka*," I murmur. The couch cushions warp as though they are melting, and I close my eyes so I don't have to see them. "The capsules are LSD. No wonder your boy Farraday could barely string a sentence together, the poor fucker."

Roxy snatches the vodka glass from my hand. I hear the faucet, and the glass is back, nudging against my knuckles.

"Water," she says. "Drink it. *Now*."

I drain it in one. I lie on the couch, staring at the featureless ceiling. Roxy tucks herself under my arm, stretching out alongside me.

I click my jaw. Ghosts are swarming on the blank space above me, waiting for me to give them a voice.

"Talk to me, Ben," Roxy says. "Just stay with me. Tell me about *your* parents."

I close my eyes again. Faces I used to know. Still there, emerging from the dark.

"They were heroin addicts," I say, "and from the age of ten, so was I. Like all junkies, I got feral when I couldn't get it. My parents would beat me black and blue if I didn't help them, so we stole. Mugged people, robbed houses, broke into cars."

I'm tripping, and this isn't a good train of thought. But talking about it is easing the pain, like some kind of psychological trepanning.

"When I was twelve, my father and I broke into a house but made far too much noise doing it. The guy came down the stairs with a knife. He went for my dad, and like a fucking idiot, I tried to get between them. I got cut up bad, but my dad got a hold of the knife. I passed out after that, and when

I woke up, I was in the hospital. They'd found the guy dead in the hall."

Roxy's fingertip moves along my scar.

"What about your parents?"

"Gone. The police went to my house and found it smashed to shit. The guy who died was a retired cop, so someone had to pay, and I didn't deny I'd killed him. No one was inclined to give me a pass, and I guess I freaked them out, so I got diagnosed as a disordered personality and stuck in an asylum, pegged as a murderer."

"That's horrendous," Roxy says, her voice strained. "Didn't you try to tell them they had it wrong?"

"Why would I bother? I was *safe* in the hospital. They got me sober, taught me to read and write, and gave me medication that kept me floating around in a numb haze. Does that sound so bad?"

"I guess not when you put it that way."

Roxy puts her hand on my cheek. It's as though my imagination has swollen and burst out of my skull, so the physical touch is a shock, and I flinch.

"How did you end up in the Bratva?"

"When I turned sixteen, the hospital trialed a half-assed out-patient scheme, so I got put on a community probation program. I absconded immediately and went to the Gurin Bratva, looking for work. My father had some vague connections with them at one time, and Pavel Gurin took a shine to me because I was a cheeky little shit. I never saw my parents again."

We fall silent for a while. I run my hand over Roxy's arm, the nap of her sweater comforting me. The acid can't have been that concentrated—already the room is settling, the furniture no longer crawling up the walls.

"Farraday is incarcerated for a horrible crime he didn't commit," Roxy says, "but like him, you can take comfort from knowing you didn't kill an innocent man. Whatever you think you are, you held back in that moment and even tried to defend your father. You can hold on to that."

I squeeze my eyes closed.

Don't go there. My brain is fucked up and this is not the time to tell her the whole truth.

"Ben?" Roxy's voice is quiet.

"Yes?"

"What does *charodeyka* mean?"

"It means 'sorceress.' It's the pet name I gave you when you bewitched me." I turn my neck so I can kiss her forehead. "I understand now, Rox. I *see* you. You already know what it means to be with me. I'm a mess, and we both know it." I put my fingertip under her chin, tilting her head back so I can kiss her. "But there's nothing and no one on Earth I'd ever put above you. If God Himself tried to harm you, I'd fucking fight Him and go to hell for it."

∽

Roxy

I'm in bed, Ben sleeping hard beside me, but I can't relax. My thoughts are tangled together, and unpicking them is like trying to unravel razor wire.

Graham is an asshole, but it's difficult to imagine him as a serial child-killer. When his son went missing, he was heartbroken and appeared on the news, appealing to the public for help. When the body was found, he retreated into himself, and his wife left not long after that.

I saw his ugly side, but I always thought the trauma of his son's murder made him bitter and angry, and it wasn't difficult to empathize.

Empathy. It's seen as a skill, a way to connect with others and share the burden of experience. But it can be weaponized and made toxic. I over-identify with people's feelings and tend to cut them too much slack, excusing their shitty behavior. Then, when they hurt me, I blame myself.

When my family fell apart, I thought it was my fault.

My father told me my mama died because she tried to keep the family together for my sake. Shame I was such a fat, pointless loser. Mama wasted her life on me, and what good was I?

I hear Graham's voice, and my father's too, spitting the same cruel words at me.

Fat. Idiot. Naive. Slut. Whore. Needy. Psycho. Fuck-up. Damaged.

And I hear Ben.

He degrades me *and* praises me. I crave it.

I need a decent therapist, not a super-possessive older man who fucks me ragged and inflames what seem to be some deep-seated daddy issues.

I close my eyes, trying to convince myself to sleep, but the deep throb inside me takes me back to what happened in the car.

Don't think about that now.

I get out of bed and pour a glass of water before picking up the sherpa throw from the couch. It's warm around my shoulders, and I open the balcony door a few inches to feel the cool breeze on my face.

Think about what you know.

The Dollmaker wants Farraday alive but unable to coordinate an appeal. Drugging him in the hospital was a clever idea. Still, it was risky, as his apparent psychosis made him unpredictable. Anyone could have asked why he wasn't getting better or taken an interest in his wellbeing. It just happened to be *me*.

I wonder why The Dollmaker didn't just *kill* Farraday in the hospital. He has access to him somehow—surely it would be better to tie up that loose end instead of keeping him quiet with a combination of a chemical cosh and threats against his family?

The killer had access to chloroform and pharmaceuticals. That's not difficult, though. Graham could get those things easily, but so could most people. Ben's profile said as much.

What else?

Graham did what he could to cause trouble for me after we broke up. He put pressure on Oliver to sack me if I didn't drop my support for Farraday, but that could just as easily be because Graham is a vindictive prick who wants to shit all over something that matters to me. Just because his mom and dad don't give him enough attention.

Yawning, I sit on the floor by the open door. I rest my head on the glass as the sounds of the city drift in.

My attacker drove a long way out of the city. The Dollmaker supposedly dumped his victims far from where they were abducted, but how do we *know* that? The kids weren't identified, so we don't know where they came from, only where they were found. There were no connections between the sites. And why bother anyway?

I'm beginning to wonder how much of the 'factual' information in the case file is actually based on Farraday's confession. The data wasn't scrutinized closely because Farraday pleaded guilty, but knowing what I know now, it would be interesting to read it with fresh eyes.

The killer hasn't come back for me yet, but maybe that's because I have Ben close by.

If I was murdered, Graham would be top of the suspect list, but he's had quite the scare. Two beat-downs in one day from Ben, and although Hillard was reluctant to let Ben walk, he at least *knows* what happened.

It wouldn't take long to find out the grizzly details of how it went down between us.

Many serial killers begin with more minor acts. Little fantasies, acting stuff out. If Graham was abusive to his son, escalated, then murdered him, it would make sense. It's a high-risk strategy, and he probably didn't think it through, but when he got away with it, he must have thought he was invincible. He has enough money to pay off whomever he chooses.

I dare not say anything to Ben—if I spin him up into a frenzy, he might do something stupid or even kill Graham, even if Ben doesn't believe Graham's The Dollmaker.

The Bratva can insist a high-profile homicide gets brushed under the carpet, but they wouldn't pull out all the stops, not for Ben. Judges would be bribed, and he'd get off lightly, but he'd still go down for it.

I lie on the floor and pull the throw over me. My eyes are heavy, but I don't want to get back into bed. If I wake Ben, he'll be able to tell I have things on my mind, and he'll drag it out of me.

I don't know for sure what I'm capable of. Nor do you.

Did Graham say that to me once? I don't know.

Dirty little slut.

Graham definitely said *that*. But those words feel different now.

Sleep is creeping up on me.

It's *Ben* who's speaking to me. In my imagination, in my memory, I hear his voice saying disturbing and beautiful things.

Good girl.

Dirty little slut.

Good girl.

Love can vanish without rhyme or reason. It just *goes away*.

But even that fear makes no difference to how I feel. I'm crazy about him. Any time together is worth the misery that will come when I'm lonely again.

I'll be his good girl *and* his dirty little slut. I'll be anything he wants if he stays by my side.

What is he willing to be for *me*?

18

The Dollmaker

I've had a hard life, never getting *respect*. I DESERVE to succeed at this, and these FUCKERS are spoiling everything.

I have to be honest—part of me enjoys the violence, even under these less-than-ideal circumstances. I enjoy watching the words make the rage that makes the punch. Fascinating and such fun to manipulate people to this extent.

But it's not hard to bring out the worst in a guy like Benedikt. I think he occupies some of the same dark spaces where I tend to lurk. He just cares more and likes it less, which is a pity. It would have been helpful if the bastard wasn't so connected because I'd have been able to keep him from getting in my way, but I'm not equipped to tangle with the Bratva.

Momma is worried. She doesn't want anything bad to happen to her only son, and who can blame her?

I have significant and vital work to do. I want to preserve my greatness and not be denied my dues.

Roxanne is no longer Farraday's cheerleader. My man at the secure hospital confirmed that. Farraday is still as mad as ever—that is, not at all—and now he has no one on his side. *Good.*

He rolled over like a little bitch when I went to him with my proposition. Any man with an instinct for self-preservation would have told me to fuck myself, family be damned. If I hadn't been so worried about him deciding to do just that, I wouldn't have started dosing the guy, but either way, he's not gonna be saying my name any time soon.

It's *Roxanne* who is the catalyst of my downfall.

Her connection to me made me feel safe. She got so close and yet never smelled the blood. Never smelled the fucking *sickness* that oozes from every pore. She understands me like no one else ever did. Served me empathy on a silver platter, and I gobbled it up.

But she had to be a *good* person. She had to *care* about Farraday and seek justice like it actually exists. She may as well search for true love or the milk of human kindness while she's at it.

I feel myself unraveling like a ball of string, running away and getting tangled up.

Oh, Roxanne. Living Roxanne. I hate to see you in this state of decay. If you dare to come to me, you'll see what power I have. I can halt time in its tracks. That man of yours will never appreciate you like I could—like I *will*. He'll watch you age and wither like grapes languishing unharvested on the vine.

I make dolls, not wine. Let me harvest you. Then I'll celebrate my glorious resurgence by growing gerberas in your fucking eye sockets.

Maybe then you'll finally be pretty.

19

Ben

I wake up to a cold space beside me and no sounds of life. For a moment, I think something has happened, and I leap from the bed, bolting into the lounge.

Roxy is asleep on the rug like a cat, the sun streaming through the window. I feel a rush of relief and sit on the couch, watching her.

A feeling is pressing on my head, weighing me down.

This woman is stealing into places I don't want her to be. The parts of my psyche even *I* don't fucking visit.

I didn't try to stop her. That's the worst thing. The acid loosened me up, but all she had to do was nudge me, and that was it. I told her everything.

No. I didn't tell the *whole* truth. Somewhere in my addled brain, the sentinel guarding my worst memories was still at his post. *Thank fuck for that.*

I told her she didn't know what I was capable of. Long may she remain ignorant. But now I've outright lied about it, right to her face.

Can I keep it from her? *Yes, I can.*

Revealing my deepest pain is a risk I just can't accept. I need to keep the upper hand, keep *control*. If Roxy knew what festers in my shattered soul, she'd want to fix it, like the good person she is.

I don't want to watch her struggle to mend what's broken. Not when I know she'll fail.

I set my coffee machine doing its thing, and the noise jars Roxy awake. She sits up and rubs her face, blinking.

"Why are you on the floor, *charodeyka*?"

She frowns. "I couldn't sleep, so I got up for a while, then crashed. I was thinking about Graham."

"Oh, fucking *were* you?" The words are louder and harsher than I intended.

She grimaces and gets to her feet, throwing a couch cushion at me. It misses by a foot.

"Don't be such an asshole," she scowls. "I mean after everything *you* said last night. I got to thinking that maybe Graham *is* behind all this. It's possible."

"Don't throw this," I say, handing her a coffee cup. "I've now gone twelve hours without fucking myself up. If you scald me, I'll be extremely pissed off."

She sits down in the armchair and tries to shoot me an angry look, but she can't help but smile.

"So I get to kill Graham Fisher?" I say. I put my cup on the table and rub my hands together. "Fucking great news."

She shakes her head. "We'd have to be certain."

I lean back and put my hands behind my head, stretching. "I hate his guts and feel like spilling them. You telling me there's more to it?"

Roxy smiles. "If you murder someone and there's no evidence other than a strong hunch, you'd go to jail," she says, stopping to sip her coffee. "And I want you here with *me*."

She's right, of course. Fucking inconvenient, but that's the problem with society's iteration of justice. Too much paperwork and not enough bloodshed.

So, how to prove it? *No, wait.* That's the wrong question. Evidence *leads*, not follows. I hate Graham Fisher and would love for him to be The Dollmaker, but that doesn't make it true.

"What do you think?" Roxy asks. "We could track down Graham's ex-wife, ask her?"

I shake my head. "She's got no incentive to talk to us even if we *could* find her. She alibi'd her husband and would tell the same story again. She could be charged with perjury if she admitted she'd lied."

"Hillard could talk to her. If we explain to him— "

"No. We need to keep Hillard out of this. He's being obstructive already, and nothing we say will likely change that. He pushed aside your concerns both before and after you were abducted. If it comes out that he presided over a miscarriage of justice of this magnitude, he'll lose his job and be disgraced. If he catches on to what we're doing, he'll give us a problem."

She grins at me. "When did you accept that The Dollmaker really is still out there?"

"When I was tripping balls on supposedly therapeutic medication." I shrug. "Before that, it was all hearsay. Like you say, gotta be certain."

The smile drops off Roxy's face, and I realize I missed her point. She thought *she'd* convinced me.

"So right up to that point, you were humoring me? Screwing me and beating up my ex, and for what? Just to pass the time?"

She wouldn't fucking say that if she had any idea what it took for me to open up to her last night.

A voice inside warns me to rein myself in. The urge to lash out at her is tremendous—I could push her away so hard that she would never want to be within a thousand miles of me ever again. It'd probably be better in the long run. She'll start to see me in a different light when the new relationship energy wears off and she realizes *this* is all she's getting .

"Whatever you say, *charodeyka*," I say. A condescending sneer curls my lip for a moment before I suppress it. "It's not easy for me to accept that I was duped. *You* could have been mistaken."

"You weren't duped." She stands up, padding toward the bathroom. "You were used, manipulated. Now you know how other people feel when *you* do it to *them*. Sucks, right?"

The bathroom door closes behind her.

Am I manipulating her? To an extent, yes.

I recognized the chinks in Roxy's psychological armor as soon as I first started talking to her. She's a girl who needs love and affection like most of us need oxygen. If I was *truly* a monster, I wouldn't have cared about the possibility of hurting her, and fucking her would have been almost too easy. She even came to *my* fucking bed, and I resisted. Sort of.

Now that she's mine, I'm leaning hard into her issues. Degradation, then praise. I know the intermittent reinforcement is messing with her head, and that's addictive in itself, especially combined with a rough and dangerous sexual awakening.

I'm mixing all this shit up on purpose because it's what *I* like, and I never considered whether it's good for *her*.

Fuck it. She screams, she squirts, and she comes writhing on my cock. How much harm can I be doing?

And besides, I can't give her up. My personality type is one of extremes, which is why I want her to be just as obsessed with me as I am with her. Just *loving* her is what any gawky kid her age would do. She needs a grown-ass man to handle her. Her nasty little tricks in the car might have been just bravado, but I doubt it.

She *wants* to play. Who am I to deny her?

∽

I'm almost done with my coffee when Freddie calls me back.

"Good morning, Benedikt," he says, too brightly. "What's up? Did you butt-dial me?"

"I need a hacker. I know plenty, but none I trust to move quickly and quietly and not sell the data on."

"Good morning Freddie, I'm good. How are you?" Freddie mutters. "I swear my fucking cheese plant has more advanced social skills than you. Do you have anyone in mind?"

I lower my voice. "Giulia. I don't have her number anymore."

"How would your girl feel about you asking an old flame for favors?"

How the fuck does he know these things? I'm going to drag it out of him one day but now isn't the time.

Shut him down and get what I need.

"Roxy isn't *my* girl. She's *a* girl and no business of yours."

"I know you're obsessed with her," Freddie laughs. "Roxy Harlowe. The woman who might just make a sick fucker like you roll over and play dead."

I'm in no frame of mind to listen to this.

"You know I don't do love, Freddie. I'm having a great time fucking her pussy *and* her mind because that's what I always do, and when I get bored, I'll cut her loose. Nothing to fucking see here, alright?"

"You're a horrible person, Ben." Freddie sighs. "Here, take down Giulia's number."

I tap at my phone keypad, entering the number as a new contact.

"Thanks," I say. I hang up before Freddie can give me any more shit.

I'm dressed and putting on my wristwatch when Roxy emerges from the bathroom, her hair in a towel.

"Who were you talking to?" she asks.

I furrow my brow. "A friend. That okay with you?"

Roxy narrows her eyes at me for a moment, then turns away.

"So I have an idea," I say, watching her as she squeezes the water from her locks. "Has it occurred to you that Farraday's wife might know her husband was framed? He's taken the rap to protect her and the baby. Maybe she's just playing her part."

Roxy drags a brush through her hair, and my mouth goes dry as her fingers weave the damp strands into the same two Dutch braids that nearly sent me feral on that hot night in Hawaii.

"You might be right," she says, "but I don't know where Lois Farraday is now. She went into witness protection because she doesn't want contact with anyone from her old life."

I'm not saying anything, but my toe is tapping like crazy.

"Moira Coffey empathized with Lois," she continues. "She went through something similar when her husband's activities were made public. Always Home donated from the victim support fund to help Lois get set up in her new life. I'm not sure how much she got, but it was quite a lot."

This is valuable intel. Time to pass it on and get things moving.

I take my cell phone from my pocket.

20

Roxy

Ben is talking to someone on the phone. *Again.*

I should tell him I was eavesdropping just now. But what would be the point? He would deny what he said, gaslight me, and tell me I was crazy. And I'd believe him just to keep the illusion that we have something real.

But I *know* what I heard.

"Giulia," Ben is saying. "It's Benedikt. I know, baby, it's been a while."

Baby? I shoot him a furious glance, but he's not looking at me.

"I need you to do something for me, okay?"

His voice is the same coaxing tone I've heard him use on me. I feel slightly sick to listen to him talk to another woman that way, and it's disturbing how quickly he can switch on that glib charm.

"Can you access the Witness Protection database? Not the standard one, I mean the multi-level encryption."

I hear the woman's voice in the speaker, and Ben smiles at her reply. "Fantastic, that's a good girl."

My eyes feel hot, and I blink hard.

He just says whatever the fuck he needs to say to get his way. I'm *right here*. Doesn't he think I'll be pissed off that he's speaking to her like that, or does he just not care?

"I need you to find a woman called Lois Farraday. Her surname at least has changed, but she used to live in downtown Manhattan. Got a bunch of money from a charity. Okay. Speak to you soon."

"Who was that?" I ask as he hangs up. "Your ex?"

Ben wrinkles his nose. "No. Giulia freelances, like me, and does a bit of work for the Bratva since the CIA fucked her over. And crime pays, of course. That's the important bit."

"You really think she'll find Lois?"

"Absolutely," he says, "but Lois isn't the only person we need to locate. Graham Fisher isn't stable. That's obvious. He has eyes on the hospital and possibly on Lois, so he might get wind of what's happening. If he's coming apart, fuck knows what he might do."

I frown. "The cops won't do anything unless Graham acts out, and by then, it could be too late. I should text Graham. Arrange to meet him or something."

Ben runs his hand through his hair as he tries to think. "No. Would Oliver be willing to babysit the guy? They seem to be friendly."

As friendly as you and the lovely Giulia? If so, I'll buy a hat.

I wrinkle my nose. "I wouldn't call them buddies. Graham was already a patron of Always Home before his son died, so I guess Oliver tried to stay on the right side of him. Donors are gods to a charity like ours." I tap at my phone. "I'll ask him if he's seen Graham. Hold on."

Ben and I stand only a few feet apart, but he never felt more distant than he does now.

I wonder how he could say the things he said to me last night, knowing he didn't *feel* them. Then I recall what he told me about his empathy—that he can turn it off when it isn't useful. He also told me that toying with people is sport to him. It's not like he tried to hide his nature. *More fool me for thinking there was more to him.*

Not a minute after I send the text, the trill of my ringtone makes us both jump. I answer it immediately, pressing the handset to my ear.

"Roxy dear, I wish I *didn't* know where Graham was," Oliver says. "He's here now. Showed up at the office bright and early. I had to cancel the drop-in session to talk him down."

Woah. Not good.

"What's he doing?"

"Ranting. Talking about how no one respects him, how he deserves better and we'll all be sorry."

"Is he still there now?" I ask. Ben looks at me, his eyebrows raised.

"Yes," Oliver says. "He's determined to ruin your life and mine. He's saying he will get Always Home audited and me personally indicted for fraud if I don't fire you. Said it wouldn't be the first time he'd set someone up. As soon as I get him out of here, I'm calling the police."

I nod at Ben and close my eyes.

Jesus. I don't want to ask Oliver to do this.

"Please keep Graham there for as long as you can. Row with him, agree with him, but don't let him leave."

Oliver lowers his voice. "Why? This man is a reprobate and a blackmailer, and I don't want his dirty hands on my charity for a minute longer. Whatever is going on here, I will back you up. Tell me."

"I don't want to pull you into something, Oliver. But I'm gonna go and see Lois Farraday. Ben can find out where she lives."

"What would that achieve? Farraday is crazy, and Lois hates him. You said so yourself. "

"Farraday is sane. The Dollmaker framed him and threatened his family's lives if he spoke out. Someone on the inside was inducing madness with hallucinogens and tanking his appeal prospects, but he's been ducking his meds and feigning psychosis. When he sees his wife safe and well, he'll have the courage to tell the truth. I need you to trust me when I say Graham is the problem."

"I catch your drift," Oliver says. I can hear his voice cracking with tears. "I'm scared for you. You're taking your man with you, I hope?"

I glance at Ben, but he's not looking at me.

No. I'm not taking Ben with me.

"No," I say. "Ben's gonna stay around here and keep an eye on the situation. I'll be okay, I promise. Just let me know if Graham leaves. Can you do that?"

"Of course I can. I'd better get back to him. He thinks I'm in the bathroom."

"You're taking a huge risk, Oliver. Thank you."

"Rox, you're like family to me," he sighs. "You lost your parents, and I never knew mine at all. People like us gotta stick together." He hangs up.

I turn to Ben. "When we find out where Lois is, I'm going alone," I say. "We know where Graham is. You need to stay here in case he does something."

Ben stares at me, and for a long moment, no one speaks.

"Fine," he says. "As soon as Giulia gives me the information, you go to Lois Farraday, and I'll park outside your workplace like a fucking idiot."

He gives me a grin. I forget myself and smile back before remembering what I wanted to ask him.

"Oh yeah." I fold my arms and tilt my head like a quizzical bird. "Who *is* Giulia, exactly? You seemed very familiar."

Ben smirks. "Jealousy looks pretty on you, *charodeyka*. No, she is not my ex. She likes me, though. It makes my life easier if I play along. She's put my request at the top of her to-do list because I have enough sense to flirt when necessary, but I'm not always sweet to her."

"So you're playing with her? Manipulating a woman into giving you what you want?"

He shrugs. "Look, I've known her for a long time, but I never had sex with her. I turned her down. She didn't expect it, so she's always chasing validation that she matters to me because it was such a kick to her self-esteem." He gives a sharp laugh. "Intermittent reinforcement is the cornerstone of behavioral psychology and all too powerful. It causes addiction on a biological level, fucking with your dopamine. You read this stuff. You know that already."

Yeah, I heard that before. But the textbook description hits differently to the cold reality playing out in my life.

Ben is talking about deliberately creating a dysfunctional attachment because it gives him control. This is *precisely* what he's done to me, but in my case, he dominated my body and my mind until I was utterly powerless to resist.

He *specifically* warned me about this. Told me he'd hurt me for kicks. That he's Machiavellian and enjoys it.

Look at how he pivots from angry to tender in an instant. His rage is on a hair-trigger, his actions impulsive, yet he's capable of deep thought and profound connection. Or so I thought.

I'm a slut, a sorceress, a fuck-doll, his good girl. He degrades me, praises me, and degrades me again.

Am I on a pedestal or face-down in the dirt? There's no way of knowing for sure. And that's the point.

He knew I'd eat up this bullshit because he saw my pathetic love-starved heart from a million miles away. He played a long game and kept me guessing. Maybe he *did* try to avoid doing this, but like the little fool I am, I threw myself back into his life and at his feet.

He doesn't love me. Never has, never will. He just knows how to bind my stupid, pliable heart to his vicious one.

He's a bad guy. But he wasn't dishonest about it. I'm here because I *wanted* to be, just like when I crept into his bed in Hawaii.

"I wish you'd lied about who you are," I say, "but you didn't. It's all games to you, and I'm just a kid, a silly little girl. You could be mine, for real, but you don't care to be. Why would you?"

Ben furrows his brow. "I don't see what the problem is here. Are you pissed that I know another woman? Because a minute ago, we were talking about your ex, the murdering sociopath." He jabs a finger at me. "*You* have a type, Rox. Don't fucking blame me for your savior complex. Do you cling to psychos because you think you can redeem them? Trying to be enough when you weren't enough for your daddy?"

He's shouting now. His handsome face is twisted into an ugly sneer, the cruel words seeming unnatural, as though someone else is saying them.

"You may as well accept it," he continues, "just as we all must come to terms with who we are. Shit happens, and it fucking changes you, so what? I don't appreciate you coming at me like I'm some kind of predator. I tried to do the right thing, but you wouldn't let it be. You took everything I had to give. Don't pretend like you didn't love every second of it."

"How *dare* you mention my father!" I scream. "You're taking my trauma—the biggest pain I've ever known—and fucking *weaponizing* it? That's low."

He throws his hands in the air. "I *am* low. Empathy, compassion. I can take it or leave it."

His phone beeps, and he looks at the screen. "Giulia has sent me Lois's address. I'll forward it to you."

He walks past me to the door, picking up his jacket. I choke back a sob, and he wheels around in the doorway.

"Roxy, if you think I don't love you, then maybe you're right. You've known love. I haven't. All I know is the thought of breaking your heart makes me sick."

I didn't imagine he loved me until this moment. He never used that word before. I stare at him but can't think of anything to say. I feel suddenly foolish and so, so young.

Ben sees my broken expression and can't look at me. He taps the toe of his shoe compulsively, making no attempt to stop it.

"If the person I am makes you angry, you should let it take hold. Work on hating me, *charodeyka*. You'll be glad one day."

"Why won't you try to be the man I believe you can be?" I say, my voice wavering.

Ben takes a step toward me, then stops. His shoulders sag as he turns away.

"I'm sorry," he says. "I don't know how."

Then he's gone.

21

Roxy

Forty-five minutes of following the GPS took me to an affluent part of New Jersey. Lois Farraday's new life didn't take her far.

I need to focus on what's happening, but I can only think of Ben.

Hearing him talk so callously about me was bad enough. But then he turned on me when I asked about Giulia. As I was starting to feel real intimacy growing between us, he poured salt into my most painful psychological wounds. And why? Because I called him out for his mindfuckery?

Ben is *not* an irredeemable mess. He's sold himself that narrative as armor, a way to justify keeping others at arm's length.

If he doesn't let his guard down and let me in, he can't hurt me. I get it. But I can't hurt *him*, either.

Love demands vulnerability between two people—it goes *both* ways.

My soft heart again, looking for excuses to forgive him. I fucking heard him on the phone. The sooner I accept his words at face value, the quicker I'll move on.

He can't claim my heart only to kick it around. I won't let him.

I pull up outside the house. *Time to get my head on straight.*

◈

Like every other in this gated community, Lois's place is smart and well-kept. It's painted in ice-cream colors, her vanilla walls complementing the wafer-pink roof. Out front, there's a small garden and a carport with just enough room for me to squeeze my car behind hers.

I ring the doorbell and immediately regret it when I hear the cry. Baby Jamie must be coming up for two now.

Lois opens the door. It takes her three full seconds to recognize me, and as the realization dawns, her mouth drops open.

"Jesus, Roxy, get inside," she hisses, hustling me through the door. "What the hell are you doing here?"

"I gotta talk to you, Lois." I nod toward the ceiling. "You need to see to the munchkin?"

"Nah, he's just complaining. He'll be asleep in no time, kid's exhausted."

She walks me through to her kitchen diner, and I sit at the table. She pours me a glass of iced tea and sits opposite me.

"I knew someone would come one day," she says. "I just didn't think it'd be you."

"Do you know about the work I've been doing with Simon?" I ask.

She sniffs. "I do. God knows why you feel the need, but I know you believe in doing the right thing, even for the wrong people. And there are few people out there wronger than Simon."

I put a hand over hers. She looks at it, then back to my face. Her eyes search mine.

"He's innocent, Lois. I know it for sure."

She snatches her hand away from me, clapping it over her mouth. "How can you know that? He confessed. It was horrible. I was there when they read it in court."

"The real Dollmaker tried to kill me, but I escaped," I say. "He knew I would eventually get Simon's case some traction, and he wanted me out of the picture."

"Oh my God, Roxanne." Lois drops her head into her hands. "But they said Simon's crazy. Too unstable to file an appeal even if he wanted to. You were trying to get his treatment reviewed, and the case re-examined, weren't you?"

"Yes. But someone is swapping Simon's medication for something that is making him worse. The real killer doesn't want Simon to move to someplace where he'll get some help, and they don't want him lucid, either. Someone framed him and threatened to hurt you if he didn't go along with it."

Lois is pale. I know it's a lot to take in, but there's no time to go easy on her.

Simon is okay. He won't tell me who set him up because he's afraid for your safety, but if you come with me, we can—"

Lois throws her hands in the air, knocking her drink over. Ice cubes skitter across the tabletop.

"That fucking Hillard!" she cries.

You have got to be kidding me.

"Hillard? *He* framed Simon?"

Lois wipes her nose with her sleeve. "I can't say for sure," she says, her voice simmering with fury. "Like everyone else, I didn't dig too deep because Simon confessed. But Hillard was tough on him. Kept him awake for days in that interrogation, repeatedly asking him the same things until Simon's mind couldn't take it anymore. They damn near tore our old house apart looking for evidence and found a jewelry box I never saw in my life, with severed fingers inside."

I am trying to figure out what to make of it. I nod, encouraging her to keep talking.

"Simon walked into the station one day and just handed himself in. He never said a thing to me about it, and I was as shocked as everyone else. He took the police to a dead body. His fingerprints were on it. There were no prints on any others, but he said he got sloppy and wanted to be caught. That doesn't seem right now, does it?"

No, it doesn't. Did the sick fucker really make Simon Farraday touch a corpse yet to be discovered, so he could lead police to it and incriminate himself?

"Hillard will go from a celebrated and legendary detective to a complete pariah if Simon's conviction is overturned," I say. "He'll get his comeuppance, and the real killer will be caught. We're sure we know who it is already, but we need Simon to confirm it."

Lois glares at me. "You mean you don't think it's Hillard who's The Dollmaker?"

~

Ben

"Where are you?"

Roxy is in no mood for pleasantries. Not so much as a hello.

"I'm still parked outside your work," I say. "Graham's car is here. Has Oliver called you?"

"No. Listen, I have to tell you something." She pauses as though trying to get her breath. "Lois thinks Hillard framed Simon, but it's worse than that—she thinks Hillard is the killer. She told me a bunch of stuff that you need to know."

"Such as?"

"Hillard is new to this area. He took control of his current precinct just as The Dollmaker murders began. Before that, he lived upstate somewhere with his mom."

"I already knew that."

"Congratulations on once again being the fucking oracle of knowledge." I can hear the venom in her voice. "Did you know he went a bit crazy, and that's why he was transferred? His dad was a rich real estate guy, but his parents were estranged, and his father stopped communicating with him a few years ago. Then his mom died, and Hillard locked himself in with her body for three days. He wouldn't come out until his colleagues threatened to break down the door. He was talking to her, writing her letters, bringing her food."

That's fucking weird. And doesn't sound like something a sane person would do, but grief is a mindfuck.

"How does Lois know that?"

"Gossip travels. Lois had a friend on the force who told her the whole tale."

"So why the fuck am I sitting here like an idiot, keeping watch over your cunt of an ex?" I snap. "You distracted me and got me thinking Graham was The Dollmaker when it may, in fact, be the cop in charge of the whole case."

"Don't give me that," Roxy says. "I want the killer caught because I care about justice. You don't care about anything. You just want to mark your territory and make sure everyone knows what's yours. Wouldn't it be simpler to just piss on me and call it a day?"

I'm surprised at how much this gets my back up. Of *course* it would be easier to obsess over her instead of...whatever this is. But I can't have this conversation now. I need a clear head and can't let her fuck with it.

"Just take Lois to the psych hospital and find out once and for all what's going on," I say.

"I called them. They say I can't see Farraday because he took me off his approved visitor list. Apparently, he's in isolation anyway as punishment for yelling at me, and he's being crazy again, so even Lois isn't allowed in for the time being."

"So they forced some so-called 'medicine' down his neck." I pause for a moment, unsure of what to do. "Look, I need to think about this. Just take Lois and the baby to Leo and Ali's. At least I know it's safe there."

"Okay, fine. Whatever you say."

Dead air on the line.

Roxy sees me for what I am. Just as I'm finding my way out of the mess that is my own head, she's pulling away because I lashed out like the impulsive, angry bastard I am.

"Rox, things aren't adding up," I say. "Let me know if Oliver calls you to say Graham has left Always Home. I'm gonna try and find Hillard."

She sighs deeply. Then she speaks.

"Please be careful." A click, and she's gone.

Leo was right. I *do* love her. Always have.

I was lost from the moment I met her. I buried it under my neuroses, afraid that I would hurt her, but she's strong as fuck. Totally capable of standing up to me.

Now it's *me* who's hurting. And I'm not used to it.

22

The Dollmaker

Where would any of us be without Alexander Graham Bell? My namesake and the man who gave us the telephone. Without him and his innovation, there'd be no way for me to have got the valuable information I needed.

That dodgy Russian fucker must have used his connections to find Lois. I can't believe it never occurred to me before.

So the lovely Mrs. Farraday is going to save the day. Ride on in to see her precious idiot husband and, with the power of true love, bestow on him the confidence to tell all. Too bad he's in a rubber room now, but he won't be there forever.

Living Roxanne has resources and brains I didn't count on. She's not intelligent, but she's undoubtedly smart for a blonde. I should have torn that whoreish hair right out of her scalp when I had the chance.

She started this whole chain of events by not accepting her fate. If she'd given herself up to me in the first place, maybe I wouldn't have gotten so riled up.

The wheels have come off now. I see it in my mind's eye as though it has already happened. Farraday's attorney will get involved, the case will be reopened, I will be arrested, the works.

Momma always said I should hide away if I was gonna do these things, but where's the fun in that? At least it'll make a good story when it finally emerges who The Dollmaker really was. Of course, Momma's gonna be embarrassed when the whole grisly tale is told, but she shouldn't have played along if she couldn't take the heat.

Maybe then everything will just...sort itself out? Like in fairy tales, when all the evil magic is undone the moment the villain is vanquished.

Fairytales are closer to life than we think—all those evil stepmothers, heroic knights, and ladies fair. But let's not forget the sad, neglected, murdered children. There are so many stories where poor little souls get hurt. Hansel and Gretel. The Pied Piper. And, of course, those lonely princesses, beset by a curse and awaiting true love.

Roxanne has her champion. Without him around, I could get to her, but he's beyond my sphere of influence.

Sleeping Beauty and Snow White both effectively died in need of love, as she will. If their princes had any sense, they'd have left the girls to their slumber. Women are nothing but trouble.

Still. We *all* have to die sometime.

I still want to meet Dead Roxanne, and eventually, I will.

23

Roxy

Leo opens the door, his gun tucked into his waistband. Lois gasps. He looks from me to Lois and back again.

"Mrs. Farraday," he says, "I won't offer to shake your hand. You need to put that little guy down?"

Lois shakes her head, clinging tightly to her sleeping baby. "He'll wake up soon. I don't feel like letting go of him."

Leo smiles at her. "I completely understand. Come and sit down."

We're getting comfortable in the lounge when Ali comes in.

"Hey, she says, giving Lois an awkward little wave, "I'm Ali. Just fixing Luna some crispies. Do you need me to get you anything?"

"I have what I need, thank you," Lois says, her eyes shining. "I can't tell you how much I appreciate you doing this."

"Not a problem. Ben called and said you needed a safe place, and there's nowhere safer than here. My Leo is itching to find The Dollmaker and murder him. I had to talk him into staying with us and letting Ben handle it."

"I can't help it," Leo shrugs. "It's who I am."

That's true. But Leo loves Ali and Luna with everything he has. He didn't know he had it in him. Ben may be the same. Perhaps he can be who he is and still love me?

My phone rings yet again. I glance at the screen and quickly slide to green.

"Oliver! Is Graham still with you? You won't believe what—"

"He's gone," Oliver says, his voice weak. "He just left now."

"Are you alright?" I ask. A coldness grips my chest. What happened?

"Well, Graham and I...it got a little bit heated." He coughs. "He had a knife. Can you *imagine*?"

"Jesus Christ, Oliver! Did he hurt you?"

"A bit." He sounds woozy. "Quite a nasty scratch, to be honest. I'm going to need to get to the hospital."

I look at Lois. *Dammit.*

"I'm sorry," I say. "I have Lois with me, and I can't leave her. If I go off on my own with Graham running around somewhere, Ben will kill me even if Graham doesn't."

"Ben's not with you?"

"No. We need to find Hillard, but he's not picking up his phone. Ben's looking for him."

Oliver chuckles. "It's alright, dear. I called an ambulance already. Bring me a fruit basket and a sensational story when it's all over."

I think of something. "Did you call the cops?"

"Yes. Hopefully, they'll pick Graham up. That might be why you can't reach Hillard?"

I have no idea whether the police will even try to look for Graham. For all I know, everyone from the Commissioner down is in on this.

"Do yourself a favor, and don't speak to Hillard if he comes looking for you. He may have a part to play in all this, and I don't want you mixed up in it."

"Okay, I won't. The ambulance is pulling up now anyway."

"Thank you for everything," I say.

"I wish I could have done more. You're already a hero, Roxy. Hang on in there and see it through."

I hang up and turn around to see Leo and Lois staring at me.

"Graham Fisher?" Lois says. "Is that who you were talking about?"

"Yeah." I blink hard, trying not to cry. "He just attacked my boss. From the look of things, I'd say Graham is The Dollmaker, and Hillard is trying to cover for him."

"That's sick," Leo spits. "For the sake of his job, this detective is prepared to let a serial killer—of *children*—go free? And an innocent man rot in jail?"

"It certainly looks that way."

Little Jamie is awake and squirming. Lois sets him on the floor, and he's away, pulling books off the bookcase.

"It's alright," Leo says. "Luna does that too. Books are just glorified building blocks in this house."

"Simon knew Graham Fisher, sort of," Lois says. "They met once when Simon went to a Gambler's Anonymous charity thing. He had a big problem at one time, and GA really helped. Fisher Pharma donates, or they used to."

"Explains how they met," I say. "Now it's a case of who gets to Graham first—Hillard or Ben."

༄

Ben

Hillard is not at the station. He isn't answering his phone either.

No one seems interested in where he is. Cops going back and forth, doing whatever they do. The desk officer says she'll keep calling him, but he's probably just busy.

No shit, he's busy. Hiding evidence, burning incriminating files, who the fuck knows?

Irritation under my collar, like hives. I felt it before. Every time I thought about Farraday.

Hillard ditched my profile, and egocentric fucker that I am, I was pissed about it. So that's what I *thought* was bothering me—that I didn't get the recognition I was due.

But I never realized that Farraday was so different from my profile. I said the killer would have a large house with a basement, and he did, but that was the only hit.

It's all there in Roxy's case notes. He's a family man, a hard and diligent worker. He has a couple of misdemeanor charges from his youth but no sexual or violent crimes. Historic mental health issue, isolated incident. Medicated ever since and lived a stable life. Loving wife.

Farraday isn't The Dollmaker, so the profile doesn't fit. But what made Farraday a target? Why *him*?

The desk lady turns to answer the phone on the wall behind her. I have a clear view of Hillard's office.

It's open.

I move quickly, ducking under the desk and past her. As I stride across the bullpen and into the office, no one pays attention to me. I quickly close the blinds and push the door, leaving it open an inch or two.

My phone buzzes in my pocket. A message from Roxy.

Graham attacked Oliver and left. No idea where he is now.

I dash off a quick reply.

Stay where you are. Don't try the prison again. Whoever has been drugging Farraday might be willing to kill him.

What a fucking *mess*. It's no wonder I didn't work it out—how many psychos are in this? At least three, including me.

Hillard's desk is cluttered. Nothing stands out. It's just piles of paper. On the walls are photos in frames and Hillard's awards for excellence, going back to the start of his career.

I thought he was a clean cop, and so did everyone else. Is he just a narcissistic bastard with enough power to hide in plain sight? It fits the profile well enough. I said the killer would be self-obsessed and grandiose, concerned with his unique wants and needs, and unable to perceive other people as human beings. Whether Hillard is the killer or just covering for Graham to save himself, it takes a special kind of self-adoration to feel justified.

One of the pictures on the wall catches my eye. I'm unsure what drew me to it, but I can't look away.

It's Hillard and Graham Fisher in black tie, standing in front of a Fisher Pharma ad board. It looks like a hotel foyer. A corporate event.

So they know each other quite well. No surprise there. That tells me nothing.

I can't stop looking, though. It's as though I've seen the picture before, but where?

Hillard.

Graham Fisher.

Fisher Pharma. That garish red logo of holding hands inside a cross. I've seen it. It appears on pill bottles and –

Shipping containers. I've seen it on a shipping container. Why? *Where?*

I squeeze my eyes shut.

Come on come on come on come on –

A crime scene photo. The final victim was wedged under a jetty at Port Jersey. Found without her fingers, just like the rest.

Simon Farraday told police where to find the body, and the fingers were in his house.

My profile said the killer would need privacy and plenty of space, most likely a large private home. Fisher Pharma ships medicines by the ton, stopping all along the coast.

I remember seeing it. Fisher Pharma in the background of the crime scene photo, on the side of a shipping crate.

Could The Dollmaker really have used a shipping container as a portable cell for his victims?

That's just fucked-up enough to be true. After all, Graham's house was searched repeatedly when his son went missing, and he always has visitors. The company presumably has any number of commercial properties he could use to hide his activities, but they wouldn't be private enough.

He's a devious bastard, but the urge to show off might be his undoing. He dumped his final victim yards away from his lair, presumably so he could revel in his own cleverness. It's the sort of thing I might do in the same situation.

I snatch the picture from the wall and smash the frame on the desk, pocketing the photo.

Time to end this.

∽

It seems to take forever to get to the port. I hit several red lights but went through every one of them.

At least one person is gonna die today. Hillard, Graham, me—who can say? But Roxy is gonna make it even if I don't. She's safely behind closed doors with my best friends. Good people that I don't even deserve.

Get angry, go on a rampage, and regret it later. You'd think I'd learn.

Roxy. The gentle, good woman that I wanted to sully.

I got what I wanted, didn't I? Too afraid to admit to loving her, so I played my stupid little games instead. I figured if she saw me in all my messed-up glory, she'd pull away from me and let me return to my loneliness in peace. The peace I knew before she haunted my heart.

But no. Instead, she met my dysfunction head-on. Our personality issues complement each other in precisely the wrong ways.

She's everything I need. I'm everything she *doesn't* need. I knew this all along, but it didn't stop me from loving her. I allowed obsession to creep in and inflame my worst excesses when I could have just admitted how I felt and risked letting her into my heart.

I park and take a stroll. There's a security guard in a booth, but he's clearly seen some shit in his time. It only takes a small roll of hundreds to persuade him to look the other way, and he tucks the money into his inside pocket without a word.

There it is. The Fisher Pharma crate is near the waterfront. Anyone else would have moved the fucking thing, but this guy doesn't think anyone is as smart as he is.

Glad to prove you wrong, fuckface.

The thing about being a psycho is you have gotta get hold of it and not let it own you. Then you can harness the darkness and put it to work. If it takes the wheel, you're joyriding, and then you're fucked. It's only a matter of time before you crash.

Jesus.

I can see Hillard. He's skulking around between containers, gun drawn.

Is he waiting for me? How could he be? He didn't know I would come here.

I pull out my own pistol and duck behind a container. Hillard is about three rows away and moving toward me.

24

Ben

I never had weapons training. Just picked up a little from dicking about with the Gurin Bratva boys when I was younger. It's possible I could succeed in winging Hillard, but chances are he'll shoot me dead before I can do him any harm.

I draw a deep breath.

"Hillard!"

"Is that you, Voratov?" Hillard sounds short of breath, and I wonder if he's freaking out. "You fucking piece of shit. What have you done to Graham Fisher?"

"So it's true?" I get low and move fast, clearing the space and getting behind the container to my right. "You're covering for the fucker. How can you do this?"

"Do what?"

I hear his footsteps speed up. I roll my body against the container and round the corner. He doesn't see me as he passes.

"I just want this shit to be over," he shouts. "I don't know why you had to get your filthy criminal hands all over it, but murdering Graham won't change a thing. I know he hurt Roxy, but more important things are at stake."

"What the fuck are you talking about?" I shout.

I peer out from behind the container in time to see Hillard emerge. I'm forced to fling myself to the ground as he fires, but then he's upon me, the gun barrel in my face.

"Is he already dead? You fucking Russians think you can just do whatever you want, don't you?"

Little flecks of spittle land on my face as he rages. It occurs to me that it will take longer for me to say the right thing than for him to shoot me in the face, but it's all I've got.

Hit him where it hurts.

"Tate, I know you're afraid. But listen to me. I didn't kill Graham Fisher. Not yet, anyway."

Confusion flashes in Hillard's eyes, but he's not letting me go. He wedges his knee firmly into my chest, the pistol pressed to my cheek.

"I got a message from Graham," he says. "He said I should come down here unless I wanted to find another dead kid."

"Were you friends?" I ask. It's bizarre to be having a conversation like this, but I've no choice but to roll with it. "I found the photo of you and Graham in your office. Believe it or not, I know what it's like to find out that someone you've known for a long time is a completely different person. You tried to cover for him, and I get it. But Tate, the guy's a child-killing freak. You can't make that go away. He tried to kill Roxy too, and you know it."

Hillard pulls the gun away from my face and holsters it. He picks up mine and tosses it away, sending it skittering across the concrete. Without saying a word, he releases me and sits down, his back against the container.

"I'm fucking tired, Benedikt," he says. "I've been in this game a long time. When did the world get so fucking ugly?" He takes out a pack of cigarettes and offers it to me. I decline, and he lights up, drawing deep. "You always know things, don't you? Even before you realize it, you have it figured out. I'm not that way. I'm a grunt. Not to say I ain't good at my job, but I have to work at it."

"Just tell me what's going on, Tate." I shuffle and sit beside him. "It's gonna end badly for you either way, you know. Farraday isn't crazy, and Roxy has his wife in a safe place, ready to go and see him. When he has his family back at his side, he'll sing loud and long until his name is cleared, and every person with a hand in this mess will go down for a long time. Make it easy on yourself."

Hillard closes his eyes.

"I swear before God, I believed Farraday was guilty," he begins. "He walked into my station, asked to speak to me, and told me he was The Dollmaker. We'd had a few cranks try that trick, so I was initially skeptical, but when I took a statement, he knew things. Things that were never made public. I took a break after an hour and had to throw up. Can you believe that?"

He takes another drag, blowing out of the thin stream of smoke. He seems relieved to be finally talking about it.

"So he said he could take me to a body, and sure enough, there she was. Some nameless little soul. We found his prints on her. Her fingers were found at the Farraday home. Lois had to be sedated when she found out."

I'm watching Hillard as he speaks. I have years of experience reading people's tells, but I detect no false notes. The man's eyes are still closed, and he's talking like he's miles away. No narrative building, no need to convince, no glances at me to see if I'm buying it. He's letting the words flow as they come, with no tension or strain. If he can lie this convincingly, he's the scariest fucker I've ever met.

"So we intended to charge Farraday with six counts of murder, per his confession. But the only physical evidence pertained to the final victim. He refused to tell us what he did with all those fingers he took, and beyond that, there was nothing. I refused to accept the possibility that his defense would argue him down to the one charge—they were hoping to duck the M'Naghten card, and had they succeeded, he'd have a fixed prison sentence and normal appeal rights. *Parole*, even."

M'Naghten is the test applied to establish whether a person is legally insane and, therefore, can't be held criminally liable. That little doozy got *me* into a cozy psych ward and prevented me from being tried for murder.

"Right up to the day Farraday walked through the door, I was playing it straight. Everyone was leaning on me, ensuring I knew it'd be my neck if I didn't catch the killer. I couldn't afford to wait for the FBI-appointed profiler to find time to do the work, and that's why I hired you, not knowing you were just another leech."

"I resent that," I say. "Okay, so you got played. The Bratva has never knowingly let a weakness go unexploited. But no one wants a serial killer running around, including the Bratva—we have children too. The profile was sound. Why didn't you use it?"

"Because I junked anything that contradicted the notion that Farraday was The Dollmaker." Hillard stubs his cigarette out on the ground between us. "I raided the evidence store, demanded secondary post-mortems, anything I could think of. Planted some material at Farraday's home. Just fibers, that kind of thing." He looks at the ground. "I felt filthy at the time and every day since, but I thought the right man had gotten what he deserved. Roxy wanted the case reviewed, so he could appeal and have a proper retrial, but the man was too unstable. When she came to me saying she'd been attacked, I thought she was full of shit. I wasn't willing to see what was in front of me."

I get to my feet. "Tate, we gotta find Graham. Did you get to the Fisher Pharma container?"

"There's a padlock on it. I was about to check, but I heard you coming down here."

I retrieve my gun, and we approach the container in silence, being as light as we can on our feet. It seems impossible that Graham might be hiding in here after all the commotion we caused, but no good getting caught off guard.

The padlock has been cut. I shift it carefully, the cold steel heavy in my palm. Hillard covers me, his gun pointing into the darkness as I open the door.

A stink of piss hits me. Graham Fisher's feet swing uselessly, his head slumped forward. The noose is fashioned from a thin wire like the Gestapo used to use. He is very dead, a wet patch darkening the front of his slacks.

A savage pleasure hits me to see him this way, tempered by regret that I didn't get to kill him. The man who killed six innocent children, one of them his own. And dared to hurt the woman I love.

Hillard stoops to the ground and turns on his flashlight. The floor of the container is littered with Polaroids.

"Children," he says, shaking his head. "Kids he liked the look of. Maybe some of them are the ones he killed already, but not all. He was building up to a whole new killing spree."

There are cardboard files strewn around, some with red stickers on the covers. I pick one up and open it.

It's a form. Parts of the text have been blanked out with a black marker pen, but what's there is weird.

Referral made re. unknown male, approx. age 7. Seen alone in Mott Haven by a street outreach team but ran away when approached.

I hear a helicopter overhead. When I go outside to look, I'm dismayed that it's the WABC news team. No doubt, vans are pulling up right now.

"I'm gonna go to my car and call it in," Hillard says. "It's a shame we won't see the bastard on Death Row, but he can't hurt anyone else."

Roxy

I'm standing in Ali's garden, enjoying some fresh air and avoiding the oppressive atmosphere in the house. When the phone rings, I almost drop it in my haste to answer.

Ben speaks before I do.

"It's over. Graham is dead."

I drop to my knees. My hand flies to the back of my head, touching the stitches.

The man who tried to kill me is dead. The same man who killed his child. A man I got close to, only to realize there was something wrong with him. I just never knew how bad the wrong really was.

"Did you kill him?" I ask, stammering as the words come too quickly. "Where is Hillard? I have to get to Farraday so he can make a statement before the cops take you out—"

"Woah." Ben's tone is brusque. "Easy. We were wrong about Hillard. He fucked up bad, but he believed Farraday was the killer. Now that he knows the truth, he's given up trying to protect himself, and his career is effectively over. It's a similar thing with Graham."

"I don't understand."

"I'm sorry to say I didn't get to kill him. It's a long and ugly story, and I dare say you'll hear it from Farraday soon. Can Lois hang on a bit longer to see him?"

I peer through the lounge window. Luna is playing peek-a-boo with Jamie as Ali looks on. Lois is asleep on the couch, her head on a cushion.

"I think so, yeah. What gives?"

"Hillard wants to take Farraday's statement himself as soon as he's dealt with everything here. It's a mess at the moment. He's got officers keeping the press back, but it'll make the news anyway. Obviously, he's got a ton to do here, but he says he'll take Lois to see her husband tomorrow."

The sun is casting long shadows. The afternoon seemed to last for days, but that's how it goes. Good times pass quickly, and bad times drag.

In the end, it was love that conquered all.

Lois Farraday loves her husband, and he loves her. Enough to let everyone, including her, believe he is a child-killer. Hillard finally knows the truth, and so will everyone else before long.

There's so much I want to say to Ben, but it doesn't feel like the right time. I want to look into his eyes. Put my hand on his face.

"About earlier," I begin. "I—"

"No." Ben's tone is cool. "You're safe now, Rox. That's what I wanted to achieve. But I can't undo the things I've said, the things I've done. I warned you, but you didn't listen."

"I heard you on the phone," I say. "You said you would cut me loose when you got bored. There's no danger now. Is this the part where you laugh and tell me it's been wild?"

There's a loaded pause. Ben is clearly trying to decide how to respond to this information.

"You know what?" he says. "You think I was honest with you, and you should have heeded my warnings. You're right. But I didn't tell you the *whole* truth. So if you'd prefer to blame me and forgive yourself, I'm happy to help."

My blood runs cold. "What do you mean?"

"I killed my father, Rox. And I'm not fucking sorry."

I can't find any words. What can I say that would make sense?

"The cop, too," he continues. "I lost my shit and slashed them to ribbons. *That* is what I am and what I have the potential to do."

I feel sick.

I trusted him with my painful past, and he wouldn't give me the same. He lied to my face to keep the upper hand. To keep the *power*.

"It's not what you did," I say. "It's the *lies* that get to me. You were right—you *do* hurt people for kicks. Does it really feel that good?"

"It feels like shit right now, if that's what you wanna hear."

I understand what he's trying to do, and I know what to say. Something I doubt he's ever heard before.

"I forgive you, Ben. Forgive *yourself*. You were a frightened kid in a desperate situation, and you made a mistake."

"You can't fucking fix me, okay?" he says. "I'm all or nothing, and this is the nothing phase. So as you said—it's been wild."

My chest burns. Is this what it feels like to have your heart shattered like bone china?

I hate the sneer in his voice, but I *despise* the self-loathing that seeps into his words. He's trying to make me fight him, hoping it'll be easier for us both if we can swap love for hate.

I refuse to stoop to that. Like when I lost my mom and dad, I would rather *feel* the pain. It means the love was real.

"I still believe there's more to you," I say. "I hope we can at least be friends. We've been through a lot together."

The silence is brief but leaden.

"Yeah," he says, without sincerity. "What will you do now?"

"I might stay here. I might go home. Haven't decided."

The silence is weighted with unsaid words.

There is no 'us' anymore. That ship hasn't just sailed—it's wrecked, smashed to pieces because neither of us were willing to be the other's guiding light.

I hear Ben's name being called in the background.

"Gotta go," he says.

He hangs up.

I stand in the garden for a while, watching as the sun fades. The moon rises in an indigo sky.

Graham Fisher will never kill again. There's no one to mourn a twisted man, scrubbed out of existence by his own hand, unable to bear the weight of his sickness. Not only is The Dollmaker's reign of terror over, but Farraday will go free.

And I'm safe. I can return to my old life and carry on as though none of it ever happened.

I start to cry.

∽

When I go inside, my cheeks are stiff with dried tears.

Luna is already in bed. Ali has set up a room for Lois to stay the night, and Jamie is sleeping in Luna's old travel cot. Hillard called Lois and brought her up to speed, and I'm grateful because the thought of talking about it anymore leaves me numb.

The news is on the television in the lounge. There's pizza and beer on the table, but no one seems to have much appetite.

Aerial footage of shipping containers, with cop cars and officers standing around. One container is taped off.

"What did Hillard say?" I ask, sitting down beside Lois.

"He apologized for what he did to Simon," she says. "It was a good talk. It's a mess down there, files and photos and all sorts, but apparently, some things have been found at this Fisher guy's house. Some weird things. He didn't elaborate."

The shot zooms in, and I see Ben standing beside Hillard.

My cell phone trills. I snatch it up, hoping it's Ben, but it isn't.

"Moira?" I say, heading into the kitchen. "Sorry, the television was on. Have you heard?"

"Yes, I just saw it." Moira sounds rattled. "The press are loving it. The Dollmaker was still at large and a trustee of *my* charity? No one's released any details yet, but Oliver told me a few things."

Holy shit. I'd totally forgotten about Oliver. The poor guy leaped to my aid without hesitation and got injured in the process, and I put him out of my *mind*?

"Oh hell, Moira. I knew Graham attacked him, but a lot was going on at the time, and I didn't know how bad he was hurt. Is he gonna be okay?"

"He took a good slash to his chest. Lost a lot of blood, but he'll pull through. They called me when he arrived at the hospital–with him having no family, I'm listed as his emergency contact."

I sink to the floor, my head in my hands.

This is my fault. I shouldn't have asked Oliver to get involved.

"I had to go home and make sure Eddie's babysitter could stay awhile," Moira continues, "but now I'm about to head back to the hospital. You wanna come with? I'll pick you up, save searching for two parking spaces."

"Thanks, Moira, that'd be great. Can you collect me up from Ali's?"

"Sure. See you in a few."

I go back through to the lounge. "I'm gonna go see Oliver," I say. "He's still in the hospital. Moira's coming to get me."

Lois sits up and stretches. "I'm gonna stay here tonight where it's safe. It's getting late, and I'm not going to see Simon tonight, but I can go in the morning."

I smile. "Okay. Will you be alright?"

Leo and Ali are snuggled up on the couch. Ali tips her head back to look at me.

"You don't wanna wait for Ben?" she asks.

"No." My voice sounds small and defeated, and I clear my throat. "We talked already, and we're done. He doesn't really want me, he was just having fun."

"Bullshit," Leo says.

"You go if you want, Rox," says Lois. "Ali is looking after me. I feel like I've known her forever already. And I'll go with Hillard to see Simon when it comes to it. All I want is to feel my husband's arms around me." Her eyes shine. "I thought the man I loved had never existed. I cried so many tears for the love I lost, for my son who wouldn't have a daddy. Being a family again feels like a miracle."

Leo and Ali exchange a smile, and I sigh. They know how it feels to fight through an impossible situation with only love to keep you going.

Not everyone gets a happy ending, but I'm glad Lois will. She deserves it.

We sit in silence for a while, watching the rolling news. Nothing changes. It's the same footage, going round and round.

The gap in the drapes brightens. Headlamps outside.

"I gotta go," I say.

Ali follows me into the hallway and hugs me, cradling my head against her chest.

"Take it easy, Rox," Ali says. "It's gonna be okay. You belong to Ben, and he to you. He'll stop fighting himself, and when he does, you'll have devotion like you never knew was possible."

∽

Moira's Porsche SUV is rumbling on the drive. She winds down the window and waves me over, pointing at the passenger side.

"Come on, hurry!"

I open the door and jump in. "Okay, okay, I'm here! What's the matter, are we—"

My words cut off at the sight of her face. Her makeup is streaked with pale lines, making her look like a marble statue. She's staring straight ahead, her hands gripping the steering wheel. She's shaking.

"Moira?" I ask. "Hey, are you okay?"

Darkness and a stifling syrupy stench. A thick wad of fabric is pressed to my face with great force.

How is this happening again oh God no—

I wrench myself away from the hands on my head, the fabric falling away. The dash is rushing toward me.

I hear a crack and then silence.

25

Ben

At first glance, my apartment looks like it always does. But it will never feel the same.

A smudge of lip gloss on the edge of a glass. A towel draped carelessly over the door. The bed is messed-up from where we tumbled around in it only hours ago.

Back when I thought we would make it together.

I want to call her, but I don't. Doing whatever I want is what got me in this mess in the first place.

The Dollmaker is dead. It didn't take much—failing to kill Roxy obviously sent Graham off the deep end. I'm glad I got a few good punches in before the cowardly fucker took himself out.

He was a man without a conscience. A man who took what he wanted, acted out when he was denied, and used other people to meet his own needs. His fantasies drove him to snuff out innocence and potential, leaving behind devastation and loss.

I don't like having things in common with a man like Graham. I told Roxy that deviance is on a spectrum, but so are many other things.

We all have the capacity to commit terrible acts. But I don't believe in evil for its own sake. What I do believe in is far more terrifying.

It's often said that evil people do fucked-up things, but that's too simple. In fact, every individual who commits an atrocity feels justified. They have their reasons, even if they are incomprehensible or based on bullshit.

When I killed my father, I told myself it was the inevitable consequence of the way I'd been treated. If you tie a dog up and kick it every day for years, you can't be surprised if it turns around one day and tears your throat out. The cop was just in the way. Hard luck for him.

For the first time ever, I *don't* feel justified. Roxy's belief in justice has reached into me, made me see things differently. When I told her what I'd done, she offered me forgiveness, and somehow that hurts more than hardening my heart ever could.

I feel fucking terrible, and for once, it's not *me* I feel sorry for.

My love for Roxy was real. I was too afraid of what that might mean, so I let the darkness inside me smother it. She was innocent, too, a woman willing to be grazed by my rough edges if it meant she could have the good parts of me.

I couldn't handle the possibility that I might be dangerous to her, so I pushed her away.

I fucked her so hard. I should have *loved* her even harder. She deserves a man who will cherish her and have the courage to bare his chest, trusting her not to stab him in the heart.

That man isn't me. I knew it all along.

I've never been more sorry to be right in my life.

I open the refrigerator and take out a new bottle of vodka, twisting off the cap. I put the bottle to my lips.

No.

Roxy said I drink too much, and she was right. She was right about so much.

I'm not gonna let my dysfunctional bullshit define me anymore. I may have squandered Roxy's faith in me, but I feel her in my heart, urging me to do better. To *be* better.

I stand over the basin, watching the vodka as it swirls down the drain.

I crawl into bed and roll onto Roxy's pillow, breathing her in. The pain hits with a hollow thump in my chest.

She's gone.

⁓

Roxy is running. She's scrambling through shadows, appearing and disappearing. I try to keep her in view, but I can't keep up, and she gets increasingly distant. Somehow, I can still see her eyes dart maniacally as she looks over her shoulder.

She's so afraid.

I look behind me. Pillars of darkness block the light, then reveal it. Roxy is crying, her thin wail of panic tearing the air.

I cast around, looking for the danger. She looks for what she fears, the thing she wants so desperately to escape from.

Other figures are running behind me in the blackness. Faces flash past me—my father and my mom. The cop I killed sometimes appears in the bright spots, looking bewildered as his chest blooms red.

Then all the others are gone, and I can't see Roxy anymore. Did she escape?

The light grows bright and sharp, like a blade, and I understand.

Roxy was running away from me.

∼

The sun crests the window ledge and casts a bright stripe through the gap in the blind, right across my face. I reach for Roxy before I remember that she's not here. She's home or with Ali or wherever.

My mind chatters as soon as it's awake, like a toddler. Tossing scraps of knowledge around, still trying to piece together a puzzle already solved.

The cops will find everything, Roxy will tell them about the acid, and Graham's filthy little drug mule will be offered a plea bargain in return for their cooperation. Hopefully, no more bodies will be found.

I never had the epiphany I was waiting for. That buzzing in my head is still there. I expect it's driven by my ego, pissed off that I didn't figure it out. I mean, Roxy and I had the fucker pegged, but before we could nail down our hunches, Graham went and killed himself.

I roll onto my back and stare at the ceiling. The blank space helps me slow my thoughts and allow the critical stuff to float to the top.

Graham Fisher. Roxy's ex, who she refused to sleep with. Killed his son but killed *two* other kids first?

There's something I'm missing there. *Park it and move on.*

Trustee for a children's charity, Always Home. He had been a big money donor for years and liked to make sure it was his name on those giant cheques.

Figures. He was a narcissist; many enjoy altruism for the accolades it attracts. He must have liked being perceived as a generous, caring man. I'll bet he got quite the kick out of hiding in plain sight. He certainly manipulated Roxy into believing he was decent, at least until she got to know him better.

Just like I did.

Don't think about her.

The buzzing in my skull is working up to a shrill pitch, as though someone is using a bandsaw on it.

Graham Fisher. CEO of the East Coast logistics side of Fisher Pharma. Wealthy, well-connected, with access to drugs. Anyone can buy LSD, but it's a different matter to swap it for real medicine. Graham must have found an employee he could manipulate.

Only child. Distant, cold father. Coddling mother. A classic combo to create a killer.

Tried to kill Roxy. Maybe it was because of her support for Farraday, but it could be because she rejected him. Men like him don't respond well to that kind of thing.

When I first gathered intel for the profile, Graham was the grieving father of a murdered son, a married man with a beautiful home that was searched from roof to foundation. Nothing of interest was found there.

There wasn't much in the shipping container either, now that I think of it. There were photos, files, and a box containing locks of soft, child-like hair, each tied with ribbon. All very incriminating. But when the cops went to his house, they found only more of the same.

What troubles me is the lack of posturing. I get that Graham was losing his shit, but his fundamental nature would not change. He got away with six murders and framed an innocent man—failing to kill Roxy sent him off the deep end, but that doesn't mean he wouldn't want the world to know what he'd done.

Once he decided it was over for him, I'd have expected to find a glorious manifesto of his mission, surrounded by his various trophies from the bodies. All those fingers are somewhere, still hidden. *Why?*

My head is starting to really hurt.

I didn't expect the killer to be a family man. It surprised me with Farraday, and it surprises me now. Why the *fuck* would a man kill two random children, then kill his *own* son, drawing massive attention to himself?

Graham's wife alibi's him. I assumed she'd lied, as though assumptions are worth a damn.

I'm too restless to lie in bed anymore. I get up and find the case file, dumping it out onto the floor. One of the pieces of paper is a list of when and where the bodies were found.

Found. Not killed. We don't know when they were killed because they weren't identified, except for Graham's son. He was the only one who was found buried, many miles away.

So he *did* start with his son. He just took more care to hide his body far from home?

No. It's still not quite right.

So what? The man was a fucking child-murderer. He might have done things for no reason. Maybe it was symbolic or something.

He was *looking* for the kid. On the news, making appeals. As soon as the body was found, he and his wife were there, wanting to make a formal identification and end the nightmare they were going through.

I remember when I first met him. The rage on his face as he talked about his son's stupidity. It was like he was lashing out at me, at him, at anyone he could. Guilty knowledge could easily do that, but so could grief.

He had zero sense of self-preservation when I went to his house the second time after he was rude to Roxy. Goading me, trying to get me to act out. Then again, in the restaurant.

Needless attention-seeking. Not the conduct of a calm, methodical sociopath.

Graham was a shitty person. I was keen to see him as a potential serial killer because I hated him. I dismissed anything that didn't fit the hypothesis. And, like Hillard, I was too desperate to make it stick.

But Graham Fisher *did* kill himself. He failed to kill Roxy. He must have realized he couldn't try and kill her again—not with me around and the cops making inquiries. But that wouldn't be enough to push him over the edge. Something made him believe he was doomed, that he'd be found out.

We'd barely *begun* to look into it. We were still wrangling with Hillard. I'd been arrested and released. Roxy had found out Farraday wasn't insane after all, and we located Lois, but Graham knew none of this. He was at Always Home, being distracted by—

Holy shit.

The shrill whine in my ears cuts out, replaced by a thundering, deafening silence. I draw a deep, shuddering breath, trying not to pass out, and lunge for my cell phone.

Roxy doesn't answer. I try Ali, then Leo, but no dice.

Snippets of memory scatter my mind like confetti. Each one I catch hold of seems to take on a new significance.

The walls of Roxy's apartment are covered in press photos of her and her colleagues. Different pictures of the charity winning awards, handing over funds to children's wards, that kind of thing.

Oliver Buckley was at the center of each and every one.

There are photos on the wall at Always Home, too. The same images, in fact. But they were scanned, blown up, and cropped, so Buckley was the main focus. Certificates in his name, letters of thanks. His good works surround him, protecting him.

He lives alone, devoting his life to his charity work. He knew Graham Fisher. He must have met Farraday through him.

My phone is ringing. It's Ali calling me back.

"Ben, I'm trying to get Luna ready for—"

"Is Roxy still with you?" I ask.

Please say yes. Please say I've gone crazy and I'm wrong and she's fine and I just need my fucking head examined.

"No. She left last night with Moira to visit Oliver in the hospital."

"Which one?"

"What's wrong, Ben?" Ali asks. "I've never heard you sound like this. Do you need me to—"

"Ali, which fucking hospital?" I cry. "Just tell me!"

"Presbyterian, lower Manhattan!"

I hang up on her and look up the switchboard for the hospital, typing the number in with shaking fingers. A bored-sounding woman answers.

"Hello," I say, trying to sound casual. "Can you tell me if you admitted an Oliver Buckley? It would have been yesterday."

She taps on the keyboard for a few agonizingly long seconds.

"There's no one here by that name," she says. "Are you sure that's the person you're looking for?"

I wasn't. But I am now.

26

The Dollmaker

Living Roxanne is now in a transitional phase. Soon-To-Be-DEAD Roxanne.

I know I'm done for, but I will go out on a high. Why shouldn't I? It's so little to ask that I be allowed my whimsy now and again, but no. Living Roxanne and her boyfriend had to SPOIL it all.

Graham Fisher was my favorite kind of useful idiot. I kept reminding him that Roxanne rejected him *and* was pushing for an appeal that could see his son's killer winning a chance for parole. It was hysterical watching him build up a head of steam over the whole thing.

At first, Benedikt was *helping* my cause. It wasn't feasible for me to try and kill Roxy again, at least not immediately, but Benedikt's possessive rage complimented my plan perfectly. All I had to do was wind Graham up and point him at Ben, and *bam*. Two fights in one day, drawing negative attention to themselves.

It was such a fun idea. Bereaved father is obsessed with ex-girlfriend, fights her new boyfriend, murders *her*, then kills himself? It would have been so *tidy*. Not as satisfying as it would have been if Roxanne hadn't escaped from me in the first place, but acceptable.

Of course, I didn't know Ben was in with the Bratva until Hillard refused to take any assault charges forward. That was a massive spanner in the works, as was Ben's insistence on staying at Roxanne's side.

Plan B was to make Graham disappear, leaving evidence suggesting Benedikt was responsible. It wouldn't have been challenging to make that stick to an impulsive, rageful degenerate like him. Hillard would then have had no choice but to arrest Ben, leaving Roxanne alone and defenseless. Then *I* could have taken my time over her, really made her *suffer* for trying to be better than me.

By the time the Bratva bailed Ben out, Dead Roxanne would be found with Dead Graham in a beautiful murder-suicide tableau, depicting an age-old story of toxic love.

But that was *before* Roxanne called and casually ruined my life with her news about Farraday.

I still can't believe Roxanne found out Farraday wasn't crazy. The sneaky bastard took it upon himself to duck his medication? It never crossed my mind that he would do something like that.

So, it follows that he told Roxanne he'd been set up, and she figured he'd spill the beans if his wife and rugrat were safe.

So Mr. Bratva used some highly illegal way of finding out where Lois was, and off Roxanne went to see her.

I never wanted Farraday dead. He's my pet. I went to *so* much trouble to keep him in his special little cage.

My weasel at the hospital called me and said Lois was trying to get in to see Farraday. It was late enough in the day to block them, but I knew Hillard would get around that by morning. So I told the weasel to kill Farraday and save us both.

He *refused*.

When I told Momma, she said I was FUCKED. She never usually swears. I think it was her pathetic way of trying to get me to stop all this, but she should have known better.

When Roxanne asked me to keep Graham occupied, it was an easy request to grant. It's not like he was going anywhere, seeing as I already killed him. I had to move quickly, taking Graham to the shipping container and stringing him up. Hard work, but I can get a lot done if I push myself.

A few minutes at Graham's house, a quick text to Hillard from Graham's phone, and that was that.

You CUNTS wanted Graham Fisher to be The Dollmaker? You got it. But it's a fucking insult to have that idiot's name associated with my work. Good thing it won't be for long. Tomorrow I'll finally get the appreciation I deserve.

All I wanted to do was get to Roxanne. I knew Hillard would be occupied for hours dealing with the suicide of The Dollmaker 2.0. Maybe, just maybe, Benedikt would think it was safe to leave Roxy alone. I laughed my ass off when I found out Ben was looking for Hillard, thinking he was in on it.

It was a mess. All I could do was hide in my favorite place and wait to see if anyone came looking for *me*.

But my life is charmed. My missteps were corrected by the universe, guiding me gently onto the path I was *meant* to walk.

Even though so much went wrong, it somehow fell into place. There was Hillard on the news, saying Graham Fisher was The Dollmaker. Benedikt Voratov in the background. I had hoped they might shoot each other and make my day, but it was still the opportunity of a lifetime.

Living Roxanne and her idiotic compassion. All it took was a sob story and a phone call, and she hurled herself into the trap.

I can't preserve this. I know that. But for a few golden hours, the unlikely duo of criminal and lawman will believe that the nightmare is over.

The world will want to understand my mind. You have not seen my like before and will not again.

It won't be long before it all comes crashing down.

I'll make the best of the time I have.

27

Roxy

I draw a deep breath as my eyes flutter open, inhaling a lungful of stale, mildew-smelling air.

It's dark, but there's a little bit of light coming from a small frosted window.

A basement. The light outside is probably streetlamps.

I'm sitting up, my knees bent. My abductor has learned from his mistake—I'm zip-tied and duct-taped. My hands are bound to my feet, left to left and right to right, and my mouth is covered. There's a painful tightness in my forehead, as though the skin is stretched too thin. A metal mesh is pressed to my cheek where I'm leaning on it.

I'm in a wire crate. The little door is locked, but the crate is collapsible. The sides are secured to each other with zip ties, but I have no doubt I could kick it to pieces in under a minute.

There is another crate beside this one. A small figure is inside, lying down.

Tears fill my eyes.

I could get out of this crate. A terrified child probably couldn't.

With that, I'm sobbing, screaming into the gag. I know I must keep quiet, but I can't. Panic clutches my throat, and I try to breathe evenly.

A low bulb pings to life. It's dim, but I can see far better.

My captor must have heard me. He'll kill me when he comes down here.

The wire of the cage has bite marks on it. Little smears of blood on the ground. I wonder how many desperate tears have soaked into this dirt floor. How many sad young lives ended in pain and terror in this lonely place?

At least six. *Two more to add.*

I glance at the cage next to me. I can see the child now—he's lying on his side, his head on his arm.

It's Eddie Coffey.

Moira Coffey's cherished little boy. Her only child. *Is he dead?*

I watch him, keeping my eye on his shoulder. It rises and falls with his breathing.

Oh, thank you, God.

I understand that I'm seeing something no one was ever meant to see. This is what The Dollmaker did with those children. Brought them here and kept them in cages as if he owned them. Why? What was he getting out of it?

A realization punches me in the gut.

I never told Ben I loved him.

The last time we spoke was horrendous. There was more to say, but it wasn't the right moment. What arrogance we had to assume more time was promised. That we could return to the conversation and clear things up.

We already spent *months* lying to ourselves.

That night in Hawaii changed everything. He disappeared, and I thought I'd lost him for good. We found one another again, and despite everything, we felt something real.

But we clung to our insecurities. Resisted the change we forced on one another. I wanted him, but it became a *need*, and I was afraid to acknowledge it. He was going through something similar, but instead of knocking down his walls and letting me in, he built them up again.

When I saw him last, we fought. The image of him turning away to leave is burned into my memory. Already it feels like years ago.

We had *so* many chances to do things differently. If we hadn't been so wrapped up in one another, we would have realized that we were wrong about the identity of The Dollmaker.

Now it's too late.

Will anyone even find me? I'm sure the cops and Ben will put it together—after all, Lois will see her husband in the morning, and the grim truth will come out. I'll be dead by then, and so will Eddie.

I close my eyes.

It's been years since I last prayed. Before it all went wrong, my mother used to pray with me, but when she died, I stopped. I didn't want to talk to God and ask Him to watch over me. He clearly wasn't going to help me. Mom had been devoted to Him, and look what He allowed.

But I *had* love. I'd rather have the memory in my heart than have never felt it.

Ben never had love and never believed he could. I missed my chance to tell him he was wrong.

Lord, please spare Eddie. He's only six, and he deserves to live. Take *me* instead. I want to be with my Mommy.

And please. Let Ben be happy. Help him to heal and grow.

Let him feel my love.

∼

I'm dozing fitfully when I hear a squealing sound. A deadbolt being shifted.

Someone is coming in.

I crane my head, but the basement appears to be an L-shape, and I can't see around the corner. Then a familiar face appears.

"Roxanne, you're awake! How are you feeling?"

It looks like Oliver, but it isn't him. Not the man *I* know. His eyes are wide and unblinking, his wide mouth twisted into a sneer.

For a moment, I wonder if this is all a very unfunny joke.

He has no bandages and no signs of injury. Of course he doesn't. Graham never laid a finger on him.

"You can't answer." Oliver tuts theatrically. "Silly me. I'll take that tape off your mouth if you promise to behave."

I nod, and he opens the door of the crate. His nails pick at a corner of the tape, and he rips it off my face in one go. I scream involuntarily, and he slaps me across the cheek.

"What the fuck did I just say?"

∽

Ben

I'm driving too fast, heading for Always Home. I don't know where Oliver Buckley lives, but if I have to kick the door down to get in there and find out, I will.

Hillard didn't pick up his phone. When I called the hospital, they said he and Lois were in an interview room with Farraday.

He's gonna call back and say Farraday named Graham. Oliver Buckley will be home or at another hospital, or it's an error.

No. The more I think about it, the better it fits. It fits like it never did with Farraday or Graham Fisher.

My phone rings as I turn onto the street. I pull over and answer it.

"Ben, we have it all wrong," Hillard bellows. "It's Buckley. The whole thing is a stitch-up *again*. Farraday confirmed it, and I questioned his keyworker too. The silly fucker buckled like a belt almost immediately. He's been buying acid, switching out Farraday's meds, and getting paid. Said Buckley called him and tried to get him to murder Farraday, but he wouldn't do it—"

I speak, cutting him off. "Hillard, I *know*. I'm about to arrive at his charity offices now."

"You are? How the fuck did you find out?"

"I didn't. In the calm after the storm, my head wouldn't stop chattering, and I got to thinking about all the pieces that didn't go together. I called the hospital, and Buckley was never admitted."

"I sent every unit I could find to his apartment, and they smashed their way in. It's pristine, nothing out of place. They're already at Always Home, too, searching the joint. Found a few things that need a good look-over, but no Buckley."

Apartment? He doesn't have his own house?

I swallow the lump in my throat. "I think he has Roxy. She's not picking up her phone. The last anyone knew she went to see Oliver at the hospital. Moira Coffey picked her up."

"Shit," Hillard says. "I assumed Roxy was with you. I'll get someone to swing by her place and Moira's too, see if we can find them. Keep it together, buddy, and don't get involved in this now. You have to keep your hands clean, so your girl can come back to you."

"Fuck you," I say, my chest tightening with rage. "I'll kill him."

"Benedikt, steady." Hillard's tone is stern. "I get it, I really do. But I'm fucked here. The best I can do is see this asshole caught, and, God willing, we find Roxy alive and well. If you start pulling your lawless Bratva vigilante shit, you'll get arrested, and my word ain't gonna be worth a damn when my superiors find out what I've done. Don't bring yourself down to Buckley's level."

"I'm promising nothing."

"The Farradays are staying together at the hospital for safety. I'm leaving now. Go find Detective Landon at Buckley's apartment, he'll keep you informed. I'll catch you up." He relays Oliver's address and rings off.

I sit still for a minute, trying to think.

There's *still* something I'm not seeing.

Roxy is missing. Oliver is missing. Moira Coffey is missing. Her little son too.

Roxy is probably already dead. I can't save her.

I'm a wretched creature. I was *before* I loved her, but now I've lost her again?

Fuck it.

I swore I'd find the person who hurt her and fucking kill him, and I *will*. I don't care what Hillard or anyone else thinks. Even if she *is* alive, she doesn't love me, but that doesn't mean I won't happily die for her.

I hear a bang and see a gate blowing in the wind.

The Farraday's old house is now derelict. A large property in its own plot, with a garden on three sides. Wooden board over the windows, but not the door.

The only thing Farraday had in common with my profile was the right kind of house. High hedges, privacy. Almost certainly a basement.

Oliver Buckley doesn't *have* a house. He couldn't have committed his crimes in an apartment—people would have heard things, seen him coming and going.

The little fucker *said* something to me. At his office, before he suspended Roxy from her job.

I'm always looking for new premises, he said. *I desperately need space to keep things safe.*

I open the driver's door.

Farraday is innocent. The cops know he's innocent. He didn't kill anyone. Very little evidence was found here back then, but it's the last place anyone would look now.

I shut the door again, shaking my head. *This is ridiculous.* I need to get hold of Leo and call in some support. I put the key in the ignition.

Then I hear it. A short, high scream carried on the wind. It cuts out in half a second, but it's enough.

I retrieve my gun from the glove box and run up the path toward the house.

28

Roxy

Oliver holds a bottle out to me, pinching the straw between his fingertips and putting it to my lips. I look at it dubiously.

"It's water, dear. I wouldn't go to all this trouble to poison you, although I'll admit I should have done that in the first place."

I take a sip. He puts the bottle beside him and sits cross-legged opposite me.

"You must know it's over for you," I say. "Simon will tell the truth, and the cops will come. Why make it worse?"

"Worse than what?" Oliver gives a hollow laugh. "I killed six children that they know of, plus Graham Fisher. Do you think sparing you and young Eddie here will make a difference? You gonna do that thing you do, demand compassion for me? Say I'm misunderstood?"

He wants to be understood. Admired, even.

I have to keep him talking for as long as possible. If he starts telling his story, he'll want to finish it.

"I always looked up to you, Oliver," I say, "but people will find out what you've done and think you're just a loser."

Risky to say that. It could go either way.

Oliver frowns. "Hmm. Do *you* think I'm a loser?"

"Not at all. It's not fun being here like this, but you must have your reasons."

Tell me all your bullshit justifications for the disgusting things you've done. Take as long as you like.

"I was lonely," he says. "Do you know what that's like? I know you do. Your Mommy and Daddy didn't love you."

Fuck you.

"They *did*, once," I whisper, "but something went wrong."

"Doesn't it always?" Oliver rubs a crimson spot on the concrete floor. "My father spoiled me, after a fashion, but he sure as shit didn't love me. As for Momma, well. She was never as accommodating, but I could get around her."

My mind is playing tricks on me. I thought I heard footsteps overheard, but no.

"You told me you never knew your family," I say.

Oliver glares at me. "You don't think maybe I told a few whoppers, Roxanne? Everything you know is a lie. Even the numbers are wrong. Back when I had help getting my hands on the little fuckers, I killed many more than six."

My blood chills at his words.

I'm gonna die here.

"I wanted to ask you something," I say. "Why didn't you have Farraday murdered? All this effort to keep the man under control when you could have silenced him forever?"

Oliver smiles. "Truthfully? He was a *trophy*. I wanted to keep him in a box, just like all those sweet little fingers, and look in on him whenever I chose." My expression betrays my disgust, and he scoffs at me. "You'd have another word for that, I expect."

Despite everything, he wants my approval. I guess he's never talked to anyone about this before.

If I deny him the understanding he craves, he may be unable to resist the urge to dig his heels in and demand it. Narcissists are like that—they want their superiority recognized. I read that someplace.

Of course, he might get mad and kill me.

Don't give up. Think your way through, as Ben would.

"To be honest, I'd call it hubris," I say, "or just plain old-fashioned conceit. Amazing you managed to keep up a murder career for so long with that kind of sloppy self-indulgence."

Oliver's nostrils flare with anger, but I can almost see the cogs turning in his head. He hates that I don't see things his way.

"You don't get it. Momma's the same. She misses the point every time." He gets to his feet and starts pacing. "Those children barely *had* lives to lose. Do you think little Max Fisher was happy? Graham was a terrible parent, and his wife didn't try to stand up to him. That boy was out of the house a lot, and he used to come by my place and have lemonade. It was our secret. We *talked*. His life was worthless and difficult, so I helped him. That's what I do, remember? I *help* children. I won awards for it."

I can't respond. I'm just staring, open-mouthed. *Does he really believe that?*

I suddenly understand. Max's body was dumped over three hours away from his home, buried in wasteland. If it hadn't been for a metal detectorist picking up his belt buckle, he might never have been found.

The reason Oliver went to all that trouble? Because Max Fisher was the *first* to die. Oliver *knew* the kid had a family. A family who *cared*. He didn't want the body discovered and identified—the trail could have led back to him. It was a sickening stroke of fate that it didn't.

"Anyway," Oliver continues, "even if I did wrong, I did a lot that was *right*. I raised millions of dollars for impoverished, neglected, lonely brats everywhere. Do you think the Almighty would begrudge me a few flea-bitten strays? He kills for fun *too*, you know. He likes to bring us into His service sometimes. An atom bomb, an earthquake—it's all the same."

I'm crying again. I'm not sure when it started, but it makes Oliver smile.

"Poor Roxanne. All you had to do was keep your fucking nose out of it, but *no*. You had to make it into a crusade for justice. Farraday is just a marionette, barely sentient. Most people are. Do you know what the Nazis called people like him?"

My vision is foggy, not just from tears but from dizziness. I shake my head to clear it, but Oliver takes that as an answer.

"I thought not. They called them *Lebensunwertes Leben*—'life unworthy of life.' Every single life I took was unworthy, to the extent that it can barely be considered murder at all. It was euthanasia. An act of *mercy*."

I drop my chin to my chest, unable to hold up the weight anymore. Oliver's voice seems to come from far away.

"He's not coming for you, is he? Love has abandoned to your fate again."

He bends down and reaches into the crate, taking hold of my chin and pulling my head up so I have to look at him. I'm reminded of Ben doing the same thing, and my heart sinks.

"You're fodder, Roxanne. But you already knew that."

Screaming from upstairs. A woman's voice. Oliver jumps to his feet and picks up his gun. He looks at the ceiling, his eyes darting as he follows the sound.

"I think your hero is here," he says. "If it were the cops, there'd be more of them."

Oh my God. Ben.

The screaming cuts off abruptly. A thud as a body hits the floor.

Oliver reaches for me and smooths the tape back into place over my mouth.

"Won't be long, dear."

Ten minutes earlier...

Ben

After the scream, I hear nothing more. All is silence.

I move slowly and quietly through the house, even though I want to run. Whether I'm being cautious or just delaying the moment when my life comes to an end, I don't know.

I don't believe I'll die at Oliver Buckley's hands. The little bastard has got it coming to him. But if he's killed Roxy, I may as *well* be dead.

All the things she showed me, and I fucking *refused* to learn. She tried to get me to understand justice. *True* justice, not the Bratva way where people get murdered, and the details are thrashed out later.

Roxy wanted evidence that Graham Fisher was the killer, but I was happy to believe it because I hated him. Hated him because he put his hands on what was mine. I should have listened to her and not allowed my anger to take the wheel.

I played right into Oliver Buckley's hands. Sure, the cat's out of the bag now, but that's down to Roxy. Her empathy for Simon Farraday and his wife gave them the courage to find their way back to one another.

I thought Roxy was naive, but she isn't and never was. Compassion isn't just a tool to her. It's a superpower.

She *knew* Simon Farraday was innocent. She knew Lois would come back to her husband's side. And she could see that Graham Fisher, though a bad person, was incapable of these atrocities. It was *me* who distracted her and forced her mind to follow the path I chose.

She didn't see the potential in Oliver Buckley, but no one else did either. The man is entirely on another plane, if he's a man at all. We may never discover what motivated him, and maybe that's for the best.

The house is not entirely empty. There are some larger pieces of furniture that Lois Farraday couldn't or wouldn't take with her. The windows are boarded up good and solid to dissuade vagrants and vandals. It's darker than I expected, and I feel my way with my feet, peering through the gloom.

A doorway here. As I move my foot, the carpet gives way to what I assume is linoleum. It cracks under my weight, making a noise.

"Who's there?"

A female voice, but I know it's not Roxy.

"I have a gun in my hand," I say. "Don't move."

I round the corner and look into the room. A gap between the boards is wide enough to let in a little of the morning sun. I'm dazzled for a moment, but as my eyes adjust, I see it's a kitchen.

A woman is sitting at a battered wooden table, staring straight ahead. Her silver-blonde hair is in a bun, her face pale and waxy in the cold light. Her hands are on the tabletop, and a quick scan suggests she has no weapons. She isn't tied up or restrained.

She has no fingers on her left hand. Each of the five stumps has been tied off with a zip tie, the loose end neatly clipped. A sticky pool of blood spreads beneath her hand, dripping off the tabletop.

The shock abates, and I recognize her.

"Moira? Moira Coffey?"

She turns her head to me slowly and smiles.

"Oh, it's you," she says, her voice light and girlish. "Have you come for Roxy?"

My grip tightens on my gun. What the fuck is she doing here?

"Yes, I have. You don't look well, Moira." I take a step closer. "Are you alright?"

"I'm fine," she says. "Have you brought anyone with you? Police?"

"No." I holster my gun and advance, getting closer. "They don't know what's happening, but they're looking for Oliver. There are cops at Always Home right now. I'm not leaving without Roxy, but you could have them here in two minutes if you run."

She sighs and looks at her mutilated hand. "Look what he's done already. He told me what would happen if I tried to run. I'm very sorry. I can't lose my son. You have no idea what I've done to keep him safe. Terrible things."

The kid, what's his name? Eddie. *Oliver has Eddie?*

"You can't trust him to keep his word, Moira. Just go get help. Do you know where Oliver is keeping Roxy and Eddie?"

"So-rree," Moira sings quietly. "I'm so so-rree."

"You don't have to be sorry, just—"

She leaps out of the chair and hurls herself at me, screaming like a banshee. I see a flash of brightness in her good hand and realize she has a knife. Where the fuck did she hide that?

She's not strong, but she's afraid. She fights like she's possessed, slashing wildly at me as I back away fast.

I grab the open kitchen door and slam it hard into her face, sending her flying, and she falls backward, smashing her head into the table as she goes down. She doesn't move again.

Sounds coming from below, heading my way. I think about moving *toward* the noises, but someone is coming to see what the commotion is, and I have no idea what to expect. I'll have the advantage if I can find some space.

I move back into the hallway and find the balustrade, following it up the stairs.

29

The Dollmaker

Oh, would you look at that. Momma's head is leaking.

She's on her front, her head turned to the side. A patch of drool coming from her mouth, and a larger puddle of red from the back of her head spreading over Lois Farraday's shitty linoleum.

Never mind. At least she's not suffering anymore. The last year or so has been hell for her. I look at her lying there and feel something, but I think it's just contempt.

Some guard *she* was. I thought the fact that my sainted half-brother is in a slaughter cage downstairs might be motivation enough. I threatened to kill the little cunt so many times, but this was the first time I ever actually *took* him from her, and she went to pieces. Literally.

I can't help but laugh. Those pieces are now in my treasure box, in their own special compartment. One of the few things I just had to bring with me when I relocated.

Momma's basement *was* perfect for my hobby. Soundproof, with lots of space. No one poking around. The cops will find it soon, and then they'll know what they are dealing with.

I had to leave my writing and my pictures. I had so many beautiful photographs. I spared a few to decorate Graham's death scene and left some at his house for fun, but there are thousands more on the basement walls. No time to collect them.

But I brought my treasures. The most important thing of all. The collection isn't complete, of course—I had to sacrifice one set to Farraday, to make sure he could back up his confession. The idea that a serial killer would take the fingers and not keep them was nonsense.

I knew it was a risk not giving Farraday *all* my treasures, but I couldn't bear to part with them, just like I couldn't bear to part with Farraday himself. Luckily for me, Hillard was a desperate man under pressure. He didn't see anything he didn't want to see.

Creaking of floorboards upstairs. I click off the safety on my gun.

Benedikt Voratov. A Bratva man, a fixer. He called me the same day he went to see Graham Fisher, long after the boy's body was found.

I was still ansty—I killed the kid because I just couldn't resist, but I wasn't sure whether his visits to my house were indeed a secret. It turned out the profiler had me on his list of Graham's acquaintances and just wanted some background color. I played it down, said I knew nothing, and the conversation was over in less than a minute. He didn't even remember my name when he came by the office with Roxy. Ignorant prick.

Something tells me he's gonna remember it *this* time.

I should have killed Roxy as soon as I heard the noises upstairs, but if I can get the drop on Ben, I can take her a present. Seeing what happens when I throw his head into her cage will be hilarious.

"Benedikt!" I yell as I advance up the stairs. "The little bitch is already dead. You're too late!"

30

Roxy

Oliver is shouting. I can't hear him clearly, but he's laughing.

If Ben kills him, I'll get out of here. If Oliver kills Ben, I'm going to die horribly.

They might kill each *other*, in which case Eddie and I will starve in this underground hellhole.

I glance at Eddie. He hasn't moved. I don't know how long he's been here, how long he's been unconscious. I assume he's drugged, but when did he last have water?

The cellar door opens, making me jump. I didn't hear footsteps overhead, not close by, anyway.

A dragging, scraping sound. Someone is crawling down the stairs. Heavy breathing, strangled gasps. There's a short cry as they fall the rest of the way, hitting the stone floor hard.

A face appears around the corner. A woman, leaning on the ground with her right hand, propped up on her left elbow. Her back and shoulder are covered in blood, her hair matted.

It's Moira Coffey.

She creeps to me, agonizingly slow, like a zombie. I'm paralyzed with terror, unable to move a muscle. As she draws nearer, I see her fingers are missing on her left hand. When she opens her mouth, her jaw judders for a few seconds, and she has to flex it to calm it down.

"Roxy," she slurs. "I'm sorry, sweetie."

My cage door is still open. Moira raises a shaking hand to my face and peels the tape away.

"Jesus, Moira. What did he do to you?"

"Who? Oh," she smiles weakly, "well, Oliver came to visit me and took Eddie, brought him here. We came to collect you, and then he..." she pauses for a long time, as though she's lagging, "...cut off my fingers. He said he would spare Eddie and me if I helped him."

She produces a small knife from her jacket pocket and busies herself with my bonds. I decide not to ask her anything more, as she needs her energy. It's a slow process as she's rapidly losing strength, but eventually, the tape is off, and the zip tie is cut away. My right hand is free, and I straighten my leg, wincing as my knee joint clicks.

Moira drops the knife, and I grab it, immediately working on freeing my left hand and foot. Moira retreats, moving laboriously. She opens Eddie's crate and crawls beside him, spooning his little body.

I'm free. I crawl out of the cage and stand, stretching my limbs. Everything hurts, and my head feels like a bowling ball, threatening to snap my neck with its weight.

I drop to my knees and reach into Eddie's cage, wanting to help, but Moira bats feebly at my hand.

"He's alive, Moira," I say, my voice cracking. "Eddie will be okay, but you might not be. You need to get to a hospital."

"I'm done," she whispers. Her eyes are closed. "The truth will come out, and I'll lose Eddie. Just get him out of here."

What is she talking about?

"Oliver is my stepson," she says. "He changed his name long ago. He's Adrian's kid from long before his father and I even met. The apple didn't fall far from the tree."

Oliver Buckley is Oliver *Coffey*?

Her eyes open for a moment. They're dull and unfocused, and I know she has nothing left.

She inhales, sharp and harsh. She uses her last breath to spit three words at me.

"Make him pay."

Her head slumps, and she's gone. I look at Eddie. Mercifully he's still out cold.

Oliver is still shouting.

I pick up the knife and make my way up the stairs.

∽

Ben

I wait in the study, the room furthest from the stairs. Oliver is taking a methodical approach, checking room by room, and yelling taunts as he goes.

My rage has calcified into a boulder of grim resolve. I'm ready for him.

It seems wise to assume he has a firearm. I'm not a world-class marksman, so I don't fancy my odds in a one-on-one gun battle. He has a distinct disadvantage, though, in that I want to kill him much more than he wants to kill me.

Come on, you sick fuck. I'm not gonna lose my shit, not this time. Not gonna call out to you, not gonna rush you so you get a chance to fuck me up. You can come to *me*, and we'll see who's the boss.

Footsteps, getting closer.

I move behind the door, gun in hand. If I disarm him, I can kill him.

One chance is all I need.

Silence. Fast thuds of retreating feet as he descends the stairs.

Roxy screams.

I hurl myself out from behind the door and sprint along the landing.

She's alive she's alive she's alive she's—

I see them as I get to the top of the stairs.

Oliver's arm is around Roxy's neck. He must have grabbed her from behind. She's gasping, kicking out, fighting to get free. He wedges the barrel of his gun against her temple, and her body sags, limp as a ragdoll.

"Don't you fucking move!" he yells at me. I freeze halfway down the stairwell.

"Toss that gun back up onto the landing," he sneers. I do it without hesitation.

"Take it easy, Buckley," I say, showing him my empty hands. "You don't wanna do this."

"Oh yes, I fucking do," Oliver says. "Your little slut should have learned not to meddle. I had everything the way I liked it until *she* started fiddling with things. And my name," he grins, "is Oliver Alexander *Coffey*."

What the *fuck*?

"As in Adrian Coffey?"

"Show some fucking respect," Oliver spits. "My father was a *senator*."

"Most people think of him as a pedophile before anything else."

"And that's the problem!" Oliver says. He's working up to a rant, and it seems wise to let him. "He was a public servant and did *good* work, like me. And he kept me calm. Brought me the occasional sad little soul when he and his friends were done, and I dispatched them. I was happy, he was happy, and the kid wasn't living in hell anymore. But Father was murdered, and I didn't get any more treats. I had to go looking for my fun, and that's when I thought of Momma, the lovely Mrs. Coffey. Let me tell you, she wasn't pleased to hear from me."

"Do you call her Mom?" I ask. "She isn't old enough."

"No, she isn't," Oliver sneers. "The gold-digging bitch just married my father and spawned the little fucker downstairs. I call her Momma to piss her off, but she always reminds me that Eddie is her *only* son. My real mom didn't bother with me. She was one of my father's whores. I grew up in foster homes until I tracked him down."

Keep talking, you egocentric idiot. You think your origin story is of interest to two people who are listening under duress.

"Moira was working hard to rehab her image after my father's hobby went public," Oliver continues, "so she wasn't best pleased to find he had a secret son with similar interests to his old man. She was on the board of trustees at Always Home, and I wanted in—I was already known for charity work, so with her patronage, it was a cinch."

"Why did she help you?" I ask. "She could have gone to the police."

"Because she knew I would take Eddie and kill him. And she's not a wonderful person either, you know. She knew about my father's proclivities but enjoyed her lifestyle, so she looked the other way. It's much the same here. She reinvented herself as a committed activist for victims of crime, a protector of innocents, just like Roxanne here. Momma knew I would use the charity's resources to find the children no one would miss. The buck stops with me as the manager. I dealt with every referral personally, remember?

"You asshole," Roxy croaks. Oliver laughs.

I'm so proud of her. There's every chance we're both gonna die, yet she's insulting him.

The cops are around the corner. The door is open. Someone needs to pass by and look inside, that's all. But Oliver has nothing to lose now. As soon as he sees a single uniform, he'll shoot Roxy dead.

Oliver is still talking, blathering on about his mission of mercy.

Fucking piece of shit. The playbook never changes. God complex. Natural order. Justification that doesn't and can never exist, except in the mind of a man who cannot accept what he is.

I keep my eyes on Roxy's face. She stares back at me, holding my gaze.

I can't save her. She knows it. But her eyes are calm, her expression serene.

I'm so sorry, charodeyka. I let you down. Don't forgive me, not this time.

Oliver howls and lets go of Roxy, dropping his gun. Roxy wheels around, keeping hold of the knife buried in his thigh, and twists it hard.

"Take that, you fucker!" she screams in his face.

~

Roxy

Oliver is reaching for me, a guttural roar of rage ringing from his throat. Ben runs down the stairs and barrels into the flailing Oliver, sending them both rolling across the floor.

"Get the gun, Roxy!" Ben cries. "Find it!"

The two men are on the ground near the wall, each trying to get over the other. Ben pins Oliver with his knee and punches him, spattering blood along the baseboard.

I see the gun near the kitchen door and try to run past the fight. Oliver's hand darts out, gripping my ankle, and I fall heavily on my face, hitting my forehead again. I look over my shoulder and see Oliver jab his fingers hard into Ben's eyes. As Ben recoils in agony, Oliver rolls out from under him.

He's coming after me.

I grab the gun and wheel around. Oliver is right there in front of me, getting to his feet, moving fast.

"You stupid little—"

I scream and fire. The bullet passes through the upper right of Oliver's chest and hits Ben's shoulder as he rises.

Oliver slumps to the ground with a groan.

I drop the gun and run to Ben, falling to my knees beside him. He's flat on his back, clutching his injury.

"I'm sorry!" I cry, my tears falling onto his chest. "Let me see, is it bad?"

He lets go of his shoulder and puts his bloody palm on my cheek. "It's a graze, *charodeyka*. Are you alright?"

"I'm fine." I cover his hand with mine. "How did you know where I was?"

"I didn't." He smiles. "But when the cops couldn't find Oliver, I figured it out. I was trying to convince myself I was wrong when I heard you scream."

I can't believe he's here. I was so sure I'd die without seeing him again.

"Roxy, listen," he says, kissing my palm. "I didn't mean all the bad shit I said. It was wrong. I knew it even then, but I was too much of a fucking coward to admit how I felt. Obsession *isn't* love, but I went from one to the other without noticing it, and it scared the shit out of me." He looks into my eyes. "Will you forgive me for being a moron?"

I tilt my head at him. "Which time? Because you were a dick to me in Hawaii, rude as fuck when I came to your apartment, and just generally hard work. You *caused* problems with Graham *and* Hillard—"

"Okay, I'm asking too much." Ben sits up, wincing.

"You gonna give me shit for shooting you?" I ask.

"Nah. We'll call it even."

Oliver is lying in a pool of blood, muttering between groans of pain.

"Hey," he says. "Hey, Roxanne. Come here."

Ben gets to his feet and takes the gun from my hand.

All he wants to do is kill the man who hurt me. That's been his goal from the start. But that was the possessive, wrathful part of him. The part that tried so hard to push me away.

I hope he still has some of that left for *me*. I fell in love with *all* of him—the bad as much as the good.

Oliver manages to raise his voice as Ben approaches him.

"You fucking stupid Russian prick. My father always said the Bratva was full of cretins."

Ben kneels and places the barrel of the gun against Oliver's eye.

"The Bratva *killed* your father," he says. "My best friend shot him. Your father was wrong, but I wonder—how smart do you think I need to be to end your pointless life right here?"

"Do it." Oliver's words trail off into a hacking cough, but he recovers enough to spit feebly at Ben. "Kill me. You don't know anything else. Criminals like you are the missing link. Civilization is just something that happened to other people, isn't it?"

"People like you?" Ben's hand shakes as he grips the gun. "You're fucking pathetic."

"So make me pay," Oliver snarls. He's laughing again. "Go on, do it."

"I won't kill you," he says, "because as much as I *want* to do it, that's what *you* want, too. I promised Roxy you'd be at *her* mercy, not mine. You want to die? Beg her."

Ben stands, keeping the gun trained on Oliver's face. He places his feet on Oliver's wrists, pinning him down.

"Come stand by me, *charodeyka*," he says. I stand at his side, congealing blood sticking to my shoes.

"I was a kid when I took two lives. One was blameless, one not so much." He sighs. "There's no taking that back. But this fucker is *not* innocent, and my conscience won't give me a moment's trouble." He stares at Oliver, but he's still speaking to me. "You're a better person than me, Roxy. I won't ask you to do it yourself, but if you want this thing dead, say the word."

The man who hurt me is bleeding rivers under my feet. Just as Ben promised.

"Hey, Roxanne," Oliver says, fixing me with a stare. "Everyone will be *fascinated* by me. Psychologists will make studying me their entire careers. I'll never be lonely again. Don't you wanna stop that from happening?"

"You know what *I* think you're most afraid of, Oliver?" He frowns at my smile. "I think you're worried that no one will give a shit, and you'll be a nobody. A sad loser, just like you've always feared. You'd rather die than risk *that*. Wouldn't you?"

Oliver doesn't answer, but I see the realization dawning in his eyes.

He enjoyed having a captive audience—literally—and talked too much. Like a fool, he gave away how to *truly* make him suffer.

Sirens. Police cars are pulling up outside. Someone must have heard the gunshot.

"Shoot me!" Oliver howls. "Don't you want your revenge?"

"Yes." I put my hand on the gun, pushing it down, and Ben lowers it to his side. "But in this case, I don't have to choose between justice and vengeance. You'll get what you deserve."

A SWAT guy peers around the front door, his gun in hand.

"Woah," he says. "Nobody move." He glances at Oliver, who is now sobbing quietly. "That's him, right?"

"Yep," Ben replies. "I'm putting the gun down, okay?" He skims the gun along the floor to the officer.

With that, the hallway of Farraday's house is full of people. Paramedics swarm Oliver, patching him up and hauling him onto a stretcher as cops rush the place, sweeping the rooms.

I'm crashing. The adrenaline in my bloodstream is falling fast, and my head is pounding again.

A cop is yelling in my face, asking me questions, and Ben is yelling back. But I can't hear them. Everything sounds like it's underwater.

"Moira and Eddie Coffey are in the basement," I mumble. "Help them."

My knees buckle. Ben catches me and lifts me into his arms, my head against his shoulder.

31

Twenty-four hours later...

Ben

The *déjà vu* is killing me.

It didn't take long for a nurse at the hospital to patch me up. The bullet took a small piece of my shoulder opposite where I was shot last time. All it took was a handful of stitches and a gauze dressing. Now I'm getting by on Tylenol and free to go home.

I'm going nowhere without Roxy.

The private room is comfortable, with a large armchair. I sit beside her and watch her sleep.

She almost passed out in my arms as we left the Farraday house and scared me shitless, so I bundled her into a waiting ambulance. The paramedic checked her over, and it was more shock than anything. Now she's sleeping it off.

I'm exhausted. My body aches all over like I fell down a flight of stairs. I place my palm on my neck, flexing as I look down at the newspaper.

It's the tenth article I've read today, but I can't let it be. My name might appear, and I need to deal with it fast if it does.

The headline yells at me in Franklin Gothic capitals.

REAL DOLLMAKER KILLER CAUGHT! SHOCK AS SET-UP AND CORRUPTION UNCOVERED.

Pictures of the Farraday house, Graham, Oliver, Hillard. And Roxy.

Hours after police attended the scene of a gruesome suicide, a story of deception, murder, and corruption has finally been uncovered.

Oliver Buckley, Managing Director of Always Home children's charity and well-known fundraiser, is in custody after the man who confessed to The Dollmaker murders, Simon Farraday, revealed Buckley framed him for the crimes.

Authorities have yet to release an official statement, but sources suggest one courageous young woman, Roxanne Harlowe, was working on getting The Dollmaker case evidence reviewed. Roxanne was abducted only days ago, but she escaped and reported the incident to the police, who were slow to act.

A picture of Roxy that I recognize from her apartment. I smile at the sight.

Police initially believed Graham Fisher, a trustee at Always Home and former partner of Roxanne, was responsible for the attack. He was found dead two days ago, alongside evidence suggesting Fisher was, in fact, The Dollmaker. Believing herself safe, Roxanne went to visit Buckley. It was then that she discovered the terrible truth.

Bit tabloid-y. Wait until they get the *whole* story.

A shot of Graham at a podium, giving a speech. It's bizarre to realize that, bad guy though he was, he wasn't even *close* to the worst. He was a bastard to Roxy and a shitty, unpleasant man, but he lost his son in a horrendous way. I wonder if it twisted him up inside and made him hateful. If so, I can understand that. Maybe go as far as empathize, though it feels unnatural.

We have yet to confirm the precise timeline, but we know that Roxanne planned to bring Farraday's wife Lois to visit her husband, hoping he would tell her the truth. Buckley became aware of this and set a plan in motion to delay the inevitable, leading the police on a wild goose chase.

Questions are being asked about lead Detective Tate Hillard, who was at the center of The Dollmaker investigation from the start. The experienced gumshoe gave hours of prosecution testimony against Farraday, and he discovered the body of Graham Fisher. It is now believed that Fisher was murdered by Buckley, who staged the scene to make it appear that Fisher not only committed suicide but was the dreaded child-killer. With police occupied, no one involved took the crucial final step of speaking to Farraday, and the delay gave Buckley what he was looking for—an opportunity to finish what he had started.

The people who snitch and info-mine for the Bratva are the same people who sell shit like this to the press. Hospital staff, correctional officers, cops, court clerks—they see things and are expected to keep their mouths shut. Why would they? Criminals and newspapers have tons of cash to throw around. This paper spent plenty.

Knowing his identity would soon come to light, Buckley lured Roxanne to him, claiming to have sustained an injury in an altercation with Fisher. Following an intervention from a friend of Roxanne, she was found alive and well at the former home of the Farraday family, which Buckley had planned to use as a new base for his heinous activities.

Moira Coffey, wife of senator and notorious pedophile Adrian Coffey, was found severely injured at the scene and later died. Her son Eddie was rescued and is recovering in hospital. The nature of their involvement is unclear at the moment.

A crappy long-lense shot of a small figure on a stretcher being carried to the ambulance.

Poor kid. We'll never know the truth about Moira's part in this mess—there's only Oliver's perspective, and he can't be trusted. Eddie Coffey is an orphan now. A boy with a painful legacy to live with.

There's that empathy again. I flip the page and keep reading.

Detective Hillard has been suspended following a debrief with the Commissioner and is expected to be summarily dismissed with prejudice for his role in the botched investigation that put an innocent man behind bars.

Hillard kinda had that coming. But the guy did the right thing in the end, and I respect him for that.

My name is nowhere to be seen. I assume Kal Antonov got the word out that, as far as anyone else is concerned, I don't exist. It probably wasn't a hard sell—the cops look bad enough right now, and the press doesn't like to get the attention of the Bratva if they can help it.

Roxy turns over to face me, her eyes fluttering open. Her hair is a rat's nest, her skin sallow, but her eyes are as beautiful and blue as ever.

She never looked better.

"How goes it, Major Tom?" I ask.

"That's what Ali said when I woke up in the hospital after you shot me. When did you start listening to Bowie, anyway? You said he wasn't your thing."

I shrug. "I've been here for hours and needed something to do. Or I've been playing his music for months because I adore you and want to understand the things you love. Pick one."

Roxy smiles and tries to sit up, but she's struggling. I hold her and reach for the pillows, plumping them up so she can settle comfortably.

"How's the shoulder?" she asks.

"I'll live." I grin. "Don't worry, *charodeyka*. You still have the upper hand. I'm the asshole here. Always was, and always will be."

"You'll have to stick around if you're gonna prove that."

Incredible that she can make jokes after everything she's been through. Once again, she ended up in mortal danger because of my stupidity.

I take her hand. "I don't deserve you," I say. "I know that. I killed my father, and when I told you the truth, I thought it would push you away for good. But it didn't. You showed me the compassion I desperately needed when I was a frightened kid."

"Why do you think I became a children's counselor?" she asks, stroking the back of my hand with her thumb. "*I* was a frightened kid, too. I would have given anything to have someone in my corner, even if all they did was listen." She sniffs, fighting back the tears. "Those kids must have been so afraid. To find themselves in Oliver's clutches, no one looking for them, no one to care whether they lived or died. Killed and dumped like junk. No dignity, no graves, no nothing. At least Eddie made it."

We fall silent for a minute. It's a mark of respect for Oliver's victims and the countless others who disappear, never to be seen again. Young lives lost and wasted.

It could so easily have been Roxy or me. We were forgotten children, too, but somehow we made it.

"I thought you'd be watching the news," Roxy says. "Have you heard from Hillard?"

"I didn't wanna put the television on in here and disturb you, but there was no way I was gonna leave you, either." I nod at the newspaper on the arm of the chair. "I've been keeping up with events, though. Hillard hasn't been in touch, but it looks like he's in the shit."

"And you?" Her eyes are full of concern. "Are you in trouble?"

"I don't exist as far as the case is concerned. The *kommissiya* might have something to say about it, so my head may yet roll for this."

Roxy sighs. "What do we do now? There's so much to sort out. I have no idea what will happen to Always Home with the manager and all three trustees out of the picture. We'll be shut down, and all those kids will lose their safe place."

"Don't worry about that now." I brush her hair away from her forehead, stopping to stroke her cheek with my finger. "The doctor said you can go home when you're ready. Your headache is just from the after-effects of the chloroform, plus the impact of your head hitting the dash."

"Home?"

I know what she's asking.

We've come full circle. Back to the start, with Roxy in a hospital bed and me somewhat responsible for the chain of events that put her there. Asking for her forgiveness yet again.

But it's different this time. I'm no longer afraid to love her. I believe in her. In *us*.

"*You* feel like home, Rox." I drop a kiss on her brow. "I don't wanna be anywhere you're not. I still don't know how to be the man you deserve, but I'm willing to *try* to be good for you."

Roxy smiles mischievously. "Not *too* good. I didn't spend months dreaming of you and all that rough stuff you love, only for you to go soppy on me."

This woman is perfection. I can't keep the shit-eating grin off my face.

"You better mean that," I say. "Because I'll try to be a gentleman if you want, but I'd prefer to spend the rest of my life wrecking you in every way I can think of. All this tension needs a release, and you look damn good to me right now."

Roxy laughs. "Right now? Can we at least get back to your place? That bathtub of yours is calling to me."

"So I'm forgiven for being the sexiest fucking idiot you ever met?" I laugh.

"Nope." She smirks. "You gotta earn it."

I look at her gorgeous face, and I'm overwhelmed with gratitude. I was so committed to my loneliness that I almost lost the woman I adore.

"I love you, Roxy." It feels good to say it aloud. "I didn't know I could feel this way, but now that I've accepted it, the world feels like a wonderful place."

"I love you too," Roxy replies. "Now let's get out of here."

32

Six hours later...

Roxy

I lean against Ben's chest, his arms around me, and let the water soothe my aching bones. There's plenty of room for us both in the bathtub, and the water is hot and deep.

Ben's hands move over my skin, massaging soap suds into my shoulders. He moves down to my breasts, working the lather over them as he cups them in his palms. My nipples stiffen as they break the surface of the water.

"So tell me," he murmurs, pinching my nipples gently, "did you ever put that dildo of yours anywhere *other* than in your pussy?"

"Sure," I say. "I put it in my nightstand drawer."

He chuckles and shifts his legs. I feel his stiffening cock between my buttocks.

"You know what I mean." He nibbles my ear. "I told you—*all* your holes are mine. But there's one I'm yet to claim."

He wants to fuck me in the ass. I've always been curious about what it would feel like, but I never dared to put more than a fingertip in there.

After everything that's happened, I want him inside me more than anything in the world. Being naked together like this is almost life-affirming. It's not just physical—it's as though we've stripped away all the armor supposedly protecting our fragile hearts. Instead, we've found the courage to be vulnerable together. Letting go of the past has given us strength we never thought possible.

I sigh as Ben's hand steals beneath the waterline, reaching between my parted thighs. His fingertip nudges between my pussy lips and finds my clit.

"I know how you fucked me when you were obsessed with me," I say, tensing my muscles as he gives me pleasure. "Now I want to know what your *love* feels like."

Ben chuckles, his cock twitching against me. "Baby, I'm *still* obsessed. I didn't think I could want you any more than I already did, but fuck *me*. I knew nothing. Loving you makes me wanna go at you harder than ever. You think you can handle it?"

"I *know* I can."

"Let's see." He pushes my shoulders. "Sit on the rim of the bath."

"It's cold!" I splash him playfully, and he pinches my nipple, making me cry out.

"Did I fucking stutter, *charodeyka*? Do as I tell you."

Ben helps me to my feet and sits me on the porcelain edge. My tits are shiny and pink from the heat of the water, and he moans at the sight. He grasps his stiff cock and strokes it, wetting his lips with the tip of his tongue.

"Pick up the soap," he says, his voice thick with arousal. "Get those pretty tits good and slippery for me."

I work up a lather in my hands before sliding the suds over my chest. Soapy trails slip through my cleavage and down my belly, my nipples peeking through the foam. Ben jerks off idly as he watches, and a sudden surge of courage strikes me.

He loves my body. I should show it off.

I reach for my nipples, rolling them between my fingertips. A breathy moan escapes me, and Ben growls.

"That's hot. What a good girl you are, giving me a show." He thrusts his hips toward me, nestling his cock between my tits. "Hold them," he says. "I wanna fuck these big tits. Look at me while I do it."

His cock slides over my slick skin as I press my breasts together, enclosing him. His mouth hangs open as he moves, the shiny tip protruding from my cleavage with each thrust.

"Keep those eyes on me, Rox."

He takes my shoulders in his hands, leaning his weight onto me. I wonder if he's gonna come on me, but he slows down, his breathing labored.

"Can't keep doing that," he laughs.

He steps out of the bath and pulls me into his arms, wrapping me with a towel. I take his outstretched hand, and he leads me to his bed. I giggle as he rubs me briskly with the towel, my skin prickling with the cold.

"Let me sort out my hair," I say.

"Fuck your hair, Rox. No, wait." He releases me from his grip, raising an eyebrow at me. "Do those sexy braids. For those, I'm willing to wait."

A minute later, my hair is plaited and out of the way. Ben grins and drags me to my feet, whipping the towel off my body.

"Perfect. Now, I don't have any lube," he says, spinning me to face him. He slips his cock between my thighs and grips my ass, pulling my body to his. "But I have my ways."

I flinch as Ben slips his hand between the cheeks of my ass, feeling for my tight pucker. He gives it a rub, and I jump.

"It's gonna be bliss to fuck that tiny hole," he says, "but I'm a patient man. I won't do it to you until you beg for it. Get on all fours on the bed, head down, and get that thick ass in the air. Spread your legs good and wide."

I assume the position, opening myself up to him. He gives a low moan of appreciation.

"You never looked sexier, *charodeyka*. I'm a lucky bastard." I feel his breath on my most intimate areas. "I'm gonna come in *all* your holes whenever I want. That's what my lovely little slut wants, right?"

He's still nasty, still disgusting. The man I love and his fucking filthy mouth degrading and praising me.

"I want it," I say.

Without warning, Ben sticks out his tongue and licks me in one movement, from my clit to my asshole. I cry out, and he grabs the cheeks of my ass in his hands, pulling them apart.

"Stay still. You act out, and I'll slap the hell out of you."

The stiff tip of his tongue spears my tightness, and I squeal. As he works me open, I feel his saliva between my legs, and my muscle tension eases.

"That's a good girl," he says. "You deserve a reward for being so well-behaved."

His fingers slip between my dripping pussy lips and slide deep inside me. I sigh with satisfaction as the full sensation gives some relief, but I need more. I reach between my legs.

Ben pulls his fingers out of me, and I gasp sharply.

"I said stay still."

He steps away from me, and I look over my shoulder to see what he's doing. He's holding two neckties and sets about tying my ankle to the bedposts.

"Shouldn't you be asking whether I'm okay with this?" I ask.

Ben shoots me a look. "If I don't ask, you can't refuse? Is that the rule? Because if so, I fucking *won't* ask. Find your damn voice. If you don't want me to do something, say so."

I don't move. He secures my other ankle, stepping back to survey his handiwork.

"So I hear no objections, Rox." He taps my buttock with the back of his hand, making me jiggle. I moan as he grips my flesh, pushing his thumb into my asshole. "Does that mean you're gonna shut up and take it?"

I nod weakly, and he laughs.

"Good. This is what you get for sassing me."

He slaps my ass cheek with everything he has, and a flash of pain heats my skin. I surge against my bonds, but I can't go anywhere, especially not with Ben's thumb inside me. He pauses to spit on me, his thumb pushing his saliva into my ass.

"That hurt you, baby?" He grasps his cock and rubs the head against my wet pussy, and I instinctively push back against him. "I know. But I think you love it."

He's right. Fuck knows why, but the sting accentuates the pleasure in my asshole and clit as he moves, teasing the tender nerves. I bump my hips back, and he pulls away, resisting the urge to plunge into me.

"You are not in charge this time," he growls. "My slutty princess wants to learn the hard way."

Princess. I like that. He can call me that whenever he—

Ben rains down blows onto my ass, one after the other, with no respite. I scream as the air splits with crack after crack as he hits me with his palm, then the back of his hand. The flesh of my buttocks is burning, but his cock sliding over my clit is bliss. My body cannot differentiate between the two sensations, so it melds them together into a full-body feeling of rapture.

"You're covered in red handprints," Ben says. He rubs his hand over me, soothing the throbbing pain. "What a glorious sight." He slides his cock up and down between my folds. "I wanna rail your pussy until you see God, but I can't let your slutty asshole go unfucked for much longer. Turn around and open your mouth."

I'm confused for a moment before I realize what he's gonna do. I shuffle until I'm facing him, my ass still sticking up in the air.

Ben stands before me, his cock level with my mouth. He takes my damp braids in his hands, wrapping them around his fingers.

"You've no idea how much I wanted to do this to you that night in Hawaii," he says. His eyes bore into mine as I look up at him. "You were driving me fucking insane."

"You should have done it." I open my mouth, and he sighs as the swollen tip of him rests on my tongue.

"I know." He shifts his hips, sliding his cock deep into my mouth. "All that time wasted. You'd better believe I'm gonna make up for it."

Ben's cock is thick, and it fills my mouth completely. He grips my braids, holding my head steady as he pushes deeper, knocking against the back of my throat. I gag hard, and he lets go of my braids, his hands flying to the back of my head.

"Take it, you nasty girl. All the way to the back, that's it. Well done."

He withdraws, his cock covered by a thick coating of saliva. He grips his cock at the base and slides along the shaft, collecting the spit, and places the flat of his palm over my face. I gasp in shock as he rubs my saliva into my skin.

"I shouldn't waste that good stuff," he says, "but I can't help it. You look so hot when you're all messed up." He grasps my braids again. "Let's do that a few more times."

I breathe through my nose as his cock crowds my throat, pulsating against my tonsils. After a few thrusts, he pulls free of me and gathers the saliva in his hand once more. As he shoves into my mouth again, he reaches along my spine and rubs the spit into my sensitive asshole.

"See?" he says. "The best lube in the world comes from you choking on my cock."

He pushes his fingers into my mouth and down my throat. I gag, and he takes his wet hand away, wiping the spit on my ass again as I cough.

He's so nasty. But this is who he is, who *we* are. Fantasizing about him warped my expectations to the point that I *needed* him to use me this way. The innocent virgin I once was is gone forever.

Ben is jerking off, his slick cock inches from my face. Suddenly, he moves, using both hands to maneuver me until I'm on my back. He pushes my legs up until my knees are by my ears, pinning them with his forearm. I shudder as his other hand roams between my legs.

"You're dripping for me," he says, parting my pussy lips. He brushes my clit before sliding his fingers through my slit, pulling my wetness into the crack of my ass. "You want me in your asshole? Eyes on me and beg for it like a good slut. I know you can do it."

I open my mouth to speak, but his look of him stops me in my tracks.

His body is tense, his muscles pumped and shining with perspiration. He looks into my eyes as he touches me, biting his lip when I gasp. Despite his words, he doesn't have the control he thinks he has. He's desperate to fuck my ass, and as much as I'm losing my mind, I wanna make him suffer a little. Didn't he say he wanted to earn my forgiveness?

"I'm not begging you," I say. I give a sweet smile. "So either you fuck me anyway, or you don't."

Ben narrows his eyes and leans down until his face is inches from mine. He stops touching my ass and leans against my thighs, his cock nudging my asshole, and puts both his hands around my neck.

I'm pinned, unable to move my body, but my arms are free. I reach for his wrists, trying to release his grip, but it's impossible. He squeezes harder in response.

"I wouldn't, *charodeyka*." His voice is soft, in contrast to what he's doing to me. I squeak ineffectually as he slides his slippery cock against my well-lubed asshole. "Your body is begging me even if you won't say it. But you will. We have the rest of our lives."

This should be terrifying. It *is*. But it's so hot. He has absolute control over me, and it feels incredible to trust him enough that I can enjoy it.

He lets go of my throat with one hand, maintaining the tension with the other. He slaps my cheek hard.

"I've been waiting for the right time to get you back for hitting me," he says.

My lips move, but I can't get the words out.

"Oh, are you finally ready to beg?" He releases his grip just enough for me to speak. "Good girl."

"Fuck you, you deviant," I whisper. "I should have hit you harder."

Ben frowns, but then I smile. He smirks devilishly.

"Do it. Come on."

I deliver a ringing slap to his face, the sound splitting the air. His head whips to the side, and he laughs, flexing his jaw.

"How many of those do you think I deserve?" he asks.

My pulse hammers against Ben's palm, and he pushes his thumb against the artery. Gripping the base of his cock, he works the tip over my asshole, nudging it open. I give a strangled gasp as his girth stretches me.

"There could never be too many," I moan. "You're a bad guy."

"Yeah, I am," he says. "I'm *your* bad guy. You're my good girl. Match made in fucking heaven."

I can't respond, not with Ben's hardness stimulating new nerves for the first time. His hips meet my buttocks, and he's buried to the hilt. I wrap an arm around each of my legs, holding them in place.

"That's it, baby. You're taking me so well. Stay like that. I'll do the rest."

I can't do anything *but* take it. His hand is still insistently gripping my tender neck, holding me down. His other hand is between my legs again, his thumb finding my sensitive clit. I grit my teeth as he pulls out slowly, my eyes rolling as he plunges back inside. He's got me so slippery that it doesn't hurt much, but the feeling of pressure is overwhelming. I didn't know it would feel so good.

Ben growls as he thrusts into my asshole. "So tight," he murmurs, his fingers tightening on my throat. "You've no idea how often I thought about fucking your fine ass."

I desperately want release, but I don't dare tell him. I roll my hips, trying to get him to push down harder on my clit, and he understands immediately.

"Oh, does my little slut want to come?" He slows his movements, almost pulling out of me, and I glare at him. "I'll allow it, but only if you ask me nicely." He releases my neck and puts his hands on the back of my thighs, holding them in place. "Come on, beautiful girl. Give me what I want, and I'll fuck your asshole until you scream."

"Please," I say, pouting. "Please let me come."

"You're so sweet," he sighs, pushing back inside me, "yet *so* needy. Just as well I want to give you my cock as much as you want to take it."

I'm not listening. I'm rubbing my clit, chasing the orgasm that is so, so close. Ben's breathing comes in harsh gasps as he speeds up, pounding my little hole.

"I'm gonna fill your ass with my come," he says. He slaps me again and again. "You pretty little ass slut. It's all for you. Every fucking drop."

He grabs my legs and slams into me, tipping me over the edge. My asshole twitches around him as he empties his load into me, my pussy spasming as it gushes fluid over his cock. A wave of ecstasy surges through my body, almost painfully sharp as my fingers still move on my clit.

For a minute, neither of us can move. His hot breath mingles with mine as he slumps over me, and I wrap my arms around his back.

Ben rolls off me and pulls the duvet over us. I snuggle into his warm chest.

He debased me. It made me feel dirty.

I never felt more cherished in my life.

"You really are a sorceress," he whispers. "I'm blessed to love you."

33

One month later…

Ben

"Did you read it all?" Landon asks. "I couldn't get through it."

There are few people at the precinct today. Most officers are on crowd-control duty at the courthouse.

Oliver Buckley's trial was surprisingly brief. He didn't try to defend himself or deny liability for The Dollmaker killings or for anything else he did. He was so excited to tell the world about his genius that he couldn't stop once he started.

The newspapers fell over one another to offer him deals, trying to get the rights to serialize the memoirs he began writing while awaiting his day in court. They really want the scrapbook police found in the Farraday's basement. The one I'm holding now.

"I read every word of it," I say, putting the book on the desk. "I kinda felt I had to. While I was keen to understand why Buckley did those things, I wasn't gonna give him the satisfaction of asking. The bastard wants people's interest. I hate that he's getting it."

"Wait and see," Landon says. "Your girlfriend got through her cross-examination like a champ, and so did you. She told me the judge has allowed her to give a personal statement before the sentencing, and I'd say she more than deserves that opportunity."

I frown. "She never mentioned that part. I was supposed to meet her afterward, but she said she'd be in the public gallery."

He shrugs and taps the scrapbook's cover. "So, what did you take from all this?"

"It shows what loneliness can do to the mind," I say. "The young Oliver was shuttled between different foster parents. He was never with them for long enough to feel a connection, and he hated the kids in those families."

That's putting it mildly. There are whole passages in the scrapbook about him bullying the biological children of his foster parents, beating and molesting them. He was moved on quickly *because* of this behavior, but that never occurred to him.

"Look here." I flick to a page filled with newspaper clippings. "He found his biological mother. The information on her is sparse, but when he was twenty, he discovered the identity of his father. Buckley felt this was the sign he'd been looking for—that he was destined to be an important figure."

"He doesn't say what happened when he and Adrian Coffey first made contact," Landon says.

"No, but what *is* clear is that although they kept the connection a secret, the senator didn't push his son away. He must have recognized some of his own deviance in the kid. Narcissists think of their children as extensions of themselves, and Adrian Coffey was keen to bring his son into his perverted world. But he didn't know what he'd unleashed."

I flip to a double-page spread written in what *appears* to be red ink. A blotch of crimson was in the top right corner, which was snipped off for forensics to check. They confirmed it was human blood, probably from Buckley's first victim.

"It says here that Senator Coffey left a child alone in a room with Oliver, telling him to do whatever he liked. I'm not gonna read the next bit aloud–"

"Yeah, I had to skip that too," Landon interjects.

"I don't blame you," I tap the page, "but here's the part where Oliver *kills* the kid. He and Adrian argue, but then a deal is struck, and a decade-long symbiotic relationship begins. The senator's victims are silenced, and Oliver gets to scratch his murderous itch. In the meantime, Oliver becomes a philanthropist, and Adrian Coffey marries Moira. The poor woman had no idea what she was getting into—the man was twenty years her senior, with a son not much younger than her."

"So when the senator was murdered, Buckley lost his supply of victims," Landon says. "Moira Coffey was a trustee at Always Home by then."

I flip to a photo of Adrian, Moira, and Eddie Coffey, taken on a skiing holiday. Moira and Eddie's eyes have been scratched out. "Buckley saw an opportunity and approached Moira, threatening to ruin her new life *and* kill her kid unless she cooperated with him. She recommended him for the post of managing director at the charity."

"And all those referrals that he personally handled." Landon shakes his head sadly. "If he found one he liked the look of, he took down the details and never filed it. Just followed the trail, picked up the kids, and that was it."

"That *would* have been it," I say, "but Buckley got paranoid about being caught. Max Fisher had been found and identified, and he was afraid the cops were getting closer. When Graham Fisher introduced Buckley to Farraday, he saw his chance—Farraday had gambling debts, and Buckley wheedled his way into his confidence, offering to help him. Then he closed the trap, and Farraday was too frightened to resist."

"Jesus." Landon shudders. "All that stuff Farraday said in his testimony. Seeing the dead girl, having to touch the corpse. Watching his wife's heart break when the fingers were found."

Simon Farraday testified with great dignity. The last time he'd appeared in court, he'd had to listen to how sick and twisted *he* was, knowing it wasn't true. Then Lois left without even saying goodbye.

Now he has her and Jamie back, and they live in Pasadena, near where Lois grew up. The family will get millions in compensation, and they deserve every cent.

"I'm just glad Buckley's scumbag took a plea bargain," I say. "The hospital said they'll be changing their vetting procedures and increasing security."

"So they should." Landon rolls his eyes. "The bastard had a prior for dealing drugs. No one checked him out before hiring him, and they let him handle medication? He also had a skeleton key and got into the cleaning stuff. Chloroform just wandered out of the building with no inventory checks."

"No kidding," I say. "You'd think the patients were running the place."

"Let me ask you a question," I say, catching Landon's eye. "How do you feel about what happened to Hillard? Did it seem fair?"

Landon sighs. "Not much in life *is* fair, in my experience. Is it fair that Eddie Coffey woke up in the hospital to find out his mom was dead? Is it fair that the kid will grow up knowing she aided his murdering half-brother, letting so many children die just so her only son would live?"

He's right. Eddie *is* safe and well, living with Moira's parents, but he'll carry this around for the rest of his life.

I can't be sure, but it's my hunch that Moira cut a deal with Oliver—Eddie lived as long as Roxy died. That's why Moira attacked me. Once she knew she wasn't gonna make it, she tried to save Roxy, but only in the hope that Roxy would get Eddie out alive.

Moira died from blood loss. I thought *I'd* caused it when I hit her with the kitchen door, but the fatal injury occurred when she fell down the stone steps leading to the basement, fracturing her skull.

"I know. But Hillard was the scapegoat for the whole mess, even though Oliver Buckley did most of the work."

Landon closes the scrapbook with a frown. "Yeah. Tate didn't deserve to lose *everything*. Although I heard a rumor that he got a mysterious payout, so he isn't doing too badly after all."

Yep. Ironic that Hillard, Mr. I-Don't-Work-With-The-Bratva, accepted an off-the-books pension from Kal Antonov. I appealed to Kal to help the guy—after all, Hillard and I *did* work together, and no one came to slap the cuffs on me when all was said and done. Hillard could have sold me out to save himself, but he didn't even try because he was willing to face up to what he did.

Kal went to the *kommissiya* with me, and we told the whole tale. Fyodor Pushkin was pissed off but conceded that Hillard was no threat to us.

Pushkin spoke to his good friend, the Commissioner, and Hillard got away with getting fired rather than facing criminal charges. I haven't heard from him since, and maybe it's for the best.

"Do *you* think Oliver Buckley is insane?" Landon asks. "That's the only question left for the court to determine now, and the sentencing decision will depend on the answer."

I don't think he's crazy. Instead of killing himself, he projected his self-loathing onto others, ending lives *he* perceived as worthless. He's a twisted, pathetic creature who murdered vulnerable children and called it mercy.

Moira and Eddie reflected the foster families Oliver despised during his childhood. He punished them for the cardinal sin committed by *everyone* in his life—they didn't see how special he was.

"I know it's tempting to say he's insane, but he isn't," I say, tapping the scrapbook's cover. "All this proves is that Oliver Buckley is a fucking loser. And deep down, he knows it."

I glance at the clock on the wall. I said I'd meet Roxy at one p.m. after the jury had retired to consider the evidence. There's no question about Buckley's guilt—not after all the horrible shit they found in Moira Coffey's basement—but what he wants is clear.

Like Simon Farraday, his play is the guilty-but-insane plea, which guarantees a lengthy secure hospital stay, relative safety, and attention. The attention he desperately wants and doesn't fucking deserve.

"Gotta go," I say to Landon. "Don't wanna miss the action."

∼

It's noon when I arrive at the courthouse. The atmosphere is febrile but orderly, the cops talking to the crowd and keeping things friendly.

Inside, the public gallery is full, the lobby packed with people eager to see the whole sorry saga come to a conclusion. Ushers are trying to convince people to leave, but no one wants to give up their space.

I can't see Roxy anywhere, but I expected that. She's in a waiting room, preparing to be called. Counting down the minutes until she gets to say her piece.

To my surprise, I see Hillard ahead of me, talking to an officer in the doorway to the courtroom.

"Hey, Tate," I say. "Can you get me in here? Roxy is about to give a statement."

"Benedikt." Hillard gives me a terse nod. "I'm just trying to get in here myself." He turns back to the officer. "Come on. We'll stand at the back. I can argue with you all day."

The officer rolls his eyes. "Goddammit. Fine. But I was never here."

Hillard and I dart past him and take up our positions along the back wall just as the bailiff raises his voice.

"All rise."

∼

Roxy

I don't look to my left, where the public and the press are sitting. My eyes are fixed on Oliver Buckley.

Not Buckley. His *real* name is *Coffey*. Oliver Alexander Coffey, the killer of countless children over many years.

It disgusts me to imagine the things those owl-like eyes have seen. He's gained weight while in custody, and his jowls rest on his shirt collar. He's not looking at me. Instead, he's looking around the room, enjoying his audience. No doubt, he plans to parcel out his confessions whenever he feels like drawing attention to himself in the future.

"Miss Harlowe," the judge says. "The jury has heard professional representations regarding the matter at hand—

whether Oliver Buckley is guilty of seven counts of first-degree homicide or guilty but insane. Before I instruct them to retire and consider the question, I invite you to make a statement."

While I waited for my call, I wrote some prompt cards to help me. I reach into my pocket for them but change my mind.

I'll wing it. If there was ever a time to be authentic, it's now.

"Thank you, Your Honor." I draw a deep breath. "I've spent a lot of time considering the nature of madness. What makes a person crazy? Can they be treated? What if they're just bad, right to the core? Can some people be essentially good but have a vicious streak, and vice versa?"

I feel Oliver staring at me. I don't want to catch his look, and instinctively, I glance to my left.

My eyes meet the clear blue gaze of the man I love, and he smiles at me.

Ben is here.

I didn't tell him I was doing this. Because as much as I'm talking about Oliver, I'm talking about Ben, too.

I clear my throat. "I don't believe *anyone* is irredeemable, but I also believe that the individual has to *want* to be a better person. Nothing that is done *to* them will make a difference. They must come to terms with the person they are and the things they have done before they can positively change their outlook and behavior." I see a couple of jury members nodding. "Deviance exists on a spectrum, and we are all capable of terrible acts. This doesn't make us crazy. It makes us human. Some people are wired up strangely, but it doesn't mean they are destined to harm others. They just have *quirks*."

"Oliver Buckley is, in my opinion, perfectly sane. He has a rationale for his actions and feels entitled to understanding and appreciation. If he were mentally ill, he would not have been able to fool the world for as long as he did. Nor could he coordinate not one but *two* attempts to frame innocent men for *his* crimes."

"Too fucking right," a voice shouts from the gallery. I look across and see Ali frantically shushing Leo. The judge glares at them both, then looks at me again.

"Please continue, Miss. Harlowe."

Ben is watching me, smiling. He gives me strength. I stand up straight and raise my head, staring Oliver down, and he shrinks back in his seat.

"Buckley doesn't deserve to be in a hospital," I say, my eyes fixed on Oliver's. "He's not crazy, and he's not exceptional. He's just a *loser*."

Oliver Buckley was the model of compliance and good manners throughout his hearings. Now, as his reckoning draws near, he can take no more.

"You stupid cunt," he says.

The judge bangs her gavel on the bench. "That's enough." She turns to me. "Anything else you'd like to say?"

"No, thank you, Your Honor," I say. "I'm done."

∼

"I'm so proud of you, *charodeyka*," Ben wraps his arms around me, "but I wish you'd *told* me you were gonna do this."

"Did you agree with what I said?" I ask, looking up at him.

He grins. "I heard you loud and clear, Rox. But I don't think *all* of it applies to me."

I kiss him. "Of course not. You *are* crazy and exceptional. And not a loser."

"I'll take it."

The lounge is tiny but private, with a cop guarding the door. It's a little oasis away from the madness outside, and we sit together for a while in silence, grateful for the peace.

I see Ali through the glass, remonstrating with the officer. The poor guy hasn't got a chance against her. Getting to my feet, I open the door, beckoning her and Leo inside.

"It's good of them to hold this hearing during kindergarten hours," Ali says, hugging me. "We wanted to be here to support you guys."

"You couldn't keep your mouth shut?" Ben asks, laughing as he shakes Leo's hand. "It's a fucking court hearing, not a boxing match."

"Are you kidding?" Leo asks. "You're lucky I didn't do worse. Ali frisked me for weapons before we left the house in case I was planning to snipe the fucker from the gallery."

Ali leans close to me. "Turns out he's into that," she whispers. "We were almost late."

I smirk. "You kinky bastards."

"Did you see Vivienne Fisher?" Ben asks. "She's here for the sentencing."

I *did* see her briefly when I arrived. Our eyes met across the lobby, and a thread of understanding passed between us.

She knows about Graham and me and what really happened to her son. She also knows what kind of man Graham was, but he didn't deserve to die. Oliver used his history with me to manipulate him with tragic results.

"I guess she wants closure," I say. "We all do."

An usher raps on the door and opens it.

"Jury's back."

∼

I sit in the gallery, Ali on my left. Ben sits on the other side, holding my hand.

Oliver Buckley's expression is one of disdain. He wrinkles his nose as though he can smell something bad and glares defiantly at the judge. The courtroom is deathly silent.

"Oliver Buckley," the judge begins. "The foreman of the jury has relayed the verdict, which is unanimous. The legality of the proposed sentence has been checked against the appropriate guidelines."

I squeeze Ben's hand so hard that he turns to look at me. He strokes my arm.

"Easy, Rox," he murmurs. "Almost there."

The judge leans over her bench and returns Oliver's glare.

"You are an ineffectual man, small of mind and even smaller of conscience," she says. "In carrying out your disgusting crimes, you destroyed young lives and sought to draw innocent people into your web, forcing them to pay your dues. You abducted and killed six children, mutilating the bodies and taking keepsakes. You presided over a nightmare that would have started all over again if it weren't for the actions of the brave individuals who brought the truth to light."

Oliver sneers. The judge smiles.

"The jury considers you legally sane and finds you guilty of aggravated murder in the first degree on all seven counts. I sentence you to life, without parole, at ADX Florence, Colorado."

"No," Oliver says.

"Evidence will be archived, except for the," she spits the words, "*biological* materials, which will receive a proper burial. Because of your notoriety, the Attorney General has permitted me to impose an embargo on the publication of your letters, memoirs, and diaries. Furthermore, no criminologists and psychologists will be allowed to engage with you directly or via correspondence." She narrows her eyes at Oliver. "You will not be an object of fascination to *anyone*, Mr. Buckley. Not now, not ever."

I slump against the seat, tears of relief rolling down my cheeks.

Oliver will live under the tightest control possible. Confined to a cell for twenty-three hours a day. No visitors, no letters, no fascinated psych students itching for the kudos of interviewing a serial killer. All he'll have are his demons, necrotizing his ego until he buckles under the weight of his inadequacies.

Now *that's* loneliness.

People burst into spontaneous applause, whooping and cheering.

"I'll appeal!" Oliver cries. "You can't do this to me. People will want to understand!"

"Nobody cares." The judge raps her gavel. "Take him down."

∽

When we leave the courthouse, the world feels like a different place. The sun is breaking through the clouds, and as it warms my face, I feel renewed.

The press swarms around the prosecutor and his team, looking for the perfect soundbite. They don't notice us passing by. Ali and Leo dash off to collect Luna, promising to call on us soon.

Hillard is waiting for us on the corner, finishing a cigarette. "This is my twelfth one today," he says as we approach, flicking the butt to the ground. "I normally smoke about ten a week."

"Tough times?" I ask.

He grins. "Not so much. How's the new counseling service coming along? I heard Always Home had to be dissolved. Too much scandal."

"Too much theft, more like," I say. "Oliver had been skimming cash for a long time, Moira too. That's how he could afford to pay people to do his dirty work. But there's still some cash left, and the IRS should release it to Ali and me so we can start again. Just a matter of paperwork."

"Bane of my life. Good luck." He nods at Ben. "By the way, I got a call from a buddy of yours. He thinks I'd be a valuable asset to his team."

Ben laughs. "Freddie's always on the lookout for people with special skills. You gonna take him up on it?"

"You never know." Hillard extends a hand to Ben. "I'll be seeing you around, Voratov. Play nice now, you kids."

We watch him walk away.

And just like that, it's over.

EPILOGUE

Five months later...

Roxy

"But where are we going, Ben?" I ask. "You're driving me mad! What kind of sadist are you?"

I didn't want to leave my fledgling charity for a surprise holiday, but Ali shooed me away, saying she had matters in hand. Managing a children's counseling service is different from just working for one, but in the three months since we started taking cases, we've gone from strength to strength. Ali still can't make coffee worth a damn, though.

The airport is busy. Ben told me to pack light, but beyond that, he wouldn't tell me a thing. My small suitcase is bursting at the seams with stuff I may or may not need, and he's still keeping me hanging.

"You *know* what kind of sadist I am," Ben says, grinning. "Ask your bruised ass. Can you sit down for eight hours without being in agony?"

"A-ha!" I snap my fingers. "We're *not* going to Hawaii. The flight time is longer than that. So where else might we—" I pause and clap my hand over my mouth. "No way."

"You got it." He points at a check-in desk. "That's us over there. JFK to Milan, then a short jaunt to Lake Como. Where we will be staying in a private villa."

I throw my arms around his neck. "How did you keep this a secret?" I ask through happy tears.

"I didn't," he laughs. "I told Ali and swore her to secrecy, so I had someone to help me plan it. I needed her to help me pick," he pauses and shoots me a glance, "a place to stay."

I'm on cloud nine. I'm finally going to Lake Como. The place where my parents were happy, back when we were still a family.

I check the departure board. "The flight isn't for a while yet. Let's get a drink and celebrate!" I put my palm on his cheek. "Sorry. Soda with a twist?"

He nods. "Absolutely. No booze for me. I never knew how much I would enjoy having a clear head."

I tap his temple gently with my fingertip. "That's because you're not running away from what's in *here*. Not anymore."

"You forgave me for everything I did and embraced everything I am." He wraps his arms around my waist and kisses me tenderly. "If you can show compassion for this monster, so can I."

I bite his lip. "You're *my* monster. Don't forget it."

Ben bares his teeth at me, making me giggle. "You're fucking damn right I am. Wanna join the mile-high club?"

∽

The villa is stunning. A neat cube of peach-colored brick, the windows edged with ornamental scrolls in the classical Italianate style. Steps lead from a paved patio to a small garden with a lush green lawn and a jetty onto the lake.

I take the keys from Ben and unlock the door, gasping at the tiled floor and modern Rococo decor. Ben smiles as I gawp.

"It's just a house, *charodeyka*."

"A house?" I wheel around as I speak, and Ben laughs at my outraged expression. "It's not a fucking house! It's a palace. A beautiful, beautiful thing."

"Takes one to know one," he says, taking my bag from my hand. "Do you love it?"

"God, yes!"

He puts my bag down beside his own. "Would you be surprised if I told you we own it?"

It takes me a moment to find my words. "Yes, I would be surprised. Because how could you possibly—"

"I'm back in with the Bratva," he says. "Of course, I'll keep my respectable public-facing image as a freelance profiler, but we're gonna be living it up from now on. Crime pays, remember? As for this place, well, Ali bought it as a gift for you. She said to tell you she paid for it with the money she found down the back of her couch."

I laugh. It's a running joke between Ali and me that she is terrible at being rich. She has the poor person's mindset and always will, but she loves to spend money on the people she loves.

"So when you said she picked out somewhere to stay, you meant she bought me a house? She's an idiot and the sweetest person I know."

"This isn't the only thing she was involved in choosing."

Ben reaches for his inside pocket, and I frown, not catching on. He drops onto one knee.

"I can't fight *every* man who looks at you, so I better make it legit."

Oh, sweet Jesus Christ fuck! How dumb am I?

"Roxy. My *charodeyka*. My love. Long ago, I told you I don't do fade-to-black romantic scenes. I guess I lied."

I'm crying. I fan my face with my hands, and he smiles.

"I love you," he continues. "I loved you from the moment we met. I was mortified to have hurt you and was terrified we'd get close, only for me to hurt you some more. You were far stronger than me. Without your good heart and faith in me —in *us*—I'd never have summoned the courage to accept the bad in me *and* the good. I'm a screw-up, but no one will ever love you like I do."

Ben holds up a black velvet box. Inside is a platinum ring, a cluster of diamonds cradling a round, brilliant-cut aquamarine.

"It matches your eyes," he says. He takes my hand. "Marry me, Roxy. Fuck everything else. I've never needed anyone before, but God knows I need *you*. What do you say?"

"I say yes."

I sink to the ground before him, and he slides the ring onto my finger. The early evening light streams through the windows, the gemstone's facets reflecting the pinkish sky.

"You know that thing you said about fade-to-black romance?" I ask.

"Yes, my love?"

"What do you think about shelving the PG-13 and shooting for an NC-17 rating?"

Ben smirks. "You're on."

∽

High hedges surround the patio. Perfect privacy. The sun-warmed stones feel good on my bare feet as I head outside to join Ben.

"I brought you a drink," I say.

Ben is sitting on a raffia couch, enjoying the view over the lake. He turns to look at me.

"*Bozhe moy*," he says. "Oh, my God. You didn't warn me."

On a dollar-to-fabric basis, the pink bikini was not good value for money. The top piece covers my nipples but little else, and the so-called briefs couldn't be any briefer. A thin strip of fuschia material hides my pussy. I have shoelaces that would provide almost as much coverage.

Ben is openly leering. I half expect his tongue to unroll like a horny cartoon character.

"Ben, you've seen me *naked*."

"I know." He takes the drink from the tray. "But this bikini is smaller than the one you wore in Hawaii."

I shrug. "You told me to pack light. I'm a good girl. I do what you tell me."

"I'll quote you on that."

Ben sips his drink and sets it on the side table. When he takes the tray from my hands, he notices the other things on it. He grins broadly.

"How is *that* packing light?" he laughs.

On the tray is my latest purchase. A treat to myself. A new dildo, a pretty one made of translucent pastel-purple silicone. Beside it is a bottle of water-based lube.

"I wanted to make sure I had space for these," I say. "I love having you inside me, but you can't be everywhere at once. And I'm nothing if not practical."

"I can see that." He puts the tray on the table and picks up the dildo, brandishing it at me. "*En garde*! Does this guy have a name?"

"What?" I chuckle. "I figured you'd be pissed off if I named it, let alone called it a 'guy'!"

"I told you, I love toys. You could name it after me."

I think for a moment and dissolve into giggles.

"Okay. His name is Benedick."

Ben raises an eyebrow at me. "I walked straight into that, didn't I? I regret everything. No name for the second-in-command."

"So what now?" I say, settling on the chair opposite. Ben puts the dildo on the table.

"Pretend I'm not here." He leans back, his hands behind his head. "Imagine you can't have me, and all you can do is fantasize while you play with yourself."

"But *I* want to—"

"You greedy slut." He slips his hand down the front of his shorts. "I'll get to you, I promise. Now *do* it."

I pick up the dildo. As I sit back down, I lift my feet onto the seat, draping my legs over the arms of the chair. I shuffle my back down the cushion until my plump pussy is on display, the pointless bikini already developing a wet patch. My fingers tug the fabric aside, and I stroke the blushing lips of my sex.

I glance at Ben. His eyelids are heavy, his hand moving idly as he touches himself. The sight of him inflames my own arousal.

I cushion my clit between two fingers, massaging it gently. There's something so lewd about doing this outdoors while my fiancé watches me. In my hottest fantasies, I never imagined this. I dip a finger into my entrance, and Ben moans.

"I'm losing my mind," he says. "I'm gonna have the sexiest wife ever."

I smile.

I can't believe how uninhibited I am, but he's done that to me. He's my first, last, and everything in between.

I close my eyes, losing myself to my movements. My clit is sensitive, and every tiny stroke sends pleasure shooting through my sex.

I pick up the dildo and rub it over my parted pussy lips, picking up my wetness. Ben gasps as I open my mouth, pushing the dildo to the back of my throat.

"That's my good girl," he says. He frees his cock, pumping it as he watches me. "You're a fast learner."

I remove the dildo from my mouth and slide it over my belly. It's slick with saliva.

"I had a good teacher," I say.

I nudge the tip of the dildo inside my soaking hole, enjoying the stretch. It's not as girthy as Ben's cock, but it still feels good. I drop my head back and push the dildo deeper, playing with my clit with the fingers of my other hand.

Ben is suddenly in front of me, kneeling between my thighs. He takes the dildo from me and slaps my ass.

"Turn over."

∼

Ben

The distant view pales in comparison to the sublime vision before me. Roxy's big beautiful ass in the air, her legs wide apart. The deep flush of her pussy, her wetness catching the evening light.

I pick up the lube.

"This will be cold, *charodeyka*." I squeeze a good amount into my palm and rub it between her buttocks.

"Oh fuck!" she laughs. "You weren't kidding."

"I'll warm you up," I say, kneading the flesh of her ass. "You just lean on the back of the chair and take it easy."

I move the dildo against her pussy, and she bucks against it, trying to get me to put it inside her. I chuckle and bite her butt cheek hard.

"Ow!" She looks over her shoulder at me, her face like thunder. "You broke the skin."

"So tell me never to do it again."

She narrows her eyes at me. "Oh, fuck *you*. Why do you always know what I want before I do?"

"I might know, but that doesn't mean you'll get it. For example," I slip the dildo inside her an inch or two before snatching it away, "you *want* to be stuffed with me and your dildo because you're a nasty little slut. But I'm gonna decide if, when, and how that happens."

The dildo has a flared base. Clever girl. She knew to buy one that could safely be used in her ass. It's smaller than my cock, so that's how it's gonna go.

I spit carefully on Roxy's tiny pucker. My saliva mixes with the lube as I use my fingers to move it all around. My fingertip pushes into her asshole, and she shudders.

"This is what my girl likes, isn't it?" I finger-fuck her ass, enjoying her little mewls of pleasure. "You want both your holes filled? Come on. Tell me what my good girl wants."

"I want you to fuck me everywhere," she says, her voice tinged with desperation. "Make it hurt, mark me, anything, but I wanna *feel* you."

"Your wish is my command."

I slide my finger out of Roxy's ass, holding her open with my fingertip so I can get the smooth tip of the dildo in there. She grits her teeth as I push past the tight outer ring of muscle and into her depths until the widest part of the dildo's base sits snugly in the crack of her ass. I step back to admire my handiwork.

"That looks so pretty," I say. I wrap one hand around her throat, her jugular pulsating under my palm. "Now, you hold on good and tight."

I shove my cock into her pussy. With my grip on her neck, she has nowhere to go, and I bottom out hard.

"You're so big," she says. "I'll never get used to you."

"I hope not."

I pull out of her and plunge back in, making her gasp. As I pinch her throat harder, I slap her ass, jiggling the dildo inside her. She yelps in surprise, her pussy clamping down on me, and I growl.

"Oh yeah. Keep squeezing me, baby. I love it."

I spank her again and again, fucking her pussy harder. I shove her head down, and she bites the back of the chair, reaching for her clit. She touches herself as I pound her, chasing her climax.

I let go of Roxy's neck, and she coughs. I wind my hand through her hair, pulling her back toward me so I can kiss her delicate throat. Part of me wants to slow down, but my hips have a mind of their own, and I growl in Roxy's ear as my climax starts to ramp up. She's sitting almost upright on her knees, bouncing on me.

"Fuck my ass with the dildo, and I'll come," she cries. "Do it, Ben, please!"

I reach between us and grab the base of the dildo, holding it still. As she moves, the toy slides out of her ass, plunging back in as she rides. I'm fucking her pussy simultaneously, sprinting for the finish.

Roxy is working her clit, panting with the exertion as she fucks herself on me and her toy. I give a deep moan as her pussy spasms, milking the come from me, and she screams, her pussy gushing all over my thighs.

I listen to her breathing for a minute, then disentangle myself from her, easing the toy from her ass.

"That was so good," she says. "Almost *too* good."

I grin. "Nothing's too good for you, my love."

∽

We sit on the jetty, our feet in the water. It's still warm, the lights reflecting on the lake as the evening draws in.

"I can see why you like this place," I say.

Roxy rests her head on my shoulder. "It's beautiful. But I miss having a home. I felt at peace here, but I lost those little things that gave me comfort every day. The things that speak of love."

I take her hand and bring it to my face, kissing her fingertips. "Like tire swings and sugar cookies?"

She sighs. "Exactly like that."

"You'll have those things again," I say. "I promise. Wherever you want to go, whatever you want to do, I will make it happen."

The lapping of the little waves is soothing. It occurs to me I can't remember the last time my toe did that nervous tapping thing.

Roxy and I went through hell to find our way to one another. She more than earned her happiness, and I'll move heaven and Earth to see she has the love and comfort she deserves. And the rough stuff to remind her who she belongs to.

I'm humming, murmuring the words of a song that seems to be permanently stuck in my head. *Heroes*, by, of course, David Bowie.

Roxy recognizes it and looks up at me, smiling.

"So, are you now a confirmed fan?" she asks.

"Absolutely." I kiss her forehead. "That one resonates with me. *You're* a hero, Rox. Do you know that? You saved my life."

I continue to sing quietly to her. She leans back in my arms, closing her eyes.

"I love you, Ben."

I cup her cheek, my lips meeting hers.

"I love you too, *charodeyka*."

THE END

MAILING LIST

Thanks for reading! Reviews are appreciated. I hope you enjoyed this book!

Sign up to my mailing list and get bonuses, freebies and offers emailed straight to your inbox.

Sign up at this link:

http://eepurl.com/h7lpFb

ALSO BY CARA BIANCHI

Thanks for reading!

If you enjoyed **Vicious Hearts**, you may also be interested in reading **Twisted Sinner**, which is Leo and Ali's story. Read FREE in Kindle Unlimited or buy on Amazon.

Also by Cara Bianchi

East Coast Bratva:

Depraved Royals

Twisted Sinner

Santori Mafia:

Bound to the Devil

Stolen by the Killer

Standalone:

Tainted Vow